WHISKEY REBELLION

AN ADDISON HOLMES MYSTERY (BOOK 1)

LILIANA HART

AN ADDISON HOLMES MYSTERY

WHISKEY REBELLION

USA *TODAY* BESTSELLING AUTHOR

LILIANA HART

DEDICATION

For Scott,

Because you're my hero and my heart.

OTHER BOOKS

Lawmen of Surrender (MacKenzies-1001 Dark Nights)
1001 Dark Nights: Captured in Surrender
1001 Dark Nights: The Promise of Surrender
Sweet Surrender
Dawn of Surrender

The MacKenzie World (read in any order)
Trouble Maker
Bullet Proof
Deep Trouble
Delta Rescue
Desire and Ice
Rush
Spies and Stilettos
Wicked Hot
Hot Witness
Avenged
Never Surrender

JJ Graves Mystery Series
Dirty Little Secrets
A Dirty Shame
Dirty Rotten Scoundrel
Down and Dirty
Dirty Deeds
Dirty Laundry
Dirty Money

Addison Holmes Mystery Series
Whiskey Rebellion
Whiskey Sour

PROLOGUE

My life was a disaster.

I sat in my car with a white-knuckled grip on the steering wheel and watched the rain pound against the windshield. I was soaked to the skin, my skirt was ripped, and blood seeped from both knees. There were scratches on my arms and neck, and my face was blotchy and red from crying. Along with the external wounds, I'd lost a good deal of my sensibilities, most of my faith in mankind, and all of my underwear somewhere between a graveyard and a church parking lot.

I'll explain later. It's been a hell of a day.

My name is Addison Holmes, no relation to Sherlock or Katie, and if God has any mercy, he'll strike me with lightning and end it all. I've had a job at the McClean Detective Agency for exactly six days. It's been the longest six days of my life, and I'll be lucky if I live to see another six. Unspeakable things, things you'd never imagine have happened to me in six days.

Now I faced the onerous task of telling Kate McClean,

my best friend and owner of the McClean Detective Agency, how I'd botched a simple surveillance job and found a dead body. Another dead body.

I should have kept my job as a stripper.

1

I've made a lot of bad decisions in thirty years of living. Like when I was eight and I decided to run away from home with nothing more than the clothes on my back, peanut butter crackers and my pink Schwinn bicycle with a flat front tire. And the time when I was sixteen and decided it was a good idea to lose my virginity at an outdoor Metallica concert. And then there was the time I was nineteen and decided I could make it to Atlanta on a quarter tank of gas if I kept the air conditioner off.

There are other examples, but I won't bore you with the details.

Obviously my judgment has gotten worse as I've grown older, because those bad decisions were nothing compared to the one I was about to make.

"Hey, Queen of Denial, you're up."

I gave the bouncer guarding the stage entrance my haughtiest glare, sucked in my corseted stomach, tossed my

3

head so the black wig I wore shifted uncomfortably on top of my scalp and flicked my cat-o-nine tails hard enough to leave a welt on my thigh. It was all in the attitude, and if I had anything to do with it, The Foxy Lady would never be the same after Addison Holmes made her debut.

The music overwhelmed my senses, and the bass pumped through my veins in time with the beat of my heart. The lights stung my eyes with their intensity, and I slunk across the stage Marlene Dietrich style in hopes that I wouldn't fall on my face. Marlene's the epitome of sexy in my mind, which should tell you a little something about me.

I'd run into a little problem lately, and let's just say that anyone who's ever said money can't buy happiness has obviously never had the need for money. My apartment had a date with a wrecking ball in sixty days, and there was this sweet little house in town I wanted to buy, but thus far the funds to buy it hadn't magically appeared in my bank account. I could probably make a respectable down payment in three or four years, but I had payments on a 350Z Roadster that were killing me, yoga classes, credit cards, a new satellite dish that fell through my roof last week, an underwear of the month club membership to pay for and wedding bills that were long past overdue. My bank account was stretched a little thin at the moment.

None of those things would be a big deal if I were making big executive dollars at some company where I had to wear pantyhose everyday. But I taught ninth grade world history at James Madison High School in Whiskey Bayou, Georgia, which meant I made slightly more than those guys who sat in the toll booths and looked at porn all day, and slightly less than the road crew guys who stood on the side of the highway in the orange vests and waved flags at oncoming traffic.

Since I'd rather have a bikini wax immediately followed by a salt scrub than have to move home with my mother, I'd declared myself officially desperate. And desperation led to all kinds of things that would haunt a person come Judgment Day—like stripping to my skivvies in front of men who were almost as desperate as I was.

The beat of the music coursed through my body as I twirled and gyrated. The lights baked my skin and sweat poured down my face from their heat. Something tickled my cheek. I caught a glimpse of black out of the corner of my eye and realized a false eyelash one of the working girls had stuck on me earlier sat like a third eyebrow on my glistening skin. I swiped at it nonchalantly, but it wouldn't budge. I ducked my head and peeled it off my cheek, but then it stuck to my finger and I couldn't get the little devil off.

I shimmied down to my knees and knelt in front of a portly man with rosy cheeks and glazed eyes that spoke of too much alcohol. His sausage-like fingers came a little too close, so I gave him a slap with my whip to remind him of his manners and the fact he was wearing a wedding ring.

I ran my fingers through his thick, black hair and left the eyelash as a souvenir of his visit to The Foxy Lady. The thought crossed my mind that he might have a hard time explaining the eyelash to his wife, but the music kicked up in tempo and I had to figure out something else to do with my remaining two minutes on stage. Who'd have guessed it would take me thirty seconds to run through all my dance moves?

The arches of my feet were screaming and I almost laughed in relief when I saw the poles on the far side of the stage. I could spin a few times and hang upside down a few seconds to take the pressure off my feet. Besides, I watch T.V. Men always seem to go crazy for the pole dancers.

My sweaty hand clasped the cold metal pole and I swung around with more gusto than was probably wise. Little black spots started clouding my vision, so I slowed my momentum down until I was walking around like a horse in a paddock on a lead rope.

I made another lap and saw Mr. Dupres, the club's owner, frowning at me. He swung his arms out and gestured something that resembled either taking off his shirt or ripping open his chest cavity, and I realized I still had on every scrap of clothing I'd walked on stage with. I threw my whip down with determination and ripped my bustier off to reveal the sparkly pasties underneath. I tossed the bustier into the audience and cringed as it knocked over a full drink into some guy's lap. Just call me the human version of a cold shower. Not a great endorsement for a stripper. I waved a little apology in his direction and tried to put a little more wiggle into my hips to make up for the mishap.

Would this freaking song ever end?

I prayed someone from the audience would have mercy and just shoot me. I spun one last time on the pole and nearly fell to the ground when I saw a familiar face in the audience.

I would have recognized the comb-over and pasty complexion anywhere, though when I usually saw Principal Butler he didn't have a stripper grinding in his lap. I kind of hoped the way his glasses were fogged would keep him from seeing me, but when he took them off and wiped them on his tie my hopes were dashed. He did a double-take and blinked like an owl before he paled.

I just wanted to vomit.

Mr. Butler practically shoved the woman in his lap to

the ground and reached for something in his pocket. He pulled out his cell phone and snapped off a picture. Not good. I guess he wanted proof to show to the school board before he fired me.

I covered myself with my arm and edged back toward the curtain. The music pounded. I waved to a few customers on the front row, their faces twisted and disgruntled at my early departure. I considered my bounty. A grand total of seventy-two cents on a bed of peanut shells lay at my feet.

Tough crowd.

Principal Butler's eyes were still glued to my chest as I finally found my way behind the thick curtains at the back of the stage. It was a darned good thing there was only a week left until school was out. Maybe the summer would give Mr. Butler time to forget he saw me in pasties and a thong and me time to forget that I saw my principal's tiny excuse for an erection.

Or maybe not.

So it turns out I'm not cut out to be an exotic dancer, and I'll be checking the employment section of the paper again.

I had to say that after the conversation I just had when I was fired from The Foxy Lady, I probably couldn't count on them to give me a glowing recommendation.

"Listen, Addison, I just don't think you're cut out for this type of work," Girard Dupres told me after my first and only routine.

I can't even begin to tell you how many times in my life I've heard those exact words. If I weren't such a positive person, I would live in a constant state of depression.

Anyway, Mr. Dupres was the guy who hired me, and he looked like a Soprano's reject—thinning dark hair, beady eyes, hairy knuckles and greasy skin. He obviously didn't know anything about hiring good strippers or he never would have considered me.

I decided it was best to look slightly downtrodden at my termination, but inside I was relieved that exotic dancing wasn't my calling. I don't think I pulled off the reaction I was hoping for, because Mr. Dupres thought it would be a good idea for me to perfect my technique in a private showing just for him. But to give him the benefit of the doubt, it's hard to have a conversation and not look desperate when you're topless and covered in sweat.

I told Mr. Dupres "Thanks, but no thanks," and headed backstage to gather my things and get dressed. I decided to keep the costume and cat o' nine tails just in case I ever had a dominance emergency, but I left the itchy wig on the little plastic head I'd borrowed it from.

I took out the blue contacts I'd worn to cover my dark brown eyes and creamed off the heavy eye makeup. I pulled my dark hair back into a ponytail, slipped on my jeans and baby-doll tee from the Gap and stepped into a pair of bright pink flip-flops. It was nice to see the real Addison Holmes once again. I'd only misplaced myself for a few minutes, but it was long enough to make me realize I liked the real me enough to find some other way to make the extra money I needed.

I'd just hide this little incident away and no one but Mr. Butler and me would ever know about it.

I pushed open the heavy metal door that led from the dressing areas to the alley behind The Foxy Lady and squinted my eyes as the sun and heat bore down on me. I slipped on a pair of Oakley's and hitched my bag up, digging at the bottom for my car keys.

If I'd been looking where I was going instead of at the

bottom of my purse, I'd never have tripped over the body. I'd probably have walked a wide path around it and wondered how someone could already be drunk enough on a Saturday afternoon to be passed out in a strip club's parking lot. As it was, my foot caught the man right in the ribs and sent me sprawling to my hands and knees.

"Ouch, dammit."

I muttered various curses as the raw skin on my palms bled. I pushed myself up slowly and took stock of my aching body. My jeans had holes in both knees and a lot of blood covered the toes of my right foot.

"What the hell?" I said as I wiggled my toes to see what the damage was. There didn't seem to be any cuts so I turned around to see what I'd fallen over.

The body sprawled out in the gap between the cars. It seemed twisted in an odd arc, but shadow shielded me from witnessing the carnage that created so much blood. If nothing else, I knew where the blood on my toes had come from. I couldn't pretend he was drunk with the dark stain spreading out across his dress shirt like a Target ad. Nor would I be able to keep my recent dabbling into the exotic arts a secret once I called the police and explained to them I'd just found my principal dead in the parking lot.

2

AFTER I'D DRY HEAVED FOR A GOOD TEN MINUTES, IT dawned on me belatedly that Mr. Butler had obviously met his end at the hands of someone bigger and badder than he was. But here I stood, alone in a parking lot in a rather shady part of town with my handbag on the ground and my body hunched over a dying rhododendron. I was practically begging to be murdered.

"Maybe I should call the police from inside," I said as loud as I dared to the empty parking lot.

I looked around nervously for signs of knife wielding maniacs hiding behind parked cars and ran to the front doors of The Foxy Lady with my hand down in my purse so the maniacs would think I was holding something dangerous like Mace or a 9mm. I didn't have either of those things, but after this experience I was going to think long and hard about getting them.

"I'm sorry, sugar. You've got to be of age to come in here," the bouncer at the door said.

I tipped my sunglasses down to the end of my nose and looked over the solid chunk of black granite. His nametag said Larry but Gigantor seemed more appropriate, with his bowling ball-like head and biceps large enough to pull semis in a monster truck rally.

At another time I'd be flattered I looked underage. But not right now. Right now, sweat gathered in unladylike creases and my stomach roiled like I'd just taken a ride on the tilt-a-whirl. Why had I thought it was a good idea to come to this hellhole?

"I need to get in there," I said as I tried to push my way past his bulk. "I've got to get to a phone."

He planted himself solidly in front of me, so I shoved my shoulder into his ribs several times to try to move him, but he didn't budge and my shoulder just ended up sore.

"There's a pay phone across the street," he said. His face was expressionless and he was obviously used to sending away pesky women who came to watch the fascinating lineup of middle-aged exotic dancers at The Foxy Lady.

"Listen, you. I just danced on that stage not more than thirty minutes ago. I'm still wearing the pasties to prove it. But now I have to get back in there and call the police."

"Whoa, honey. I don't care if you're the Saturday night headliner. Nobody calls the police in this place. If Mr. Dupres got a little frisky after your show then we'll settle it between you and me, but we ain't calling no police. Maybe we can go get some dinner and get the details worked out."

Gigantor smiled and two gold teeth glinted against the sunlight. I had an out of body experience as he ran a meaty finger down the side of my face.

I was left with no choice. I did what any girl would have done when faced with a dead principal and a randy bouncer. I kneed him in the balls and watched him tumble like a redwood in the forest. I heard his head hit the ground with a thud as I ran to the bar.

"Somebody needs to call the police," I said to the bartender. "There's a dead man in the parking lot."

"Calm down, lady. I don't think you killed Larry. A kick in the balls is nothing to get your panties in a twist over."

"Just do it!" I screamed. "And pour me a double shot of Jack Daniels."

I was well on my way to being snockered by the time the first patrol car showed up. Mr. Dupres had come out of his office once the news that the police were on their way reached his ears, and he ordered Gigantor to keep people away from the body until the police showed up. He gave free drinks to his customers to keep them indoors and had all his afternoon dancers come back on stage for an encore. Thankfully, I wasn't asked to participate.

Mr. Dupres came over to me once he got his customers settled, grabbed my arm and my drink, and led me away to a private table.

"Now you just let me do all the talking, Ms. Holmes," he said as he sat down across from me. "I've dealt with this kind of thing before, and I can tell you're pretty shaken up."

I shrugged and finished the rest of my drink. Warmth spread through my body, and I didn't care if he wanted to do all the talking. Probably the less talking I did the better off I'd be. Who would believe that a small town teacher fell over her dead principal in the parking lot of the place she'd just taken her clothes off? Not me. I'd never believe such a story.

The bartender came and put another drink in front of me and I gave him a sloppy grin. I'm a cheap drunk. Usually a half glass of wine puts me down for the count.

I noticed Gigantor had come back inside and was

talking to two uniformed officers, both of them writing quickly in little notebooks. Gigantor turned his head, scowled at me, and then pointed a finger in my direction.

Uh-oh, I was guessing by the scowl that Gigantor was still upset with me for kicking him in the balls. Probably the giant lump on his forehead where he'd hit the pavement wasn't making him feel so hot either. I giggled out loud and then kicked Mr. Dupres under the table when his hand crept up my thigh.

"Stop it, you pervert." I tried to slap his hand away, but everything was starting to get a little blurry. "This is all your fault. You think I'm easy just because I got naked on your stage? Well, I'm not. I teach world history for goodness sake. I'm a respectable member of my community." I tapered the sentence off on a keening wail that was bound to gather all the dogs in the neighborhood. I was a terrible drinker and an even worse whiner.

"Hey, I can be respectable," he said, patting my head awkwardly as tears streamed down my face. "It doesn't look like it, but this place has a pretty decent income. I've got a nice house with a swimming pool. You'd like that, wouldn't you?" he said, sounding more frantic the harder I cried. "Of course, I'd have to divorce my wife before I could move you in."

I was about to ask him if he could divorce her in less than sixty days and if he'd be willing to assume my considerable debt when a man started making his way towards us. I'd seen him come in and talk briefly to Gigantor and the bartender, and I could tell by the way he moved that he was the one in charge. He stopped briefly to speak to the two officers who had taken Gigantor's statement and then started making his way towards me.

He moved with a predatory grace and skimmed just

over six feet. His skin was swarthy, hinting of some Mediterranean ancestors, and his hair was almost black and cut close to his head, though it still managed to curl just a bit on the top. His face was shadowed by a growth of beard and his slacks and jacket were rumpled enough to let me know that he'd already had a long day on the job. He dodged the customers and the half-clothed waitresses who threw themselves into his path with ease.

As he moved from the shadows and closer to me I could see him better. His face was hard and chiseled, his expression one I'd seen on other cops' faces. My father had carried that look in his eyes until he'd died last year—the look of someone who'd seen too much and didn't trust anyone.

Then the man looked at me and I forgot to breathe, but probably part of that had to do with the fact that my nose was clogged with snot. Amid the darkness of his hair and skin was the palest, most beautiful pair of blue eyes I'd ever seen.

Heat gathered in my belly and it had nothing to do with the whiskey. I tried to see my reflection in the metal napkin holder at the center of the table, but it was distorted. My forehead looked huge, my ponytail was lopsided, my eyes were red and my nose was swollen. Or maybe it wasn't distorted. It would probably be best if I didn't look at myself again. I grabbed a couple of napkins from the holder and blew my nose, making a great honking sound that Mother Goose could be proud of.

"Addison Holmes?" the man asked and flipped open his identification to reveal a shiny gold badge.

His expression was somewhere between incredulous and pitying, but I had visions of handcuffs and satin sheets running through my head. I glanced discreetly at his hand to see if he wore a ring.

No ring.

He couldn't possibly be gay. Fate wouldn't be that cruel.

Maybe I still had a chance.

I realized I was clenching my fists when they started to sting again, so I relaxed and noticed they still had blood on them. Whiskey first, first aid later. Only I'd forgotten the first aid.

The detective was obviously waiting for me to say something, but I couldn't remember if he'd asked me anything. "I'm Addison Holmes."

"I'm Detective Nick Dempsey. You're bleeding, Ms. Holmes," he said as he took a chair and sat down at the table.

"I fell."

I grabbed a couple more napkins from the holder and looked down at my hands. I didn't have any water, so I dipped the napkins in my whiskey, thinking that at least my hands would be disinfected. I sucked in a breath as the alcohol touched the open wounds. I would have cursed a blue streak but I couldn't catch my breath.

Tears gathered in my eyes, but I blinked them away so I wouldn't look like a sissy in front of the hot detective. Not that he was likely to give me the time of day anyway once he found out what I'd been doing at The Foxy Lady. Men like this guy didn't have to frequent strip clubs to see beautiful naked women. He probably had a whole herd of beautiful naked women lined up on his doorstep.

I wasn't feeling so good all of a sudden, so I laid my head down on the table and decided to have a pity party. Not to mention I didn't want to embarrass myself further by throwing up on the detective's shoes.

Maybe the whiskey wasn't such a good idea.

"I know this is a difficult time for you, Ms Holmes." His voice was soothing, velvety smooth, and I'd bet it was hell on women when he used it in the bedroom. "Would you mind if I asked you some questions?"

I was about to tell him he could ask me anything he wanted when Mr. Dupres opened his mouth. "I don't know about that, Detective. Ms. Holmes is one of my best employees and I feel as her manager that you need to direct your questions to me." Mr. Dupres patted my arm, staking his claim.

My head snapped up hard enough to make me dizzy. "What?" I gasped in embarrassed horror. "But you just fired me."

I looked over at Detective Dempsey and caught a glimpse of his bemused expression before he carefully masked it. I looked at him imploringly, begging him to understand with my eyes.

"Umm, wait, that isn't what I meant to say. You see, Detective, I'm not really a stripper. I was just a stripper this afternoon because there's this house I love, but I wasn't very good at stripping, and then I got nervous because my principal was getting a lap dance and it was gross. And then Mr. Dupres fired me, and I was kind of glad because my mother would kill me if she ever found out I'd done something like this, and probably the school board wouldn't like it much either because I teach ninth grade world history. And after I got fired I went into the parking lot to go back home and I tripped over Mr. Butler and his blood got on my toes so I threw up."

Detective Dempsey and Mr. Dupres were both looking at me like I was insane, so I laid my head back down on the table and closed my eyes. I have a couple of relatives who have been declared certifiably crazy, but I never thought until now that it was something that would pass on to me. I mean, it's not really a big deal. This is the South. In the South we're all proud of our crazy relatives. We like to put them right out in public so everyone can see them. I just wasn't quite ready to go on display myself.

"Mr. Dupres, I'd appreciate it if you'd give me and Ms. Holmes a few minutes alone. Maybe you could go get her a cup of coffee," the detective suggested in a tone that wasn't meant to be argued with.

"Sure, sure. I'll be right back." Mr. Dupres scurried away like the rat he was and returned only moments later with a steaming cup of something that looked more like black swamp water than coffee, but I took the cup gratefully. He hovered behind us just within earshot and tried to make himself look busy. Being shut down due to a dead body in the parking lot would probably be considered bad for business, so I could understand his concern.

"Did that all sound as stupid as I think it did?" I asked.

"I think you've been under a tremendous amount of stress today, Ms. Holmes. Maybe you could start again from the beginning," Detective Dempsey said. "I'm not sure I caught everything you said." He looked me over from head to toe like I was a specimen under a microscope.

"You don't look like you miss much. You probably caught the gist," I said a little waspishly. I was embarrassed. Or mortified might have been more accurate. And Detective Dempsey was an easy target for my self-disgust.

I sipped the coffee through the straw and knew before I did that it was going to burn my tongue.

"You see, I needed another income, and I saw an ad in the newspaper this morning for The Foxy Lady. I decided to give it a shot since it's in Savannah and the chances of running into anyone I know in a place like this and in a city this size are low. Of course, I should have known better. Murphy's Law and all that," I said, flinging my hand in the direction of the stage and accidentally tossing the bloody napkin that had been on my hand onto the table of men seated next to us. I grimaced and muttered an apology as they shot me dirty looks. Detective Dempsey's face was void of all expression, but I swore I could see the beginnings of laughter sparkling in his eyes.

"Keep going," he said.

I looked for the eye crinkles or a slight quirk of the mouth, but I couldn't see anything in his expression other than cool disinterest. "There's not much more to tell. I saw my principal in the audience, got fired and fell over him in the parking lot, in that order."

Detective Dempsey took out his notebook and started writing. "You said earlier that your principal was getting a lap dance. Did you know the woman?"

"No, but I didn't get to meet all the girls when Mr. Dupres hired me. I literally got hired and was handed a costume. I've only been here a couple of hours."

"Would you recognize her if you saw her again?"

"Maybe. She had a lot of blonde hair, some of it may have even been hers, a dog collar and her attributes were um...," I cupped my hands out in front of my chest. "Fake. That's pretty much all I got."

"What about other customers? Was it crowded? Was there anyone else in the audience you recognized?"

"It wasn't exactly standing room only. The tables down front were full, but I didn't recognize anyone. There was a couple making out in one of the corner booths that I noticed because a bouncer had to intervene before they had the chance to give their own public show. I couldn't see the man's face because it was hidden in shadow and all I could see of the woman was a blonde ponytail bobbing up and down. The other tables were pretty empty other than a few pathetic looking men scattered around. It was hard to see the back of the room from the stage because of the lights."

"Did you see anyone else in the parking lot?"

"No, but I wasn't really paying attention. I was looking for my keys. That's why I tripped over Mr. Butler."

A sob caught in my throat and I looked down at the table. I wanted to go home, and if Detective Dempsey had given me anything that had remotely resembled sympathy I would have broken down on the spot, but he kept his voice at the same level, unexpressive, and asked me the same questions over and over again. I was willing to bet when it came to playing good cop/bad cop, Detective Dempsey was always the bad cop.

I had no idea why I found the thought exciting.

"We're going to need you to make a formal statement down at the station. It will take a little time to talk to everyone around here, so tomorrow or Monday at the latest will be fine."

"But aren't I a suspect? Aren't you supposed to tell me not to leave town?"

"I think you watch too much television, Ms. Holmes. It should be pretty easy to get your whereabouts from the security cameras on the inside of the building."

"Hmm," I said. I hadn't thought about that, but I wasn't exactly at my best at the moment. I looked at him and pleaded with my eyes. "No one can know about this, Detective. I made a bad decision, but I have a lot to lose."

"I'll talk to Mr. Dupres myself and make sure he doesn't give your name to the press, and there's no reason for me to include your employment here in the report, only that you found the body."

"Thank you," I said, and truly meant it.

"Are you good at taking advice, Ms. Holmes?"

"Not especially, Detective Dempsey."

His lips quirked a little. "I'm going to give you some anyway. You look like a nice kid from a nice family. Go back to your teaching job and stay away from places like this. It doesn't suit you."

I knew everything he said was true, but that didn't mean I particularly liked hearing it. It was like rubbing salt in an already opened wound, and I didn't need some cop coming along to tell me that I'd done something stupid.

"I'm thirty years old, Detective Dempsey. I stopped being a kid a long time ago, and sometimes decisions have to be made that aren't particularly pleasant, whether people like you approve of those decisions or not. Now if you're finished I'm going home."

I scooted out of the booth and grabbed my bag, prepared to make a grand exit when I felt his hand under my elbow.

"Let me have a patrol car drive you home, Ms. Holmes. I'd hate to have to arrest you for drunk driving."

I could see the laughter in his eyes, even though his mouth was in a serious line. I would have jerked my arm out of his grasp, but I was afraid I'd fall over.

Men like Nick Dempsey are extremely irritating to independent women like me. They like to be in charge and they always think they're right about everything.

The depressing thing is they almost always are.

THE DRIVE BACK TO WHISKEY BAYOU WAS SOMBER TO say the least, but at least the officer taking me home didn't make me ride in the back of the squad car. That would have fueled the gossip flames of the few remaining tenants that were still in my apartment complex.

I checked behind me to make sure the officer in my car was driving responsibly, and when I was satisfied he was, I turned back around and tried to find a comfortable position on the torn vinyl seat of the Crown Victoria.

I noticed the *Now Leaving Savannah* sign and knew I'd be back home within minutes. Whiskey Bayou is a nice place to live. It's a small town of about three thousand people surrounded by swamps and slimy creatures that bite. It's an acquired taste, but picturesque in the daylight. And since it takes less than ten minutes to drive north to Savannah we're not completely cut off from civilization. It just sometimes feels that way.

We turned right on Main Street, just past the two-storied, red-bricked crumbling buildings and the giant sign that said *Welcome to Whiskey Bayou—The First Drink's on Us*. An old depot that housed a train car graveyard sat on the left and a small diner, grocery store and park were on the right.

The Whiskey Bayou residential area was constructed around the Walker Whiskey Distillery, which was built sometime in the 1800's. When I was in college, I found out the Walkers were distant cousins of the Holmes, so I did my best to learn everything I could about whiskey just in case I was the last remaining relative someday and had a chance to inherit. Mostly everything I learned about whiskey was that it gave me a terrible headache and made my mouth dry.

The roads around the distillery looked like something a drunken council member would plan out, with crooked streets, some of which dead-ended for no apparent reason, and roundabouts that seemed to have no exit once you were on them. I remember once when I was a child, my mom going around in circles for what seemed like hours until my sister, Phoebe, finally threw up all over the back seat.

The officer who was driving me home seemed to be in the same predicament, and we went round and round until my eyes crossed and my stomach lurched. He finally flipped on his lights and broke several traffic laws once he saw the tinge of green my face had turned.

My apartment complex was just south of the residential area of "downtown" Whiskey Bayou. It was built on swampland, which was only part of its many problems.

The building was a square of four stories made of crumbling orange brick, single-paned windows—most of which were cracked—and stairs that divided the building into two halves. The parking lot was no better than rubble and sad looking shrubs lined the cracked sidewalk. The inside wasn't a huge upgrade, but the rent was cheap.

"Geez, lady. You live here?" the cop asked.

"Home sweet home," I said as I got out of the car. "Just park my car as far away from the building as you can. I wouldn't want it to get damaged if the building collapsed in the middle of the night."

"Right," he said, not sure if I was joking.

I was. Kind of.

"Thanks for the lift," I said and turned towards the building. Mr. and Mrs. Nowicki were both peeping out their window on the first floor, so I gave them a wave and headed up the stairs.

I was on the fourth floor. I hated being on the fourth floor. The plus side was that I was in damned good shape from hauling groceries, textbooks and whatever else I could carry from Pottery Barn up four flights of stairs. The bad news was that things like rain and tree limbs came through my ceiling first.

I noticed the yellow slip of paper taped to my peeling front door as I stuck my key into the lock. It was another eviction notice, warning me that I had to be out by the deadline under penalty of law.

No problem.

I'd think of something.

I tore the note off, pushed open the door with my total body weight because the humidity caused the wood to swell, and made my way to the bedroom where I fell face first on the bed.

I couldn't take much more in a day. I'd stripped, found a dead body, committed assault, gotten drunk, ogled a hot detective, despised the same hot detective, been escorted home in a police car and gotten another eviction notice. And it wasn't even dinnertime.

I was asleep before I could tell myself that things could only get better.

3

SUNDAY

I'D BEEN TAKING A LITTLE HIATUS FROM CHURCH FOR the past six months, so when Sunday morning rolled in with a crash of thunder and the plop of water as it hit the random buckets I had placed around the apartment, it seemed like the perfect excuse to miss one more Sunday service. I snuggled back under the covers and dozed until noon. Besides, my mother would be there, so she was representing me by default.

My reasons for steering clear of the First United Methodist Church in Whiskey Bayou had nothing to do with God, the new banjo player they hired to accompany the choir or the fact that Reverend Peters frequently took too many sips of the communion wine.

It had to do with the fact that my wedding took place there six months ago.

It was a beautiful Christmas wedding. The church was

decorated in yards of tulle and red roses, the cake was five tiers of confectioner's heaven and seven bridesmaids were decked out in ruby satin. My dress had cost a fortune and was decorated with thousands of tiny seed pearls and a fifteen-foot train. The wedding was perfect.

The only thing missing was my fiancé.

While I'd been waiting to walk down the aisle, my fiancé Greg had been boffing Veronica Wade, the home economics teacher from my school, in the back of the limo that was waiting out front.

My ex-brother-in-law was the one who'd caught them in the act, and Derek "the Dweeb" Pfeiffer has never been one to handle situations delicately—like when he left my sister so he could find himself and inspire people through his rock. And let me tell you, Bon Jovi he is not. Of course, my sister should have known better than to marry someone who would give her the name of Phoebe Pfeiffer.

Derek didn't think about keeping the news of Greg's infidelity in the family and handling the matter quietly. He went directly to the videographer so the whole thing would be caught on film and made an announcement to the attendees from the vestibule.

Greg and Veronica raced off in our limo and used our honeymoon tickets to frolic in the Bahamas for two weeks, while I faced a crowd of two hundred. I didn't get married that day, but the non-wedding got a hell of a write-up in the Whiskey Bayou Gazette, and I still have wedding cake in my freezer, which is always a plus.

A glance at the clock showed me I'd sufficiently slept in long enough to miss church. I rolled out of bed, suddenly wide awake, and threw on a robe. I weaved my way around buckets filled with water on my way to the kitchen, and went through the routine of making coffee, ignoring the red flashing light on my answering machine while I waited for the coffee to percolate.

"Come on, come on." I shifted back and forth on my feet impatiently. I couldn't take it any longer, so I poured half a cup and drank it down quickly, sighing as the cobwebs cleared from my mind.

I refilled my cup, opened the refrigerator door and stood there a few minutes, wondering what I could do with one egg, a slimy head of lettuce, two bottles of ketchup and a six-pack of Corona. I closed the door with a sigh and made a note to stop by the grocery store.

The red light from the answering machine was making my eye twitch, so I forgot about eating and went to play my messages.

I hit the play button and fell back into an overstuffed chair to await the inevitable.

"Addison? Are you home? This is your mother."

She always says that, like I'm not going to recognize her voice.

"Why did a policeman bring you home? You're not in trouble are you? Make sure you let me know if you need bail. I was thinking about buying a new washer and dryer. Why aren't you ever home?"

Click.

I did some deep breathing and relaxed further into the chair while I waited for the next message.

Beep.

"Addison? It's your mother again. I wanted to remind you about services this morning."

There was a small stretch of silence after this announcement and the disapproval came through the recording loud and clear.

Click.

Beep.

"I saw you yesterday," the voice said.

I sat up straight and spilled hot coffee on my hand. "Ouch dammit."

"I watched you dance for me on stage." The voice was distorted and I couldn't tell if it was a man or a woman.

The spit dried up in my mouth and my flesh pebbled with chills, despite the fact my air conditioner wasn't working.

"Naughty, naughty, Addison. I never would have guessed you're such a bad girl. I wonder what the fine, upstanding citizens of Whiskey Bayou would think if they knew your secret."

I'd been wondering the same thing myself and had come to one conclusion—it couldn't be good.

"But don't worry. Your secret's safe with me. For now. And my condolences on Bernard Butler's demise. He must have been in the wrong place at the wrong time. Just like you."

A shrill laugh came through the recording that had chills snaking down my spine, and fear like nothing I'd ever experienced caused my skin to go clammy with the sweat and had spots dancing in front of my eyes.

The banging at the door made me shriek and drop my coffee mug onto the rug, spilling the rest of the contents. I looked for the closest weapon, but all I saw was a bunch of decorative pillows and a dozen or so candles that I used when the lady in the apartment below mine makes deep fried tofu.

"Open the door, you lazy bitch."

I let out the breath I'd been holding with a nervous laugh. I knew that voice. I scrambled to my feet and wondered how I'd ended up crouched in a little ball between the sofa and the wall. I braced my hand on the doorframe and tugged on the knob. The door pulled open with a creak of rusty hinges and swollen wood.

"You've got to get out of this place. It's a disaster waiting to happen," Kate McClean said as she breezed by me and threw a bag of donuts on the short bar that's attached to my kitchen.

Kate was short, about five-foot-two, though she'd argue with God Almighty himself and insist she was an inch taller. Her chin-length blonde hair was cut in an easy to maintain style and her face was scrubbed free of makeup. We were the same age, but if I were meeting her for the first time I'd think she was still in high school. She'd already changed out of her church clothes into her habitual outfit of torn jeans and a white t-shirt. She avoided the water buckets and peeling linoleum like a pro and poured herself a cup of coffee.

"Which is why it's being condemned," I said as I finally shouldered the door closed.

I opened the bakery bag and breathed in the fresh scent of warm pastries and decided my mom must be representing me pretty well at church because God sent donuts instead of making me eat slimy lettuce.

"Forget the coffee," I told her. "It's after noon, and everybody knows if you eat donuts after noon you're supposed to wash them down with beer."

"Hmm, I'd forgotten that rule," she said.

I handed Kate one of the Coronas and grabbed another for myself.

"Your mom wanted me to make sure you were still alive since you haven't bothered to return her phone calls," Kate said. "And she wanted me to let you know that she saved you a seat next to her this morning just in case you decided to show up."

"Ah, it's so nice that my mother can send the guilt through you. I can't even get decent Chinese food delivered here, but guilt—"

"Hey, what are friends for?"

"Donuts and shopping."

I ate a powdered donut then an apple fritter so I could get a healthy serving of fruit in for the day.

"I saw Greg this morning," Kate said after a while.

"Good for you. Did he get struck by lightning?"

"Not that I know of. He's been sitting in the front row every week. Maybe he's trying so hard because he wants you back. Veronica wasn't with him this morning."

"Ha, there's no way he wants me back, and I wouldn't have him anyway. He's sitting in the front row doing heavy repentance because I heard he's losing clients by the handful. Apparently, it makes people a little uneasy when their insurance agent is caught cheating."

"Hmm, I hadn't thought of that," Kate said.

"Besides, he and Veronica are most definitely still together. She tries to corner me at school on a regular basis so she can give me the explicit details."

"What a bitch," Kate said.

"You'll get no arguments from me. I go out of my way to avoid her now because she brought pictures of them in the act and left them in my school mailbox."

To say that Veronica Wade and I have a history is an understatement. Every woman in the world knows there's always one girl you go through school with that makes life miserable. It's the same girl who dumps water on you and tells everyone you wet your pants. The one who ties your shoelaces together and puts itching powder in your gym clothes. Juvenile bullying at its finest. But then high school comes along and things start to change. Body parts develop and teeth become straight. Tanning beds, nail salons and highlights are discovered. And suddenly the attention shifts.

I'd always been the scrawny kid with freckles, an overbite, and frizzy hair. Veronica had been the delicate piece of dandelion fluff with a cherub's dimpled smile and sparkling blue eyes. The one who could charm herself out of any situation with her cuteness. But the cuteness wore off by the time she hit freshman year as she grew taller and started to resemble something more along the lines of a beanpole. Breasts and hips never found a home on Veronica and the dandelion fluff hair turned dark at the roots. My mother liked to say that Veronica was as ugly as homemade sin. Needless to say, Veronica didn't take the changes high school brought gracefully. Meaning the stuff she'd done to me in elementary school was nothing compared to what she did to me in high school.

And maybe I didn't help matters any by relishing in the newfound attention my own breasts brought me. I might have accidentally put dead fish in the trunk of her car and slipped the wrong answers to a test inside her locker, but it was only because she started it. If she hadn't put superglue on my oboe reed (the results of which ended in very painful surgery on my part) or loosened the bolts on my desk so it fell apart as soon as I sat down (also resulting in pain), then I never would have even considered having such a long standing rivalry with Veronica Wade.

She was my archenemy. My nemesis. We were Elizabeth Taylor and Debbie Reynolds. Or Tupac Shakur and Biggie Smalls. It got to the point where the school counselors automatically put us in separate classes just to avoid the aftermath. That we'd both ended up teaching at the same school we'd spent the worst years of our lives in was irony at its finest. The fact that Veronica went away to college and came back with massive breasts, white-blonde hair, a new perky nose, cheek bones that could cut glass and a giant chip on her shoulder seemed to go unnoticed by most people. But not me.

"So what did you do?" Kate asked.

"I told her to lay off the Twinkies because her ass looked huge in one of those pictures."

"Good thing she got those breast implants to even everything out."

Kate and I finished off the last two donuts with a lot of finger licking and sighs. I couldn't think of a better way to start a Sunday afternoon.

"You know what you need, Addison?" Kate asked. "You need to get back out there. Ever since the wedding you've gone into hiding. You haven't dated anyone and the only people you ever spend time with are your widowed mother, your fourteen-year-old students and me. You know, Mike's cousin just broke up with his girlfriend, and he's always been attracted to you."

Mike was Kate's husband of two years, and I'd met Mike's cousin. He wasn't my type at all, which is mostly the story of my life, a.) because he looked like one of my students and b.) because he couldn't control the copious amounts of spittle that came from his mouth whenever he said a word that began with S. I was belatedly coming to the conclusion that I was nobody's type.

"I don't have the time to date right now, Kate," I said, trying not to hurt her feelings.

"Nonsense, I'm not taking no for an answer on this one.

I'm giving you an intervention to save you from becoming a lonely old maid. You're one step away from adopting a herd of cats. Trust me on this."

I didn't argue with her because I'd found myself standing outside of Grueber's Pet Shop last week looking in the big front window at all the kittens.

"Are you going to tell me why you really came by?" Changing the subject seemed like a good idea.

"Damn, I thought the donuts would lull you into complacency so I could be sneaky about it."

"I'm your best friend. Best friends can't be sneaky and get away with it."

"Well, I'm a private detective. It works differently with me."

I rolled my eyes and waited for her to get to the point, though I was pretty sure I already knew what it was.

"I hear you had a pretty eventful day yesterday," she said carefully.

"It depends on what you mean by eventful." I wasn't sure if she was talking about the dead body or the stripping. I didn't want to give myself away. There were some things that even best friends shouldn't know about.

"I'm talking about the fact that you stumbled over the body of your principal in the parking lot of one of the seediest titty bars in Savannah. The Foxy Lady parking lot has seen more criminal activity in the last month than Whiskey Bayou has seen in a hundred years."

"Well they didn't exactly advertise that fact in the newspaper," I mumbled. I would pick the most dangerous strip club in Savannah to get a job at.

"What was that?" Kate asked with an arched eyebrow.

"Nothing," I said. "It was just bad luck. I've got to go

give a statement at some point, but I'm not a suspect of anything."

"Of course not. You're the worst liar I've ever met. The police would know in the first thirty seconds of talking to you whether you killed him or not. Just make sure you don't put off giving your statement. It'll just piss off the detective in charge if he has to come hunt you down."

My nipples came to attention, and I shivered as I thought about Nick Dempsey. I was going to have to see him again, no matter how mortified I was at my behavior from the previous day. A small part of me was looking forward to our next meeting. The other part of me wanted to move to Alaska and forget Nick Dempsey had ever crossed my path.

"Don't think I haven't noticed how you've avoided telling me what you were doing in that parking lot. I still have a lot of contacts you know. I could find out if I wanted to."

"I'm going to plead insanity at this point. All you really need to know is that I'll never be able to make a career as a professional dancer."

"I knew that already," Kate said. "I saw you at our senior prom."

"Huh. I guess since you're so smart about all these things you can tell me how to get a second job that will pay me a lot of money in a very short period of time."

"Maybe Mattress Mattie will let you rent out a room by the hour. It is the oldest profession after all, and she always has cars in front of her house."

"You're not helping. I'm almost desperate enough to consider it. Look at this place. I have to be out of here in sixty days, and I'll set up a tent in the back of my classroom before I move back home with my mother. I have water leaks and clogged drains and plaster falling from the ceiling into my T.V. dinners."

"I don't understand why you need money so badly. You've got a good job with the school, and it's not like this place is costing you a lot to live in." Kate looked around at the crumbling walls and warped floors, obviously not impressed with anything she saw. "I guess your car payment is probably pretty hefty, but it's a sexy car. You've got an image to maintain after all."

"Yeah, and I have the speeding tickets to prove it," I said, more depressed than ever. Leave it to Kate to paraphrase my life in just a few seconds. "There's a vacant house for sale on Hutton Street I want to buy, but I don't have enough yet for the full down payment. I paid an initial five thousand dollars just to get things started. I've done all the paperwork and assured John Hyatt at the bank that I'd have the rest of the money by the end of sixty days."

"That's not a lot of time," Kate said.

"Thanks for reminding me. I appreciate the help."

I was an idiot for thinking I could get that much money in such a short period of time. My eye twitched so I grabbed another beer from the fridge and pressed it to my lid to relieve the pressure.

The great thing about living in a small town is that institutions like banks make certain allowances that most big mortgage companies never would. Like not making sure I actually had enough money before allowing me to purchase a house. It's a love-hate situation, because John Hyatt, the bank president, also has a bad habit of telling everyone in town how much you qualify for and what kind of shape your checking account is in. I'm one of those people who live paycheck to paycheck. I might live in a dump, but my car is new and I always have good shoes. There are worse things in life.

"It probably wasn't a good idea to tell John Hyatt you'd be able to get the rest of the money that soon," Kate said. "You know how he has that superiority complex and likes to make sure the little people know where they belong. He'll make up a horrible story about you and spread it around town if you don't keep your word. Remember when that awful rumor about Mary Gantz went around? He told everyone she'd defaulted on her car loan because she was paying so much in medical bills to treat a stubborn case of gonorrhea."

"*He* started that rumor?" I asked, shocked. "She's still in therapy over the scandal it caused. What a horrible man."

"Exactly my point. Don't cross John Hyatt. How much are you short?"

"About five thousand dollars, which is why I need another job."

"If you need one that badly, I could let you do some surveillance work for me at the agency. We're a little overburdened at the moment. Adultery and fraud are up this month."

Kate had been a police officer for two years before deciding she wasn't a team player, so she quit and opened her own private investigations office between Whiskey Bayou and Savannah.

The McClean Agency was one of the most popular in all Georgia. Kate had kept friendly relations with her contacts in the police department, and she still got to carry a gun. Sometimes I was a little jealous of the gun. It made her look really cool and important whenever we went out to dinner somewhere. All I ever got to carry around was a bunch of ungraded term papers.

"I'm glad business is good for you," I said, perking up at the thought that someone else's misfortune could be money in my pocket. "What would I have to do?"

"It's a pretty easy job. I'll give you some files on the people we've been hired to investigate and you follow them around and take pictures. You're not licensed so you can't meet with clients and you'll have to keep accurate records so I can write the reports. We'll put you on the payroll as an independent contractor and pay you a hundred dollars a night. You only have to make sure the targets don't see you."

"A hundred dollars a night! I bet Mattress Mattie doesn't make a hundred dollars a night."

"Mattress Mattie doesn't have teeth, Addison. I don't think you can compare the two."

"Whatever. I'll take the job. If I do work for you in the evenings and eat Top Ramen for every meal, I might just be able to pull this off. This is great. Thanks."

"What are friends for? Stop by the office after school tomorrow and you can fill out the paperwork."

I was going to be the best employee the McClean Agency had ever seen. Sam Spade would be no more than a name by the time Addison Holmes had made her mark. The sigh must have tipped Kate off to my thoughts.

"You're totally having delusions of grandeur, aren't you?"

"Maybe a little," I said, pouting.

"Why don't I show you how exciting detective work is? Finish your beer and get out of your pajamas."

"You won't regret this, Kate."

"That's what you said when we were in the tenth grade and you talked me into sneaking out and borrowing my mom's car to go to Brad Cooper's party."

"Yeah, but she never did find out how that dent got on her fender."

The rain was still pouring when we left my apartment and headed out to the parking lot. Kate had no problem with parking in range of falling bricks, and after I looked at the car she was driving, I could see why she wouldn't care.

"Nice car," I said, eyeing the taupe Taurus with immediate dislike.

"The first rule of thumb is to always blend in to your surroundings."

I looked at my shiny red Z and back at Kate's Taurus with a shake of my head.

"Are you sure you don't want to take my car?" I asked. I grimaced as the sticky stuff on the door handle attached itself to my hand.

"No, I just told you we need to blend in. People have a tendency to notice flashy red sports cars. Especially one that says HISTORY on the license plate."

"All right, all right, show me the ropes," I said. "Who are we going to bust?"

"No one," Kate said with an eye roll.

We headed into Savannah at a boring, law-abiding speed and it was everything I could do not to fidget in my seat and sneak glances at the speedometer. We turned into a sub-division of middle class, ranch-style houses built in the seventies. There were cars of various makes and models parked along the street, and I was ashamed to say Kate was right. My car would have stood out like a sore thumb, even with the added cover of the rain. She parked behind a minivan that had "Wash Me" written in the dust on the back window and then shut off the engine. I cracked my knuckles, not used to sitting in silence with Kate.

"So if the first rule is to blend in," I said, "what's the second rule?"

"The second rule is that we do not confront or apprehend," she said. "Not ever. And the third and most important rule is that we never break the law. Your only job is to watch, photograph and take notes for the file. That's ninety percent of what we do. We rely on the facts and our instincts to get us out of trouble if the need arises. Then it's case solved and we file it in the drawer."

"Cool. I've got great instincts."

To give Kate credit, she did keep her face perfectly blank after I made this statement. I had terrible instincts, and no one knew that better than Kate.

Kate had always been the serious one, bordering on anal, and then she evened it out by having a sense of humor so dry it was almost too late to laugh by the time you thought about what she was saying. Kate never got into trouble. Unless she was with me.

While my body was finishing my homework and doing chores, my mind was thinking of different ways Kate and I could have the best adventure possible. Whether that be taking apart her parents' television to build a robot to do our chores or stalking a teacher home so we could see if he was really a superhero in disguise. About the time we reached our senior year, Kate was finally able to tell me no and think of creative ways to keep me from doing anything too over the top or just plain stupid.

I owed Kate a lot.

I was startled back into reality as the Taurus sputtered to life and Kate drove out of the neighborhood.

"Where are we going?" I asked, confused. "We just got here."

"Addison, we've been here for half an hour. I've taken

pictures and given you a full rundown of what you can expect when you're on your own. You, however, have been humming the theme song to *Growing Pains* and checking the mirror to see if your roots are showing."

She was right. I was hopeless. Sitting still was not one of my strengths.

"You're a good friend," I said, patting her on the arm.

4

MONDAY

"YOU LOOK LIKE YOU'VE HAD A ROUGH DAY."

I winced at the chirpy voice that was, in my opinion, the equivalent of fingernails on a chalkboard.

Rose Marie Valentine teaches choir in the room next to mine, and unfortunately her singing voice is even worse than her speaking voice. The walls are thin at James Madison High School, and sometimes I wish I could teach kids about the Battle of Little Bighorn in a padded cell. If only life were that easy.

Rose Marie was the last person I wanted to talk to today. In fact, I didn't want to talk to anyone. I wanted to be the invisible woman today, and I figured if I wished it hard enough, kept my eyes closed and didn't say anything to acknowledge her presence, she'd just go away and leave me floating in an invisible cloud of depression.

"Are you all right, Addison?"

So much for luck. I slowly brought my head up off my

desk and peeled away the term paper that was stuck to my cheek. I could tell by the smears on the page that I'd have a big fat F marked in red on the side of my face. A merry band of hammering men were pounding away in my left temple, and I was pretty sure I'd hit rock bottom around my third period class. Technically, things could only get better.

Once his family had been notified, the news of Mr. Butler's death had spread through our small community like wildfire. I'd been fortunate that my involvement in finding his body hadn't gotten out yet, but I wasn't holding onto too much hope my luck would continue.

Teachers had been roaming the halls all day with red-rimmed eyes and the school counselor had been available for all students and faculty who were having a difficult time coping with the situation. I personally wouldn't take advice or comfort from James Madison's counselor if I had an ingrown toenail. My mother went to school with him, and she said he used to tie firecrackers to cat's tails and light them when he was a kid.

"Addison?"

"I'm fine, Rose Marie. I just have a little bit of a headache."

What I was really thinking was that it wasn't such a great day to go into the police station and give Detective Dempsey the statement he was so hot and bothered for or to start a new job, but then I thought of the little house on Hutton Street and decided to suck it up.

I opened my eyes and saw more than I wanted to of Rose Marie. She was dressed in hot pink capris and a pink and white striped sailor's top. What they say is true about large women not wearing horizontal stripes. Her permed blond hair was teased high around her head, and she always wore two perfect dots of rouge on her cheeks. I had the sudden urge to take out my makeup sponge and show her how to blend.

"Bless your heart," she said in a syrupy accent thick enough to spread on toast.

Rose Marie wasn't a bad person. She was just someone who took a great deal of energy to deal with, like a toddler or a Great Dane.

"I just can't believe Veronica said those things to you at lunch today," she continued. "I don't believe for a minute that someone posted naked pictures of you on the Internet, but I'll go home and check for you this afternoon just to make sure."

"Thanks, Rose Marie. You're a true friend."

"I'm sure you'd do the same for me," she said. "I wouldn't be surprised if Veronica posted those pictures herself." Veronica had experience in posting naked pictures of me on the Internet, so I wasn't completely surprised by her bombshell during lunch. She'd done the same thing our senior year after I'd been voted Most Likely to Succeed by setting up a camera in the girls locker room. I like to think she wouldn't have bothered with such a thing if she'd known in advance that my greatest successes would be teaching high school history and being the president of the Whiskey Bayou Yoga Association. But here we are again.

"She's always been vindictive and spoiled," Rose Marie continued. "I heard she seduced her mother's third husband when she was sixteen and blackmailed him with the tape because he didn't buy her the car she wanted."

"I heard that, too," I said. I knew for a fact Veronica had always been vindictive and spoiled. Just like I knew the moment she came back to town she'd set her sights on Greg Nelson. It was me who was naïve enough to think he'd ignore her advances since he was so madly in love with me.

"I tell you, you girls have been entertaining this town for twenty years, but it's not just a simple case of female rivalry anymore. In my opinion, Veronica's out to draw blood. I'd watch my back if I were you."

"Well that makes me feel better," I said.

God bless Dairy Queen. When life lets you down, they're always there to pick up the pieces with the help of twenty-percent butter fat.

I'd gone home to change into what I considered to be "spying on adulterous spouses attire." Which included a short black skirt, a George Michael concert tank top that said FAITH in hot pink glitter, a pair of flip flops, an oversized straw hat, and large sunglasses to help hide my identity. I'd wiped the red marker off my face, but I still wasn't in top form, so I stopped for a banana split to calm my nerves before driving to Kate's office.

I was multitasking, steering with my knees while eating my ice cream as I weaved in and out of traffic on Harry Truman Parkway. My stereo was cranked and Lynyrd Skynyrd was vibrating the fillings in my teeth.

I savored each bite of ice cream and hot fudge and almost missed my exit because I was lost in semi-orgasmic bliss. I was in the far left lane of traffic, so I punched my horn to warn the people around me and zipped over two lanes. A black Ford F150 swerved when I cut him off at the exit, and I winced and waved an apology as I headed down the exit ramp.

In my rearview mirror I could see the truck parked at a funny angle on the side of the road and all four of its tires smoking. Whoever was inside looked to be okay though so I didn't stop to lend a hand.

I glanced back at the road in time to see the stop sign, so I slammed on my brakes and jerked as my body slammed against the seat belt and my head hit the steering wheel. Fortunately, I'd finished my ice cream because the plastic container was now face down on the floorboard.

I made the rest of the drive to Kate's office in peace with no more close calls and decided it would probably be best if I didn't indulge in one of my greatest weaknesses while traveling at a high rate of speed from now on.

The McClean Detective Agency was run from a two-story, red-bricked building that was more than a hundred years old. There were black shutters on each side of all the windows, green ivy growing riotously across the front and large white columns flanking the front door. It was on the corner of a block filled with similar looking buildings that housed law firms, doctor's offices and tax agencies.

The street was packed, so I parked at the end of the block and walked to the building. My head was throbbing by the time I made it up the stairs to the second floor.

I waved hello to Lucy Kim, Kate's secretary, and as usual hurried past her desk as quickly as possible. The woman scared the crap out of me. There was something in her eyes that made it very clear she was way more than an average secretary. She looked really crazy and deadly at the same time. She always dressed in black and the highest heels I'd ever seen in my life. Her hair was straight as rain down her back and her lips were always the color of blood, like she'd just finished feeding.

I shivered when she just stared at me with a blank expression instead of saying hello in return. Like I said, she scared the crap out of me.

I nodded to a few other familiar faces and knocked on Kate's open office door before sticking my head inside. Kate sat at her desk, piled high with papers, and still managed to look professional and cool.

"Hey, come on in. I was wondering if you'd changed your mind after yesterday," she said, standing up to give me a quick, but preoccupied hug.

I looked down at Kate's practical blazer and white stretchy shirt tucked into dress slacks in no-nonsense gray and shook my head. I'd never been able to get her to see the importance of colors and accessorizing. I could see her shoulder holster when she moved back behind her desk, and I wondered if I got my P.I. license if Kate would let me carry one too.

"I got held up in a little traffic on the way here," I lied. "What is this suit you're wearing?"

"Don't start, Addison. I'm a private detective, not a supermodel," she said, exasperated.

Kate looked me over from top to bottom. "That must have been some traffic because you've got chocolate sauce on your shirt and a bump the size of the Grand Tetons on your forehead."

My forehead was a little sore, but I ignored the pain. I was more concerned about the small glob of chocolate on my left breast. It was an exercise in self-control that kept me from leaning down to lick it off.

"Dammit, this is vintage George Michael."

"Look on the bright side. No one will be able to see you since you'll be hiding out in your car the whole time."

"Good point. You know, I have some serious reservations about your secretary. Have you done a background check on her? I bet she's an assassin for hire or maybe even a vampire. I bet she's the head vampire, not one of those lowly minions that have their minds warped during the transition."

Kate looked at me like I was an idiot and rolled her eyes. "I think *your* mind's warped. Lucy is very good at her job, but I wouldn't stand in her way if I were you. I'm lucky to have her."

"Well, I tell you, something's not right about her. I saw her at the supermarket a couple of weeks ago, and it surprised the hell out of me to see milk and eggs in her grocery basket. I figured she had the blood bank make deliveries right to her door."

"Has anyone ever told you you're weird?" Kate asked.

"All the time," I said, giving one last glance at the chocolate sauce on my shirt. "Okay, hit me with everything you've got. I'm ready to catch some bottom feeders."

"Since you weren't listening yesterday when I was passing along my infinite wisdom, I'll repeat everything. The most important thing you need to remember is that you're not out to *catch* anyone. Your only job is to trail each subject and snap a few photos. If you run into any trouble whatsoever, I want you to drive away. Period. And we *never* break the law."

I nodded my head furiously, trying to convince her that I would never be so stupid as to get in the middle of anything dangerous or marginally illegal, but she knew me too well. Disaster was my middle name, and it showed a serious lack of judgment on her part that she'd even offer me a job like this. But for a hundred bucks a night, I could be agreeable to almost anything.

"We also have a confidentiality clause you need to sign. Most of our clients are from out of town, but we give local residents our promise to be discreet as well. There could be times when you'll recognize somebody."

"I can talk about it with you though, can't I?"

"Absolutely. I always enjoy hearing the juicy tidbits. But you can't tell your mother."

Kate must have read the intent on my face because a

guilty flush washed over my skin. I had planned to do just that. Old habits were hard to break, and gossip in a small town was the same as breathing. My mother would never forgive me if she found out I knew other people's dirty secrets and didn't share them with her. That was grounds for being cut out of the family will.

"Oh, all right. I promise not to tell a soul. Except for you, of course."

"Here are three of our most recent cases. All of them are allegedly cheating on spouses or significant others. I would take them home tonight and read them through before you start tailing them. It'll make your job easier in the long run to have all the information in your head."

I flipped through the files. There was a doctor from Savannah, a librarian from Thunderbolt and a banker from Whiskey Bayou.

"Whoa, this is a file on John Hyatt," I said.

"Yeah, you remember Fanny Kimble?"

"A couple of year older than us, head cheerleader, president of the math club, homecoming queen and valedictorian. Black hair down to her ass, big blue eyes and built like a supermodel—all leg and no breast. How could I forget Fanny Kimble?"

"Well in a few months she's going to be Mrs. John Hyatt. The only problem is she thinks he's cheating on her. She suspects it's a relationship he had before they ever met that has continued over the past couple of years. She's found expensive lingerie a time or two and receives hang up calls when she spends the night at his house."

"But how could he cheat and get away with it?" I asked naïvely. "He works at the bank and lives on the busiest corner in town. You'd think someone would notice."

"Which is why you'll need to talk to the neighbors

when you get a chance. Besides, just because we live in a small town doesn't mean the people there don't have secret lives. Look at Greg, for example. He'd been sleeping with you and Veronica for two months before you were supposed to get married, and you never had a clue."

"Thanks for reminding me," I said. "I think I'll leave on that pleasant note and go earn some money."

Before I could gather all my things there was a terse knock and a powerful presence at the door that made the hairs on the back of my neck stand up and heat shoot straight to my unmentionables. I looked down to make sure my clothes were still on and hadn't melted away at the first sign of such masculine vitality.

"Sorry I'm late. You wouldn't believe the day I've had. I caught two homicides this morning, and then some drunk woman ran me off the road and a nail punctured my tire. I should have given her a ticket, but I couldn't drive on a flat."

Uh-oh. I recognized that voice now, though it was more expressive than the first time I'd heard it. I looked up into the familiar face that hadn't yet noticed my presence. He was an electric force standing in the doorway of Kate's office, and a quick spurt of jealousy rushed through me as I wondered how they knew each other.

Nick got his first glimpse of me and narrowed his eyes. "I should have known it was you," he finally said, shaking his head. "I thought I recognized the car, and my first impression of you was that you don't seem to think things through too well."

"Hey, that's not fair. You don't even know me."

"For which I can be eternally grateful, since I just changed a tire on hot asphalt that was baking my internal organs at a hundred and thirty degrees."

48

"Why is your flat tire my fault?" I asked. "I honked. You should have gotten out of the way, but you sped up instead."

"I was trying to get out of your way. You're a menace to society. You shouldn't be let out of a padded cell, much less issued a license to drive a vehicle."

"I'm a very nice person, dammit. I've just been under a tremendous amount of stress lately and my life has gotten slightly misdirected."

"Well, thanks for trying to bring me down with you. I deal with the scum of the earth on a daily basis, and I can't remember the last time someone irritated me as much as you do."

Nick's voice hadn't risen in volume since he'd started lecturing me. It had gotten softer and the words more terse and deliberate. I noticed the vein bulging out in his forehead and thought it looked a little dangerous.

"You need to take some anger management classes before you explode or something from keeping everything inside," I said. "It wouldn't hurt for that granite face of yours to show some emotion. Your bedside manner sucks. You didn't even ask me if I was okay or make any personal observations when you questioned me."

"Lady, I was there to investigate a murder, not participate in social hour. Besides, you were drunk. I was just trying to get you to tell me what you knew before you passed out in my lap. And speaking of Saturday, why the hell haven't you come in to give your formal statement?"

"This is perfect," Kate said before I could argue in my defense. "I've never known two people that make more memorable first impressions than the two of you. It's absolutely perfect."

Nick and I were both looking at Kate like she'd lost her mind.

"Kate, I think your headband's too tight. It's cutting off the circulation to your brain," I said.

I stood and gripped my small stack of file folders to my chest, hoping to hide the chocolate sauce I'd spilled on my boob, and got ready to make a grand exit.

"I'm out of here, Kate. I'll read these through and start the surveillance tomorrow night. I don't think I'm up to starting tonight anyway. It's been a hell of a day, and Mr. Personality is giving me a headache."

"Kate, please tell me you're not giving this nutcase a job. She couldn't find her way out of a paper bag. How the hell is she supposed to follow a suspect around unnoticed? She has the subtlety of a neutron bomb and the luck of Jimmy Hoffa."

"All right. That's enough. Who the hell do you think you are?" I asked, poking my finger into his chest hard enough so he took a small step in retreat. He narrowed his eyes menacingly.

"I'm a cop, and I could have you arrested for assaulting an officer," he said, taking hold of the finger I had pressed against his rock hard pectoral muscle and pushing it away. "Want to see what it feels like to be cuffed and put in the back of a police cruiser?"

A shot of heat spread from my loins to all my pleasure points, my eyes widened and my breath caught at the image, and I could tell he wasn't entirely without imagination either as he realized where our conversation was leading.

"If you two will give it a rest, I'd like to give my clients the illusion that this is a place of business," Kate said in her best intimidation voice.

I was caught off guard because Nick smiled at Kate's attempt to restore order. Damn those laugh crinkles in the corners of his eyes. I'd just had more of a sexual rush in the last ten minutes than in the whole two years I'd spent with Greg. My sympathies went out to Veronica. She could have Greg with my blessing.

Kate looked at me in exasperation. "I told you not to delay giving your statement, Addison. Why don't you follow Nick back to the station and get that taken care of? There's no point delaying the inevitable. Don't argue," she said, as I was about to do just that.

She turned her attention to Nick. "Addison and I have been best friends since the first grade. She's going to work for me for a little while as a personal favor. You two will probably run into one another on occasion, so my only request is that you don't shed blood in my building. It's damn hard to keep a good business reputation nowadays, and blood is hell to get out of industrial grade carpet."

I nodded stiffly in the jerk's direction and gathered up as much dignity as I could find. I was running a little low today, considering everything I'd been through up to that point, but I was a southern woman and I could be dignified in my sleep. For the most part. Despite my mother's best efforts, sometimes I fell off the wagon a little.

"I'm not the one you have to worry about. I can get along with anyone. It's obviously Detective Sugar here that needs a lesson in manners."

I thought that was a great exit line, but I didn't get out the door fast enough to miss his parting words.

"Is that chocolate on your shirt?" he asked with a leer.

I very maturely shot him the finger and decided it probably wouldn't hurt to grab another chocolate fudge sundae before giving Nick my statement. It was bound to cool off my overheated body.

5

TUESDAY

THE LAST WEEK OF SCHOOL WAS ALWAYS A DRAG, AND with Mr. Butler's death things were in even more of an upheaval than usual.

The funeral was scheduled for the following day at eleven o'clock, and I knew nothing short of my own death would excuse me from missing the event. The school would be closed for the day in honor of his memory.

In all honesty, I was still waiting for the truth to come out about my involvement in finding his body, but so far luck was on my side. Detective Dempsey had kept his word, much to my surprise. I wasn't used to dealing with men that had integrity. Of course, things were still early yet.

Whoever left the message on my machine hadn't called back, so I'd decided to pretend it was a prank and not take the matter too seriously. It definitely wasn't something to get Kate or Detective Dempsey in an uproar over, so I didn't bother mentioning it to either of them. They both had a tendency to overreact about things like that. Not to mention I'd probably have to sit through another afternoon of questioning like I had the day before when I'd been pressured into giving my statement. Detective Dempsey most certainly liked to dot all his I's and cross all his T's. An annoying habit in my opinion.

When the school bell rang at three-thirty on Tuesday, I grabbed my bags and ran to the teacher's parking lot, ready to earn some real money. I was forced to stop as I saw someone leaning against the side of my car with her arms crossed over her ample bosom. I growled low in my throat and narrowed my eyes.

"I'm in a hurry, Veronica. I don't have time to listen to your sexcapades today."

"What a shame," she said. "I'll have to send you the video."

"Slut."

"Bitch."

Her smile was devious and I knew she was waiting for the right time to spring something unexpected on me. I unlocked my car with the remote, and when she still didn't budge I wondered if I was going to have to physically remove her. Not that I was totally adverse to popping her one in the jaw, but probably the teacher's parking lot wasn't the best place to do so.

"You won't be so cocky once you're out on the street and your apartment is torn down."

"Give me a break," I said. "Do you honestly think I haven't found a place to live yet?" I looked her in the eye and dared her to dispute my claim. I halfway had a place to live, which by my way of think was better than nothing.

"Oh, do you mean that cute little house on Hutton Street?" Veronica asked coyly. "I was just talking to John

Hyatt about that house the other day. I was thinking it would be the perfect place for Greg and me to live after we're married this summer."

My vision hazed and I saw red. "Is there a reason you're trying to make my life miserable? Surely we can agree to stay out of each other's way for the rest of our lives."

"Don't pretend you don't know why things have to be this way between us. There's not enough room in Whiskey Bayou for the both of us, and I can promise it won't be me who runs out of town with my tail between my legs."

She walked to her own car two spaces over and gave me a little wave with the tips of her fingers and a sly smile as she drove out of the lot.

It took every ounce of self-control I possessed not to run her off the road as I sped out of the parking lot. I was going to have a talk with John Hyatt. Veronica Wade could steal as many men as she wanted to from me, but she wasn't going to get my house.

Whiskey Bayou Bank and Trust was diagonal to the Walker Whiskey Distillery and across the street from the fire station. Very convenient unless you needed to get money out at peak traffic time or during a fire.

Like the rest of the buildings on Main Street, it was a combination of original architecture and modern convenience, but there was something about the bank that gave me an icky feeling.

I'm pretty sure it was the smell. It was a weird combination of Pine Sol, money and old people that made my stomach churn every time I crossed the threshold.

I saw several people I knew and waved hello before I made my way to the back offices of the loan department. Kimberly Bowman was manning the desk out front, long red nails typing rapidly and the phone stuck between her ear and shoulder.

I went to school with Kimberly. She used to be Kimberly Johnson, but she married Tim Bowman right after high school and gave birth a short three months later. She only blanched slightly at the sight of me, which told me right away that something was wrong.

"Addison, what a surprise," she said, her smile a little too bright. "John's not in at the moment. Could I take a message?"

John Hyatt was a bottom-feeder of the worst kind. Oh, he was Mr. Big Smile in front of potential customers, but my mother had told me once that she suspected he was an abuser of epic proportions. She said our mailman of twenty-five years had told her he'd been putting a lot of those unmarked manila envelopes in John's mailbox. Everybody knows the unmarked envelopes mean there must be something dirty inside, otherwise there wouldn't be so much secrecy.

Just as Kimberly fed me this line I saw the slatted blind in the big glass window of John's office move slightly and a pair of hazel eyes appear.

"That's not true. I just saw his eyes, and I want to see him. I'm a customer at this bank and have every right to see my banker."

Kimberly was standing between me and my goal, wondering whether or not it was worth the broken fingernails to keep me from the office door, so she did the wise thing and got out of my way.

John, greasy smile in place, opened the door before I could steamroll through it. His light brown hair was neatly combed back and his face was freshly shaven. He wasn't a big man, barely taller than my own five feet eight inches, and he was whipcord lean. It was his commanding personality that made him seem larger than life. That and the fact he wore inserts in his shoes to make himself taller. He was only a few years older than me, but he was a respected member of the community, like his father and grandfather before him. I was going to change all that.

"Addison, how are you? Don't you look lovely today?"

"What the hell is going on around here, John? I want to know why Veronica Wade thinks she's going to buy my house."

He licked his lips nervously. "Now Addison, sometimes these things happen. This is business. In the real world the bottom line is all that anyone cares about."

"Don't you dare patronize me. I was told I had another sixty days before I had to come up with the rest of the money. That's the bottom line. I know how Veronica Wade works, and I hope for your sake that the sex was worth it because by the time my mother finishes spreading rumors about you, you'll be lucky to get a nice cushy job at the McDonald's down the street."

He sucked in air through his nostrils. I was revved and ready to go. I probably looked a little like the queen of the damned, but I didn't care. I didn't do mad well. Some women had a really effective mad, but once I got started all the blood rushed to my cheeks and the tears came to my eyes. I hardly ever cried. Unless I was angry.

I wiped my cheeks off and pointed a wet finger at John Hyatt.

"We had paperwork. I gave you money."

He held up his hand and managed to retain the air of authority and confidence he'd had before I walked through his door. "If you'd read the fine print, Ms. Holmes, you'd see that both parties have the option of backing out at any time during the sixty day waiting period. This bank has certainly done nothing wrong," he said smugly.

So maybe I hadn't had the time to read all the fine print, but you could bet your bottom dollar I was going to check into it as soon as I got home. And I wasn't ready to let John Hyatt off the hook just yet.

"You have not heard the end of this. Small town banks are only as good as their reputations. You're a worthless worm of a man, John Hyatt, and someday the way you treat people is going to come back and bite you in the ass. I will get my house. You shook on it, gave your word on it. You know what that tells me, John."

John shook his head no. Sweat beaded on his upper lip.

"It tells me your word doesn't mean shit," I said. I made sure to slam the door on the way out, and I ignored the stares and whispers as I left.

There is never such a thing as too much drama in Whiskey Bayou.

My anger didn't diminish as I headed back to my apartment. I was going to catch some cheaters in the act, and by God, their infidelity was going to pay for my new house.

I changed into black yoga pants and a matching tank top and pulled my long hair through a Savannah Sand Gnats hat. I filled my backpack with bottled water and trail mix and grabbed a Sudoku book to fill the time.

Now I was ready for a stakeout.

I jogged out to my car and took it as a sign from God that my life was taking a direction for the better since the sun was out and there wasn't a rain cloud in sight.

When I got closer to my car I realized that something was taped to the driver's side window. The picture distorted and of poor quality, but I got the gist.

It was a picture of me on the main stage of The Foxy Lady. I looked like I knew what I was doing in the still photograph, hanging upside down on that pole like I'd been born to be a stripper. I remembered precisely when the photo had been taken and by whom. Mr. Butler had been alive and well when he'd immortalized me on film. The problem was Mr. Butler wasn't so alive and well now, which meant he couldn't have been the one to tape the photo to my window.

I looked around but didn't see anyone skulking about or looking guilty—not surprising since anyone standing in the parking lot of my apartment complex for more than five minutes had a ninety percent chance of being hit by falling debris. The problem with this latest development was that the most likely person to have Mr. Butler's phone was his killer. And now the killer was taunting me. Never a good situation to be in.

I folded the picture and stuck it in my bag in case I ever decided to take up scrapbooking and got into my car. One stupid picture left by a killer wasn't going to slow me down. No sirree. My life was headed in a new direction, and this new direction was going to have nothing to do with strip clubs or dead bodies.

I decided to do a bit of snooping for John Hyatt's fiancé before I went into Savannah. I drove down Main Street and took a left on Whiskey Road. John Hyatt lived on the corner in a large three-story plantation house with an expansive front yard and beds of flowers everywhere. Scarlett O'Hara would have loved John Hyatt's house.

There was a three-car garage attached to the house on the street side, and a wrought iron fence surrounded the Hyatt compound. It seemed like a lot of space for one man, but he'd inherited it from his parents and seemed to enjoy the lavish lifestyle it represented. There was a white van parked in the driveway that I knew wasn't John's, so my curiosity level went up a notch.

I looked through John's file one more time to refresh my memory. Fanny Kimble and John Hyatt had been engaged for thirteen months, and their wedding was scheduled for October of this year. That seemed like a long time to be engaged to me, but I wasn't really an expert on relationships. Fanny was a true southern debutante, so a wedding that would eventually cost more than the governor's inaugural ball might take longer than normal to plan.

Fanny stated in her interview with Kate that she was only allowed to stay the night on Mondays and Thursdays, and John had to pick her up from her house so the neighbors wouldn't gossip if they saw her car parked in his driveway all night.

"Hmm, a cautious man, John Hyatt. Reputation is everything."

I drove down the street and turned around in the cul-de-sac. I pulled into the driveway of John Hyatt's neighbor and got out of the car, surveying the neighborhood as nonchalantly as possible. It was a wealthy neighborhood of men that worked sixty-hour weeks and socialite wives who spent all their time in Savannah shopping. The houses were deserted at this time of day.

Except for Victor Mooney's house.

Victor Mooney had never worked a day in his life and thrived on the drama of others. Nobody knew where his money came from, but he had enough to buy himself a new Cadillac every year and donate money to projects when he wanted them named after him.

He had the door open for me before I made it to the front porch, and I hoped my hunch would pay off.

"Good afternoon, Mr. Mooney," I said with my company smile in place—the smile that dripped sincerity and showed a lot of teeth. It was a southern technique perfected at birth.

Victor Mooney was in his late sixties and resembled a freshly scrubbed pot-bellied pig. His skin was pale and pink and his round belly sat on two stubby legs. He always wore red suspenders and carried peppermints in his pockets.

"Addison, what brings you here on this beautiful day? A girl your age should be out leading some man about by the nose, not visiting with dirty old men."

His cheeks pinkened and I wanted to pat the top of his bristly white head. His blue eyes twinkled as he bent down to kiss my hand. He led me into his living room by the elbow and sat me in an uncomfortable Queen Anne chair that was made for midgets.

"I'm actually doing a favor for a friend of mine," I said, deciding to be completely honest. "Do you remember Kate?"

"Of course I do. You girls sure did get into a mess of trouble when you were younger," he said, chuckling. "She's got that detective agency up near Savannah, doesn't she?"

"Yes, that's right."

"And you're working a case and want my help." Mr. Mooney's face was brimming with excitement and it was hard not to get caught up in his enthusiasm.

"Yes, but whatever we discuss needs to stay between you and me." I knew I was breaking all kinds of clauses in the contract Kate had me sign, but surely she'd understand as long as the end result came out okay.

"Oh, yes, yes, of course. I'm considered somewhat of a

confidant in Whiskey Bayou. I know all kinds of things about people that I've never told a soul. Did you know that Harley Baines uses Viagra?"

"No," I said, trying to get the portly city councilman out of my head.

"And Maggie Murchison can't get pregnant because her husband had a vasectomy three years ago," he went on.

"Oh, poor woman." There was no way I was keeping that bit of information from my mother. Roger Murchison deserved to be lynched for that act of treachery.

"What about John Hyatt?" I asked.

"Ahh, yes. I should have known he was your target. I hear he's decided to let Veronica Wade buy that house he promised you." Victor clucked his tongue in disappointment. "I have a good mind to go down to the bank and withdraw all my money. I'd rather keep it in a shoebox under the bed than deal with a dishonest banker."

"Does Mr. Hyatt have people in and out of his house frequently?" I asked.

"Oh, yes. It's like a circus over there all the time. There are always cars in and out."

"How can you see the cars in the driveway if the garage is on the other side of the house?"

"I can see almost the whole street from my third floor balcony," he said sheepishly. "The white van belongs to Maria Vasquez. She cleans his house and does the laundry three days a week. And on Mondays the lawn service comes out and tends to the mowing and weeding. And on Friday mornings a man comes to clean the pool. It's all very scheduled, like clockwork."

"What about Monday and Thursday nights?" I asked, thinking of Fanny's statement that those were the only two nights she was allowed to stay over.

"Oh, he goes to pick up his fiancé around six-thirty. Sometimes they go out to dinner, but they're usually back by eight or so. Those are the only nights she sleeps over. He takes her back home around seven-thirty the next morning."

"Do you ever see any other women at the house?"

He stopped and looked at me, and for the first time I wondered if he was going to lie to me and cover for John Hyatt. He finally sighed and shook his head. "I don't understand why a man who has a beautiful woman at his side would go out looking for something else," he said with disapproval. "There is another woman, and it seems like she practically lives there. I don't know her name, but she's got long blonde hair and a large chest. She parks a white Lexus in the garage and sneaks in and out at all hours. I wish I could give you a better description, but the only time I ever see her is if I catch a glimpse through one of the upstairs windows."

"That's all right, Mr. Mooney. You've helped me a lot," I said as I stood to go. "Maybe you could keep watching for me and keep a log of the times you see this woman. If you know what you're looking for maybe you can get a better description."

I handed Mr. Mooney a card with my number on it and said goodbye. I knew two facts: Veronica Wade had somehow convinced John Hyatt to give her my house, and Veronica had long blonde hair and a large chest. It was too soon to believe in coincidences, but the evidence so far was pretty damning.

I sped into Savannah casting nervous glances at my clock. It was three minutes till five as I parked my Z at the corner of Jefferson and West Gaston and waited for Barry Crumb to leave his office for the day. I sighted through the lens of the Nikon Megapixel Digital Camera Kate had left in my mailbox at school, just to make sure I had a clear shot of the door.

In all honesty, I had no idea how to work the camera. It had way too many buttons and moving parts for me to feel comfortable using it, but Kate had assured me all I needed to do was point and shoot.

I opened Barry's file and looked at the 5x7 shot of him paper-clipped to the inside and shuddered. I tried hard not to dry heave at his photograph, but it took more will power than I possessed. Why anyone would want to sleep with Barry Crumb was a mystery to me.

Dr. Crumb was an OB/GYN with an office in the heart of Savannah, so he did a brisk business. He wasn't having financial troubles, just the opposite. Business was booming for Dr. Crumb. But his wife of thirteen years had a suspicion that Dr. Crumb was spreading his love around, and apparently it was my job to find out one way or another.

I checked my watch one more time. 5:15. His car was still in the lot, so he hadn't slipped past my attention while I was getting settled in with all the necessary comforts. The thought did cross my mind that I might need a new car for my new career, but James Bond seemed to get by okay with a flashy sports car so I could too.

The sight of my target brought me out of my daydream. "Bingo."

I sighted Dr. Crumb with the Nikon and took a couple of quick photos to make sure the thing worked. He got into his new Lexus convertible and checked his appearance in the rearview mirror.

I put the Z in drive and kept about a block behind him, making sure to keep a couple of cars between us. I followed him down Montgomery and flipped on my blinker as he turned right on West Bay. My adrenaline pumped and my heart pounded as I swerved around some pedestrians, never taking my eyes off of Dr. Crumb.

I called Kate on my cell phone as I followed his Lexus into the Hyatt Regency parking lot.

"Have you seen this guy?" I said by way of greeting. "That's not even a face a mother would love. How is this guy bagging chicks?"

"It takes all kinds," Kate said. "Plus, his wife told me he has other attributes that can't be seen on first impression, if you get my drift."

"Huh," I said and disconnected.

I took a couple more shots of Dr. Crumb entering the hotel and sat back into my waiting position. I'd found that sitting still by myself was much harder than sitting still with Kate in the car, so in about half an hour's time I'd eaten all my trail mix, finished two Sudoku puzzles and graded thirty quizzes.

The summer sun was still high, and I started to wonder how Dr. Crumb could have sex in the daylight. Greg and I had never done it in the daylight. If we were going to do it at all, it had to be right before *The Tonight Show* came on. Greg had it down to a science. He'd finish at exactly 10:29, roll over and flip on the T.V. Though, quite frankly, even though the sex was terrible, there were times I missed having a man sleep over. Greg never complained about having to get up in the middle of the night and plug a hole in the roof when he slept over.

"Okay, don't go there." I was through thinking about Greg.

I slid out of the Z to stretch my legs and cure my boredom. I jogged in place, did some stretches and looked at my watch again. 6:42. So apparently Dr. Crumb had some staying power.

I was on my third set of leg stretches when I saw Dr. Crumb come out of the hotel. And he wasn't alone.

"Holy shit."

I jerked my car door open to get the camera and somehow my head and the door made contact.

"Ouch, shit, why me?" I rubbed the spot furiously and grabbed the camera with my other hand. I hunkered behind my car and wiped my still watering eyes before looking through the lens. I'd hit my head in the same damn spot I had yesterday.

"Gotcha."

I snapped a couple of photos and was especially proud of the one I got of him in a torrid embrace. Mrs. Crumb was going to be extremely surprised. Dr. Crumb didn't have a girlfriend. Dr. Crumb had a boyfriend.

I guess I could see the appeal of looking at something a little different when all you did was inspect vaginas all day.

I was a little torn about catching Dr. Crumb in the act. I held the potential to ruin thirteen years of marriage by showing his wife a few photos. On the other hand, he was cheating and I really needed the extra paycheck. Technically, I wouldn't be ruining his marriage because Kate would be showing the photos to Mrs. Crumb.

Guilt absolved.

This revelation deserved a trip to Dairy Queen. It was just after seven and I hadn't eaten dinner. I parked the Z and went inside, hoping they'd give me a bag of ice for my throbbing forehead if I ordered enough food.

"Geez, lady. What did you do to your head?"

So much for hoping no one would notice.

"I had a little accident. I'll take an Oreo Blizzard and a bag of ice, please."

LILIANA HART

I collected the ice cream and headed back to my car with the ice pressed to my forehead.

"Ahhh—"

I pressed the electronic remote and screamed as a hand squeezed my shoulder.

"What the hell are you screaming for?"

Oh, I so did not need this right now. I tried to make a quick deal with God, swearing I wouldn't miss church for the rest of the year if he'd just make this man go away.

"Hello—Addison?" He snapped his fingers in front of my face a couple of times. "What are you doing?"

"I was praying that God would make you go away."

Nick laughed and the sound turned my insides to jelly. It was deeply masculine and shivered all the way down my spine. It had to be because I had a head injury. There was no other excuse.

"And what do you mean, why am I screaming? You don't just walk up to a woman in a parking lot and grab her. I thought I was being mugged."

"I called your name, but you were so busy making orgasmic noises with your ice cream that you didn't hear me."

Heat washed over my face. He was right. I had been making orgasmic noises. I loved ice cream. A lot.

"I'm going home. My head hurts and I can't think fast enough to spar with you tonight. What are you doing here anyway?"

"I was getting gas across the street, and it was hard to miss the flaming red blur and squealing tires as you sped into the parking lot. It must have been an ice cream emergency."

I must have hit my head harder than I'd thought because the next thing I knew everything went dark, and

66

when I woke up I was in a place I'd never been before, and it smelled fabulous.

"You smell so good," I said, taking a big whiff of Nick's neck. I think I might have accidentally licked him, but I couldn't be too sure.

"Well, I do try to shower everyday," he said, leaning my head back so he could look me in the eyes. "That's a pretty nasty bump you have there. Do you want to tell me what happened?"

His face was close enough that his breath feathered my lips, and I sighed as I felt the familiar stomach clutch of attraction. You'd think my body and my brain would be in agreement over the fact that Nick was all wrong for me, but my body insisted on being stubborn.

"I hit it on my steering wheel yesterday when I ran you off the road."

"That would explain why you looked so crazy in Kate's office. Maybe you jarred something loose."

"And then tonight I ran into my car door when I was trying to get to the camera to take some pictures. I think I hit it harder than I thought."

I looked around, realizing I was sprawled on the ground of a Dairy Queen parking lot. A small crowd had gathered to stare at me, while others walked by like they saw women littering parking lots every day. Nick's arms felt better holding me close than I wanted to admit, so I was reluctant to tell him I was okay to stand up when a sudden thought came to me. I jumped up and groaned as the ache in my head intensified. "Where's my ice cream? Is it okay?"

Nick looked at me a little incredulously, but obviously saw the determination in my face and looked around for my ice cream.

"Sorry, kiddo. The ice cream is toast. If I would have

known how much you wanted it I would have let you fall to the ground and grabbed it instead."

"Well, shit."

"Looks like. Sorry."

"Why are you being so nice to me? I thought you were the tough guy without a heart."

"Don't let my concern fool you. I saw Kate's camera on the seat and knew she'd be pissed if it was stolen while you were lying on the ground unconscious."

"Gee, thanks." I stood up shakily and got into the driver's seat, wondering how many times I could embarrass myself in front of the same man. The answer wasn't comforting.

"I'm going to follow you home. You still look a little shaky."

I normally would have told him thanks, but no thanks, but I was still feeling a little unsteady.

"I'd appreciate that."

We made it to my apartment with no major mishaps, and I decided to park close to the stairs and take my chances with falling brick crushing my car. I wanted nothing more than to crawl up the stairs and fall into bed.

I was surprised when the car door opened and Nick was there to help me gather my things and push me up to my apartment.

"You're ruining your tough guy image."

"I just like to make sure there are no dead bodies on my watch."

"You're such a giver."

I unlocked the front door and Nick shoved it open for me so I could stumble inside. I fell face first onto the couch and decided everything would be okay once the room stopped spinning. I heard Nick rummaging around in the kitchen and rolled over so I could see what he was doing. The light hurt my eyes, so I lay there with them closed and hoped he would leave soon.

A bag of ice mysteriously appeared on my forehead.

"Ahh—thank you."

"I don't know why I have this insane urge to take care of you," Nick said. "It seems like you're used to having these things happen to you."

"Yep. Someday I'll tell you about my sophomore year of college. This is nothing compared to that."

"Are you holding up okay?" Nick asked.

I stayed silent because I wasn't sure exactly what traumatic event he was talking about. There had already been so many.

"About finding your principal dead in a parking lot," he clarified.

"As well as can be expected. The funeral's tomorrow."

"Yeah, I'll be there with a few other undercover officers." He squeezed the back of my neck between his thumb and forefinger and I felt like purring. I was a little tense for some reason.

"Have you found out anything about Mr. Butler's murder?"

"We looked at the video tape from the parking lot, but the location of the stabbing was just out of range of the camera. We're in the process of identifying everyone we see on the tapes from inside the club as well as the license plate numbers from the parking lot."

"Stabbing?" For some reason not knowing how Mr. Butler had died made it seem less real. I hiccuped into a couch pillow and squinted my eyes closed. "What the hell was he doing in that place?" I asked, not expecting an answer. "What the hell was I doing there? If he hadn't seen me on stage he never would have left so soon."

"This isn't your fault, Addison. You were both just in the wrong place at the wrong time. It happens to everyone."

Surely he didn't expect me to believe that things like that happen to everyone. I was a freak of nature, probably cursed at birth by Rumpelstiltskin or some other crazy shit. If Nick Dempsey had any indication of self-preservation, he would run like hell in the opposite direction and never speak to me again.

"Is there anything you need me to get you before I leave?"

"There's some aspirin in the kitchen cabinet above the coffee pot, and there's a half pint of hazelnut ice cream in the freezer."

"It seems to me you have an obsession with ice cream. Maybe you need to get a man to help control these urges."

"I had a man. He left me for the home economics teacher. I'll pass, thanks."

I heard him rummaging through the freezer and sat up a little. Nick wasn't such a bad guy.

"Looks like Dr. Crumb is guilty," he said, pausing by the table with all my stakeout paraphernalia on it. "Nice photos."

"Thanks. I'm sure it'll give Mrs. Crumb a surprise, but it's better to know for sure than to always wonder."

I took the aspirin and knocked it back with a spoonful of hazelnut ice cream.

"Sounds like you know from experience."

"Nah. I was pretty much blindsided."

"Then he obviously wasn't the right man for you. I think I'd notice if someone that mattered seemed like they were drifting. Why'd you want to marry a guy like that, anyway?

I kept my eyes closed and decided I had a better chance of getting him out of my apartment if I just answered the question. "It's not like he started out as lying, cheating scum," I said. "He was charming and smart, and I was almost thirty."

"Ohhhh," he said laughing. "Old maid status."

"Shut up. In the city being thirty and single is no big deal, but in Whiskey Bayou everyone is expected to marry and reproduce shortly after graduation. You have no idea what it's like to walk down the street and have people look at you like your ovaries are no better than dried prunes."

"You're right. I don't."

"Greg was exactly what I was looking for in a man. He had a respectable job and he would have been a good father."

"And he was cheating scum."

"Yeah," I said depressed. "That, too."

"You never mentioned passion. Where was the spark? You can't spend fifty years of your life admiring his charisma and intelligence."

"Spark doesn't last," I said, getting irritated because I knew he was at least partially right. "It's never a good idea to let hormones make the important decisions in life." I opened my eyes and finally looked him in the eye. His cocky grin was not reassuring.

"Maybe next time you should look for someone who gives you better orgasms than a pint of Haagen Dazs."

"Get out," I said, wishing I had the strength to throw something in his direction.

"Hey, look on the bright side. Right at this moment a

whole room full of cops are watching you take your clothes off on tape. I'm sure you'll find a man in no time after that."

"Out," I said and pointed toward the door. I ignored his laughter as he let himself out of my apartment. I tried to console myself with a bite of ice cream, but I realized he was right. I did have better orgasms with frozen desserts than with a man.

As far as I was concerned, real orgasms were myths anyway. And any man watching me strip on that tape would probably suffer from erectile dysfunction for the rest of his life.

I decided to take back the nice thoughts I was having about Nick Dempsey. He was still a jerk, and I'd had more than my fill of jerks lately. Greg and Nick were packaged differently, but I had a sinking feeling that they were very much the same on the inside.

6

I WOKE UP TO MUSIC BLARING AND MY HEAD POUNDING. I slapped feebly at the alarm, because I had no desire in my present condition to listen to Paul Simon singing about some woman who had diamonds on the soles of her shoes, and made my way to the kitchen for more aspirin. I caught my reflection in the toaster. My forehead was an interesting shade of purple, yellow and green.

I staggered into the shower and let the hot water and steam work its magic on my body. Of course, the hot water in my apartment lasted for exactly four minutes and thirty-two seconds, so I've learned to be efficient once under the spray. Adequate shower time was definitely a priority in my new home.

I turned off the water, got out and wiped down the fogged mirror with a towel.

Eeek!

I should have let it stay foggy. The yellow and green on my forehead had disappeared at some point during the shower, and all that was left was dark purple and black and a big lump. It was an appropriate color for attending a funeral.

I was a little relieved to see the lump. I'd read somewhere once that it was always important that a lump form when you had a head injury because if it didn't it meant your brain was bleeding on the inside.

I was good to go.

My hair was wet and plastered around my head, and a brilliant idea popped into my brain. I needed bangs. Bangs would solve all of my problems. They'd give me a new look and cover my massive lump. Problem solved.

I snipped at a few strands of hair and was satisfied I'd achieved my new look. I did a full makeup job and blow-dried my hair. The bruise was still showing after all that work, but there wasn't much else I could do.

I winced as I heard a deep rumble of thunder loud enough to rattle the panes in my windows. I heard a crash of glass and went searching through the apartment until I found the broken shards on the floor of my bedroom. The thunder had rattled a few panes right out of the window, so there was a gaping hole in my bedroom, though it did bring in a nice breeze.

"Great. Don't you know I don't have time for this today?" I asked God. Not that he was probably going to help me out since I hadn't visited him in a while.

I swept up the glass and taped a garbage bag over the hole with duct tape. While I was in cleaning mode, I made my bed, vacuumed the floor and put the cans of beets, salmon and sauerkraut in alphabetical order in my pantry.

They were the same cans that had been there since I'd moved in, and I'd already decided I'd leave them to be demolished with the rest of the building when I moved out. But that was no reason not to be tidy. Or perhaps I was stalling.

At ten o'clock I dug through my closet until I found my funeral suit. It was the same black suit I'd worn to my father's funeral and overwhelming sadness took hold of me so quickly that I shoved it back in the closet and looked for something else.

The only other black dress I had in my closet was a 1950's wool day dress with a flared skirt and thin black belt. I'd found it on the clearance rack at Neiman's for a quarter of its original price, but it still had the tags on it because there was never a good time to wear wool in Georgia. As soon as the fabric got wet I was going to feel like I was being suffocated by a wooly mammoth, but I pulled it off the hanger anyway.

I skipped the pantyhose, slipped on a pair of three-inch strappy sandals, grabbed a pink rain slicker and shoved a bunch of Kleenex in the coat pockets.

I parked my car in the parking lot and slogged my way up to the doors of The Blessed Sacrament Catholic Church behind all the other mourners. Funerals were attended by all in Whiskey Bayou. All the businesses closed except for the Good Luck Café, and that was only because they had to be prepared for the onslaught of mourners that would hit the tiny restaurant after the burial.

The church was packed to its full capacity by the time I found a seat on a back pew. Both balconies were filled and the choir loft was crammed with singers in white robes. Mr. Butler's casket was mahogany and draped with a white cloth, and the casket was closed to keep the guests from having an up close and personal look at what a body looked like after an autopsy.

Mr. Butler's family walked in a procession from the back of the church to the front pews reserved for family. I didn't recognize any of them because Mr. Butler had been a transfer from a Savannah high school several years before, and he'd kept his Savannah residence instead of moving to Whiskey Bayou. There was a younger version of Mr. Butler at the end of the procession, which I assumed had to be a younger brother. He had the same sandy colored hair and slight build.

Unfortunately, genetics hadn't been kind to the Butler brothers because they all looked like Mr. Burns from The Simpsons, and after seeing their mother lead the procession down the aisle it was very obvious that her boys got their looks from her.

The youngest brother turned as he passed my pew and gave me a look of such startling hatred that I sucked in a breath and flushed in embarrassment as the people sitting around me began to titter nervously. I slunk back in my seat and wished I'd worn one of those big black hats with the netting on them.

"We are here to today to celebrate the life of Bernard Ulysses Basil Butler."

I took out a Kleenex and covered my face so no one would see my smile. How could anyone name a poor, helpless baby that?

I kneeled and sat and sang and kneeled some more with the rest of the mourners. I didn't even start crying until the woman next to me started blowing her nose and hiccupping. We kneeled again and prayed some more, and I listened as Mr. Butler's family and friends told stories about the man they loved.

I'd been right about the young man who'd given me the hateful look. His name was Robbie, and he was the youngest of the five Butler brothers. I had an uneasy feeling in the pit of my stomach as soon as he took his place at the podium.

"My brother was a good man," Robbie said in a shaky voice. His eyes were rimmed red and filled with sorrow. "He was a man who touched the souls of everyone he met."

I couldn't help but think how Mr. Butler had been touching the soul of the woman that was giving him the lap dance, but that probably wasn't what Robbie was talking about.

"Bernie was my brother. And my guardian angel. He always protected me, no matter what the cost. But he had no one to protect him when his life was so viciously taken."

Robbie's eyes found mine and stayed steady, the hatred not a figment of my imagination as I had first hoped.

"Bernie was my guardian angel, but he was also human. A human who made errors and bad decisions. He fell victim to the beauty and seduction of a Jezebel. A woman who might as well have stabbed him in the heart herself."

The crowd was looking around nervously, trying to see who Robbie was staring at so intently. I was doing the same thing. I wanted to see a Jezebel just like every other person in the room.

I could hear Mrs. Butler openly sobbing from the front of the room and the choir was shifting anxiously, prepared to burst into song at a moments notice.

"Bernie was a victim. This woman teased him with her body and led him astray with promises of immoral acts.

Those of you that know Bernie and have heard the gossip know that he would have never been at an establishment like the one he was murdered at unless he was lured."

Robbie's gaze had never faltered from mine during his speech, and it hit me like a bolt of lightning that he was talking about me. I was the other woman. The Jezebel.

My eyes widened and he gave me an evil smile. Why would Robbie think that I was involved with Mr. Butler? The only thing I could think of was that he knew my secret. But how? And it still didn't explain why he thought we'd be involved.

"I ask each and every one of you to be the guardian angels over the people you love. Protect them from evildoers and harlots, and don't let the task fall to your neighbors, because how well do you really know the person sitting next you?"

Robbie Butler left the podium and took a seat next to his mother, putting a comforting arm around her frail body. The rest of the church sat still in silence with the fear of God upon them. If my knees weren't so sore I'd think I was sitting in the middle of a bunch of Lutherans caught at a Baptist tent revival. As far as eulogies went, it left a lot to be desired.

I sat and kneeled and prayed for another half hour before the pallbearers carried Mr. Butler down the center aisle. I kept my head down and looked at my feet as the family followed slowly behind the body. I wasn't up to seeing Robbie Butler's accusing glare again.

The rows began to file out and everyone was invited to walk next door to the cemetery. Umbrellas popped up and I used the crowd of people as cover to sneak to my car and get away.

I'd been called a harlot, a Jezebel and a seducer of men in the House of the Lord. Just because no one knew it was me Robbie had been talking about didn't mean the barb didn't sting. If I was going to be accused of being a slut, I damn well wanted the sex to back it up.

It was after noon by the time I got back to my apartment. I changed into a short, black denim skirt and an electric blue halter top to make myself feel better about the lump on my head and looked for something to eat, but the lunch fairy hadn't visited while I'd been gone.

When the rain still hadn't stopped by three o'clock, I ran downstairs and borrowed a couple of boxes of double fudge brownie mix from Mrs. Nowicki so I would stop worrying about Robbie Butler, my principal's murder, the money for my house and Nick Dempsey—not necessarily in that order.

"Okay. I'm just going to have to tough this out. The cheating scums of the earth can't be caught if I'm afraid of a little rain."

A *little* rain might have been under exaggerating just a bit. It was a torrential downpour that no sane person would go back out in. It was a hell of a day to dig a grave.

I wrapped the brownies up, exchanged my sandals for a pair of cute pink galoshes with daisies painted on them and put on my pink raincoat. I was glad I'd been lazy and parked close to the building once I saw how high the water was rising in the parking lot. Galoshes weren't helpful in a swimming pool.

As I suspected, there was no one crazy enough to be out in the weather but me, so the drive to Kate's office was made fairly quickly, considering I was mostly driving blind.

"I smell brownies."

I had barely gotten in the door when Kate and ten other people started making their way towards me. All of Kate's employees were former law enforcement of some kind, and they were like Pavlov's dogs over day-old jelly donuts, much less homemade brownies.

"I only made two dozen so you'll have to share."

"That's not the way it works here," Kate said, grabbing two. "This office is about survival of the fittest."

I grabbed two for myself and handed the rest of the brownies over before I was accidentally eaten. I followed Kate to her office and brought the camera and notes I had collected on Barry Crumb.

"That bruise looks painful."

"Dammit. I didn't think anyone would notice."

I peeled off my raincoat and hung it on the coat rack in the corner of Kate's office. Kate was a big film noir fan, so everything in her office looked like it just came out of a black and white movie, right down to the slatted blinds and black lettering on her office door.

She was wearing a pinstripe suit today, as equally shapeless as the one she had on the last time I saw her, and sensible flat shoes. I guess the jacket had to have plenty of room to hide her gun.

"I like the bangs by the way. And the outfit makes for a nice diversion," Kate said.

"Thanks. Obviously not diverting enough if my forehead was the first thing you noticed when I walked in."

"Well, technically I noticed the brownies first. And maybe I noticed the bruise because Nick stopped in this morning and told me what happened last night."

"I don't think I like Nick. Nick has the sensitivity of a clod of dirt."

"Well, he's a man. But he is a damn good cop. He seems to have developed a little bit of a soft spot for you."

"Oh, yeah. I could tell that right off last night when he told me he only stayed around to help me because you'd be pissed if I got your camera stolen."

"If he didn't care a little he would have let you fall to the ground and taken the camera with him to make sure it was safe."

"Okay, so Nick's a saint. I'd just as soon he achieved sainthood by bothering somebody else. I've already dealt with enough jerks in my life."

"Oh, so you're telling me you weren't attracted to him when he first walked in yesterday? I've known you too long to not know when you're hot for someone."

"Sure I was attracted. The man's a god. He just has the personality of a troll. If I could keep him from talking and then have my way with him everything would be fine, but I have a feeling he's a hard man to shut up."

"You're letting this deal with Greg make you cynical." ·

"I know. I'm just so pissed off about everything. My life is spiraling down the toilet."

I blew my new bangs out of my eyes and wondered what I could have been thinking. Now I'd have to go through that awkward growing out stage.

"How was the funeral?" Kate asked.

"Long, sad, boring. The usual," I said. "And Mr. Butler's brother got up in front of the whole congregation and called me a harlot, but other than that it was the same old, same old."

"What?"

"Well, he didn't actually say *That Addison Holmes is a whore beyond all reasonable doubt*, but he was looking right at me when he gave the eulogy about his brother being seduced. He really looked like he hated me. It was scary."

I thought about the anonymous message I'd gotten on the phone and the photograph taped to my window and wondered if Robbie Butler could be the guilty party.

"If he didn't call you by name, then you've got nothing to worry about. Maybe he has a glass eye and couldn't look at anyone but you."

"You could be right. But I've always thought glass eyes were kind of expressionless, not hate-filled and menacing."

"Like I said, don't worry about it. You've got bigger problems with John Hyatt and Veronica Wade. Not to mention the fact that it's been a while since you've had sex."

"I don't understand why relationships are so difficult for me," I said. "I'm not hideous. And I've got a steady income."

"It'll come, honey. When you're not even looking for it. Don't settle just because it's something you want. You'd have been settling with Greg. Just look at me and Mike. I never wanted to get married, but then I almost shot him and he almost arrested me and then we fell in love and put the handcuffs to good use."

Mike had been a detective for five years when Kate went into the academy, so they hadn't run in the same circles. They'd met by complete accident when Kate had caught Mike skulking around her apartment complex looking for a kid who'd just knocked over a liquor store. Only Kate didn't know that. She'd thought he was a burglar and knocked him over the head with her Smith & Wesson 9mm pistol. Mike had retaliated by taking her off guard when he regained consciousness and handcuffing her to the pipes on the outside of the building. The fireworks between them hadn't stopped since.

"I was over Greg the minute he cheated. I'm just

looking for someone fun. Someone that I can talk to and relax with and have crazy sex with. I'm sure you're right. When my soul mate comes along I'll know it."

"Which is why I've set up a date for you tomorrow night," Kate said. "He'll be by to pick you up at seven. Wear something slutty."

"I don't want to go on a blind date. Who did you set me up with? It's not Mike's cousin, is it? Because I really don't think we'll suit. He's an infant."

"No, it's not Mike's cousin. It's a surprise. Just be ready at seven and keep an open mind."

"Oh, yeah, that sounds promising."

I polished off the rest of my brownie and remembered why I had come to begin with. "Speaking of cheating bastards, look at the photos of Barry Crumb. I caught him red-handed, so to speak."

I handed Kate the camera and sat back with a satisfied smile on my face, my feet propped up on the corner of her desk. All was right in the world of justice.

"This is such a cool job, Kate. I have to thank you for giving me the chance to do this. It kind of takes the pressure off of my life to see how crappy everyone else's is."

"These are good shots. It's enough to give to Mrs. Crumb anyway. I'll leave it in her hands what she wants to do about it though. Who are you going after next?"

I decided not to mention that I'd already broken the rules by having Victor Mooney keep an eye on John Hyatt. Kate wouldn't understand my reasoning. What I really needed was a partner. It was hard to be in two places at one time.

"I've still got open files on Gretchen Wilder, John Hyatt and Harry Manilow. The Wilder file seems pretty interesting. From its size it looks like she's been a client for awhile. You'd think her husband would want to save the money he spends hiring you and just file for divorce. She's obviously not going to stop having affairs."

"Neither one of the Wilders are going to stop having affairs. They keep us on retainer to photograph each other with different partners. And the more graphic the picture the better. Apparently it's their version of foreplay."

"So why am I even wasting my time if we know for sure she's cheating?"

"Because they pay us an exorbitant amount of money to provide the proof for them. We're not marriage counselors or divorce attorneys. We just do what we're paid to do."

"People are weird," I said shaking my head. "That takes all the fun out of it for me."

We both paused in our conversation at the knock on the door, but it opened before Kate could invite whoever was on the other side in.

"Looks like I missed out on the brownies," Nick said as he put a stack of files on Kate's desk. "Maybe I could talk you into making me some more since I was so nice to you last night."

I took my feet off the desk and tried to give the appearance that I could be somewhat ladylike when the situation demanded. I didn't trust the look in his eyes.

"That sounds like a fair trade. Thanks again for your help."

I could be nice when I wanted to be. It's just that there was something about Nick that made me want to be contrary.

"I'm out of here, Kate." I grabbed my coat off the rack and shrugged it on. "I've got the Wilders to satisfy."

"Remember, the juicier the picture the better."

"Yeah, yeah, I know. See you around," I said to Nick.

"Hey, wait a sec," he called back before I could reach the door.

I waited for him wearily as he approached, wondering what he was going to say to piss me off this time. I inhaled swiftly and held it there as I watched his hand move towards my breast. My whole body was on fire with one small touch of his finger, and I watched him smile in satisfaction at my reaction and bring the small piece of brownie that had fallen on my shirt to his mouth.

"Mmmm—good brownie."

There was a small part of me that wanted to punch him in the face, but mostly I just wanted to rip my clothes off.

I didn't dignify giving him a response because I couldn't get my tongue to work. I grabbed my things to my chest and walked out the door, shoulders straight.

"Stupid jerk, stupid, stupid—idiot."

I wasn't sure if I was talking about Nick or myself. Probably a little of both. I stood on the sidewalk in front of Kate's office and let the rain sizzle off my overheated body. I didn't need these complications in my life right now. Want, yes. Need, no.

There was plenty of time before I had to act as a marital aid to Gretchen Wilder, so I decided to follow up with John Hyatt. I thought the best course of action was to see if I could catch sight of the mystery woman who was spending so much time at the Hyatt mansion. School was out for the day, so if the mystery woman was Veronica as I suspected she might be there already.

I used my cell phone to call the bank. A woman answered, but I didn't recognize her voice.

"May I speak to John Hyatt, please?" I asked, crossing my fingers that she didn't recognize my voice and just hang up.

"I'm sorry, but Mr. Hyatt is attending meetings today. He won't be back in the office until tomorrow. Would you like to leave a message on his voice mail?"

"No thanks, I'll just call again tomorrow," I said and hung up.

I left Savannah at light speed and headed back to Whiskey Bayou, sure that John Hyatt and the mystery tart, a.k.a Veronica Wade, were about to get caught in the act.

Once I got into town I was glad to see that the weather was still keeping everyone indoors. I drove down Main Street ten miles over the speed limit, passing the train depot, The Good Luck Cafe, the whiskey distillery and the fire station before I took a left and headed into the residential area of Whiskey Bayou. I had a plan, and it might even be a well-thought-out plan.

My parents had lived in the same small, cottage style house their entire married life, and when my dad died last year my mom got two German Shepherd puppies to keep her company.

People always comment on my parents' house because it's so out of the ordinary. "It looks like a fairy tale from Hansel and Gretel or Snow White," they'd always say. That weirded me out as a kid because who would want to live in a place where an old woman shoved kids into her oven? I'd gotten over it for the most part.

I pulled behind the 1969 Dodge Charger my mom had bought off eBay with the insurance money she'd gotten after my dad died—it was an exact replica of the "General Lee" from the Dukes of Hazzard.

I sloshed my way to the detached garage at the back of the house. My dad had been an avid collector of nothing and everything, so I knew my best chances of finding what I was looking for were in the garage.

The walls were lined with tools, some of which had never been used, and there were shelves filled with fishing lures and golf clubs, two sports I was pretty sure my dad had never played. There was a telescope in the corner he'd bought when I was going through my astronaut phase and a Samurai sword he'd bought at a flea market. I found what I was looking for in a box marked hunting gear. Go figure.

I dug through layers of bright orange vests and about a hundred bottles of buck urine before I found the binoculars. The houses on John Hyatt's street all backed up to Magnolia Park. If I was lucky I'd catch a glimpse of the culprit through the windows from long distance.

I realized once I turned into Magnolia Park and weaved my way through mud holes and giant trees that my plan wasn't as well-thought-out as I'd imagined.

On a bright sunny day, what happened inside John Hyatt's house would be an open book—the entire backside of his house was glass and looked out onto the pool. But in a deluge of rain with zero percent visibility it was pretty much a bust.

"Come on, Addison. To be a private investigator you have to think like a private investigator. Think, think, think," I said. "What would Nick do?"

Nick would probably suggest that we make good use of the back seat or tell me to find a different job. Subconscious Nick was no help at all.

I started the car back up and weaved my way out of the park. I pulled my car right in front of John Hyatt's house and got out.

Addison, Addison, Addison. What the hell are you doing?

I had no idea what I was going to say once I got to the door, or what I would do if I actually was confronted with

Veronica, but I was lousy at the wait and see game. I was all about the action. In my mind, I was Lara Croft trapped in Mayberry.

I stood on the massive front porch and rang the doorbell. I could see Victor Mooney from the corner of my eye looking out the window and giving me a thumbs up. My heart was pounding and my breathing was a step away from hyperventilation.

"Lara Croft doesn't hyperventilate," I announced, just to make myself feel better.

When the front door opened slowly with a creak, I thought I would pass out from the anticipation. I put my head down to control the dancing spots in front of my eyes, and also to give Veronica a different place on my head to hit if she was going to attack me. My forehead was still sore.

I opened my eyes and saw a very nice pair of Manolo Blahniks with turquoise feathers that I'd envied from afar the last time I was at Neiman Marcus in Atlanta. My gaze raised to a pair of shapely legs and then higher to a black pencil skirt, a turquoise halter-top and long dangly earrings.

"Can I help you," a husky voice asked, and I was finally able to look at the face of a woman with splendid taste in clothing. Her hair looked like spun gold and hung in waves to her shoulders.

How could I have thought this was Veronica? Veronica had a great body, but she dressed like a fifty-dollar hooker and her hair was only blonde because she went to a salon every six weeks like clockwork. The woman in front of me was no Veronica. This woman had class.

"Great shoes," I said, meeting a pair of curious hazel eyes. "I'm sorry, but have we met before?"

You'd think I'd remember meeting a woman like this one, but I was drawing a blank. Maybe she was someone I went to school with that changed from an ugly duckling into a swan.

"No, I don't think so," she answered politely.

"Is John Hyatt home?

"No, he's not. Can I help you?"

I stuck out my hand and felt like a fool. The princess and the pauper had never had much meaning before now. "I'm Addison Holmes."

"Ahh, Ms. Holmes. I've heard a lot about you." She left it at that, and I was pretty sure nothing she'd heard about me had been good because she moved her body across the front door like I was going to race inside and steal all the silver.

I knew there was only one way to handle the situation, so I swallowed my pride and did something I'd always hated to do. "Just tell him that I came by to apologize." My tongue swelled over the lie, because I'd be damned if I really meant any apology to that weasel, but no pain, no gain, right?

"I'll do that," she said and started to close the door in my face.

"I'm sorry, but I didn't get your name."

"Loretta Swanson. I'm Mr. Hyatt's estate manager. Try to stay dry," she said and closed the door.

Was she kidding? I was going to need a canoe if this rain continued on much longer.

I got back in the car and thought for a minute. Loretta Swanson, an estate manager that Fanny Kimble hadn't mentioned once when Kate had questioned her. Did Loretta make it a point to not work the nights that Fanny was staying over, and better yet, how was it even possible that both women hadn't stumbled across each other in the thirteen months of John and Fanny's engagement. I needed to talk to Fanny Kimble.

There was something that bothered me about Loretta Swanson. You wouldn't think a typical estate manager would be able to afford six hundred dollar shoes. Loretta was someone that John Hyatt treated like a queen. And my gut told me Fanny had a good reason to be jealous. I was going to have to bite the bullet and have another visit with John Hyatt. I might even have to apologize to him for real to get the information I wanted.

Gretchen Wilder was a sex-crazed librarian, but the Thunderbolt Public Library didn't close until seven o'clock, so I had time to swing by my mom's and mooch dinner before playing peeping Tom.

My mom wasn't the world's best cook, but her pantry was always stocked and I was willing to bet there was no slimy lettuce anywhere in her kitchen.

I once again parked behind the General Lee and sloshed my way to the back door. The rain was lessening, which was good now that I was soaked to the skin, and I wiped my feet on the doormat before opening the door to the kitchen.

The smell of Lemon Pledge and coffee that had sat on the burner all day hit my nostrils. I was chilled and shivering, my hair hung in my face, and I was willing to bet my waterproof mascara was smudged under my eyes.

"Addison?" my mother said. "Is that you?"

"Do you have a lot of strange, wet women walk in your back door on a daily basis?" I asked sarcastically.

My mother clucked her tongue like mothers do and went about laying down towels on the floor so I wouldn't drip. Mom was a pretty woman, barely fifty, and looked exactly like I would in the next twenty years—long dark hair that had no gray thanks to Clairol, dark brown eyes and olive skin. She was a little wider in the hips and a lot more blessed in the bust, but if I ate a steady diet of Hostess Cupcakes I could probably graduate to a C cup in the next ten years.

"Let me get you a pair of clean sweats and underwear," my mother said.

"Just the sweats. I'm not wearing your underwear. That's weird."

"You can't go around without undergarments on," she said scandalized. "What if you were stopped by the police on your way home?"

"They might let me out of a ticket," I said, teeth chattering.

If my mother was upset about me not wearing underwear, I shuddered to think what her reaction would be if she ever found out about The Foxy Lady.

"Where did I go wrong?" she asked as she went to get dry clothes. I didn't have an answer to that question, but I was pretty sure it wasn't her fault. I think I was wired differently from birth. Maybe she smoked pot or something while she was pregnant. It would sure as hell explain what was wrong with my sister.

"Have you ever done anything questionable in your life? Something you regretted?" I asked my mother when she came back in with a pair of dark grey sweats, socks and old running shoes.

"Of course. But the choices we make shape our destiny. I wouldn't change anything I've done because I wouldn't be who I am today."

"Hmmm. That's pretty wise." If I hadn't stripped at The Foxy Lady I never would have met Nick. Not that we had a relationship. I had trouble determining from one encounter to the next if he wanted to throttle me or kiss me. He could have a girlfriend or a dozen kids for all I knew.

Nick Dempsey was a master at sending mixed signals, and I was acting like a love-puppy looking for any attention at all. Very lame. I needed to forget Nick Dempsey and move on.

"I hear you've got a date tomorrow night," my mom said.

I'd forgotten about the date Kate had set up. "That's right," I said, not sure where this was leading.

"I'm glad you've finally gotten over Greg. He'll come to regret the decisions he's made someday. You'd have made a wonderful wife."

I'm sure my mother said that with no prejudice whatsoever. I personally think I'd make a terrible wife. I hate to do laundry and I never have food in my refrigerator, though I can cook when meat and produce magically appear. I like to sleep in the middle of the bed and I don't like to budget. Not very wifely at all.

"It's just a friendly date, mom. Don't reserve the church just yet."

"You never know when you're going to run into your soul mate. Just make sure you wear underwear. You don't want your date to think you're easy."

I rolled my eyes, grabbed the warm-ups and headed to the bathroom. I showered under blistering water for a luxurious ten minutes, dried off and put on clean clothes—without the underwear my mother had brought for me despite my protests.

When I came back to the kitchen I was warm and in a more positive frame of mind. My mother put a hot bowl of vegetable soup in front of me and I inhaled the aroma. My mom could make soup from a can with the best of them. She sat across from me with her own bowl.

"You know, your question about me having regrets got me thinking. Did you know I spent a lot of my young adult life on buses, traveling across the country, rallying for different causes and protesting anything and everything?" Her smile was nostalgic. "I was a crusader—always ready to defend the weak and fight for a good cause. Those were the good old days. I used to be a free spirit, you know, before I met your father and decided to settle down and be an accountant."

"So you gave up your free spirit to marry Dad? That doesn't sound very fair."

"Oh, it was an adjustment for both of us. His mother hated me. Still does, the old witch. You should have seen the two of us, me in my gold platforms and your dad buttoned to his chin in that sexy uniform. I don't have any regrets, but putting on panty-hose for twenty years was the hardest thing I ever had to do. I was completely satisfied to stay at home and work in my garden, but they didn't pay cops much back then, and I had to go to work. Your father, rest his soul, was a tight-assed Republican, and I'd never been with someone so straight-laced when it came to issues in the bedroom, but we were a unit, your dad and I. We had good years between us."

My mom doesn't usually like to talk about the past, and I knew talking about my dad made her sad, but I felt like we were really having a great bonding moment. It was just the thought of anything to do with my parents and conception and bedrooms that I had trouble keeping my gag reflexes under control.

"I'm afraid there's more of me in you and your sister than your father was hoping," she continued. "I can at least be thankful you have a steady job and have never been to jail. Unlike Phoebe. Though you seem to have a bit of a problem with your temper. I don't know where you get that from. I had a dozen people call me yesterday to tell me what a scene you made in the bank. I was mortified."

"Well, John Hyatt shouldn't have gone back on his promise," I defended.

"You're right about that, but a southern lady does not go around town causing scenes and stirring up gossip. A true southern lady can out manipulate General Lee when it comes to revenge. We'll think of something. Just try to be more circumspect in the future."

"Gotcha. Revenge is good. Gossip is bad. If only you'd told me these things in my formative years so I wouldn't keep screwing up."

I found myself in a familiar situation as I sat in the dark with my binoculars glued to my face hoping to catch Mrs. Wilder in *flagrante delicto*.

Basically, I was stalling. I knew what I had to do to get the job done. I just didn't particularly want to do it. I pulled the anorak I'd borrowed from my mother over my head and zipped the camera in the front pouch so it wouldn't get wet. I was going to have to get up close and personal to deliver what the client wanted. The rain hadn't let up like I'd hoped and was still going strong. There was flash flooding all around the area. I could have used this as an excuse to go home and bundle under the covers, but according to Mattress Mattie you couldn't make money in bed by yourself, so I had no choice but to get wet and dirty. Two of my least favorite things to do.

I was parked across the street from a small bungalow on Peters Street in Driftwood. Driftwood was a twenty minute drive from the Thunderbolt Public Library where Mrs. Wilder worked, but that's the direction she and her boy toy headed after meeting in the parking lot of the library.

And when I say boy toy, we're talking literally. Mrs. Wilder knew how to pick 'em. I had to give her credit for that. The kid couldn't have been more than twenty. They'd been inside the bungalow about half an hour, which more than stretched my limit for sitting inside the car.

"Surely that's enough time to get things started."

I tightened my hood and pushed at the car door. The wind had picked up and it took an effort to get it open. I kept my head down and trudged across the street, losing my balance twice in the gusts and nearly falling on my face.

I heaved a sigh of relief when I made it to the side of the house. The brick wall blocked most of the wind and rain and let me catch my breath. Lights were on all through the house, and I peeped around to look at the driveway one more time just to make sure I had the right house. Mrs. Wilder's black Jeep Cherokee was parked next to a red pickup truck. It was the right house.

I jogged in place for a few seconds and gave myself a pep talk. "All right, it's now or never."

I crept along the side of the house and started looking in windows. The first window I came to was an office of some sort, and it was empty except for a couple of boxes and a cheap metal desk. I exhaled a shaky breath and crept on, thanking God with every step that it was pouring down rain so no one could see me make a fool of myself.

The next room was the kitchen. There was an open bottle of wine on the counter and two empty glasses sitting next to it.

"All right. Getting closer."

The third window I came to was kind of small and set high up off the ground. I could see the light shining through, but there was no way I could see in without standing on something. I looked around frantically for a box or a table. No such luck. There was, however, a big oak tree that was growing right in between the bungalow and the house next door. If I climbed out onto the branch I would be able to see in.

Now, I was no dummy, so I decided the best thing to do before killing myself in a tree was to make sure I couldn't see them from another window. Unfortunately, that wasn't the case.

The tree was my only option.

I'd never actually climbed a tree, so working for Kate was teaching me all kinds of new things, except I'd always hated to get dirty and nothing much had changed in my advanced age. All I can say is thank God for yoga because otherwise I'd be in real trouble.

I jumped up and grabbed hold of the lowest hanging branch and brought my legs up to wrap around it so I was hanging upside down like a possum. I was miraculously able to swing myself up into a sitting position and from there I hoisted myself up to the next branch.

"Piece of cake. I should have been a gym teacher." If only it weren't for those horrible blue wind suits they had to wear.

I pushed myself with my legs as far as I could go towards the end of the limb and balanced while I dug the camera out of my front pocket.

Note to self: Next time get the camera out before you're lying on your stomach.

"Oh man. Holy cow."

I'd hit the jackpot. The high window definitely looked into the master bedroom. I couldn't really tell if I was looking at Mrs. Wilder or not since I didn't have a close up photo I.D. of the parts I was looking at, but I was pretty sure I was at the right place.

It was like looking at a car wreck. All I could do was stare and hope there were no injuries. I'd never seen sex like this before in my life, not like I had a whole lot to judge by, but I was pretty sure that Mrs. Wilder was my new idol. And I had no idea how she was hanging from the ceiling, but it seemed to be getting the job done.

"Damn. Pictures."

I brought the camera up and started snapping pictures like a woman obsessed, afraid to look away in case I missed something. I don't know how long I was in the tree, but I know I got an education I never got in health class.

They looked to be winding down, and I realized I was pretty turned on and my body was frozen in one position. I must have been there longer than I'd thought.

I looked up again just to make sure my cover was still safe and was surprised to see they'd started again.

"Wow, good for you guys."

I had to say I was a tiny bit jealous, considering my sexual exploits revolved around The Tonight Show, and no matter how much I wanted to continue, Greg's recharging period was about twenty-four hours. Maybe I should have gone for the twenty-year-old. Of course, Greg had been having sex with Veronica too, so I could be judging his staying power unfairly.

My thoughts automatically veered to Nick. I'd be willing to bet he didn't need any recovery period. He was probably one giant hormone with a permanent erection.

I slowly untangled my legs and held in a yelp as thousands of tiny pinpricks ran rampant over my skin. I juggled the camera in one hand and tried to keep my balance, but it was hard to balance something that was dead weight.

I'm pretty sure the thunder drowned out my scream as I hit the ground. It didn't look like that far of a fall when I was standing on the ground looking up, but the breath was knocked out of me and I was pretty sure the ass was ripped out of my sweatpants, either that or I had explosively wet my pants.

Maybe I should have worn the underwear after all.

I lay on the ground for a couple of minutes and closed my eyes, hoping that when I opened them I'd be at home in bed and waking up from a nightmare.

Nope. That would be too easy.

I pushed myself slowly to my feet and whimpered all the way back to the car. The good news was that I had saved the camera. The bad news—well, the extent of that had yet to be seen.

I opened the door to the Z and got in gingerly, holding my torn sweats together and favoring my knee. I put my head down on the steering wheel and wished I had the strength to weep, but all I managed was pathetic whimpers that damaged my pride more than it already was.

"Getting caught as a peeping Tom is a misdemeanor fineable up to thirty days in jail and a five hundred dollar fine."

I screamed at the voice coming from the next seat over and what was left of my adrenaline went into overdrive.

Attack first. Think later.

I don't think my adrenaline was up to the fight because before I knew it both my arms were behind my back and a familiar voice was trying to calm me down.

"What the hell is wrong with you? Do you always attack innocent people? You're crazy," Nick said, shaking the fillings loose in my teeth.

"I'm crazy? Me? You don't just get into someone's car and scare the hell out of them and then call them crazy for being scared. Let me go!"

"Not until you calm down. And why didn't you look to

see if anyone was in your car before you got in? That would have been the smart thing to do."

I was seething inside. I knew what Nick said was right, but that didn't mean I wanted to hear it. As far as I was concerned, I was right too. I got really still and waited for him to release me, knowing I'd probably end up going to jail for the rest of my life, but I didn't really care. I'd heard the prisons had good doctors, and I could learn how to crochet. Maybe I could even get my Master's Degree. Prison sounded like heaven at this point in my life.

As soon as he let me go I went into Tae Bo mode and landed a solid punch to his jaw before he restrained me again. Now I had sore knuckles to add to my other list of injuries. But boy was it worth it.

"Ouch. Son of a bitch," Nick said, wiggling his jaw with his hand. "You need to be locked up." He paused and looked down at my sweatshirt. "Are you wearing a bra?"

"Get out of my car. Now."

"I need to talk to you about something if you can be normal for thirty seconds," he said. "I didn't follow you all this way so you could take swings at me. I'm trying to run a murder investigation, which is a hell of a lot more important than getting your jollies by watching live porn. Can you be an adult and talk to me?"

"I don't think so. Take a goddamn number or make an appointment. I don't care what you do. Just get the fuck out of my car!"

"Oh, I get it. It must be that time of the month."

I was pretty sure he saw the steam coming out of my ears at that point, so he opened the door quickly, looking for an escape route. I floored the gas pedal before his feet hit the pavement and felt great satisfaction as I saw him stumble onto the ground on his hands and knees. The smell of exhaust and burnt rubber was the only reminder I had been there.

It had been a hell of a day, and I didn't think ice cream was going to make it better, but I was willing to give it a try anyway. And then I was going to chase it with a shot of vodka.

7

"ARE YOU ALL RIGHT, MS. HOLMES? YOU DON'T LOOK so good."

I'd been hearing this same question every time the bell rang and a new class walked in the door. The answer to the question was simple. Hell no, I wasn't all right.

I'd lived thirty years without doing as much damage to myself as I had in the last five days. I'd broken a leg once trying to stand on my bicycle and pretend I was a circus performer, and I broke all the fingers in my left hand when they were accidentally slammed in the car door, but those incidents were nothing compared to the pain I was currently feeling.

My head was down on my desk and the white noise of my students' voices was lulling me to sleep. For every teacher, there was always one class that made you want to stick forks in your eyeballs.

This was the class.

It was seventh period, the last class of the day, and it was filled with second year freshmen, athletic rejects, and girls that needed to buy stock in kneepad companies.

This was the same class that when I asked who Benjamin Franklin was, only one kid raised his hand and said he was the dude on the money. I figured this kid should know all about Benjamins because he'd been busted twice for selling marijuana in the janitor's closet during lunch.

Sometimes teaching made me feel like I was really making a difference in kids' lives, but mostly it was depressing as hell. They were all bigger than me, meaner than me, and every one of them probably had a weapon of some sort in their baggy pants.

I put a movie in and punched play, but didn't dare turn the lights off because I didn't want to contribute to the teen pregnancy rate.

I was seriously considering getting down on the floor to stretch out my aching muscles, but I knew I'd never be able to get back up again. My knee was swollen to the size of a grapefruit and my ribs were bruised from my fall from the tree. The good news was that the bump on my head had faded to a dull purple. To top it off, the treble choir next door had just started singing a *Grease* medley for the end of the year production. I could hear Rose Marie's warbling voice over the choir, and it was everything I could do to stifle a laugh and protect my battered ribs.

I'd pretty much seen everything in the eight years I'd been teaching. I'd seen students cheat their way through my class, dealt with parents who thought their children should be given a free pass in life, found used condoms in the teacher parking lot and caught students smoking weed in the bathroom. If I could find one student who would loan me a shot of whiskey to help me get through the rest of the day, I'm pretty sure my life would be complete.

I'd barely stretched my aching body out on the couch when I heard three hard knocks on my door.

"Come in," I croaked. I wasn't about to move from my spot on the couch.

"Are you nuts? You can't just leave your door wide open for anyone to come in and murder you. There *are* people in this world that are crazier than you are."

The sight of Nick walking though my front door was enough to make me forget about my injuries. He was wearing worn jeans with holes in them, a white t-shirt, and a navy blue windbreaker that said HOMICIDE in bright yellow on the front pocket. His gun was strapped to his hip and he looked good enough to eat.

Lord, that was one fine man. He made my tongue swell up and my limbs weak, but I was made from sturdier stuff than to let a man like Nick Dempsey cloud my brain with lust. My brain had never been clouded with lust when I'd been with Greg, but he'd seduced me with his outgoing personality and intelligence. I should have realized he was trying to get me to buy insurance instead of getting me in the sack, but it was a mistake any woman could make.

"Damn, it's you. I was hoping it was Jack the Ripper coming to put me out of my misery. You don't happen to have your gun on you, do you?"

"Of course I have my gun," Nick said, giving me a look that said, *why wouldn't I have it, I'm a cop.*

This guy was way too literal. I needed someone with a sense of humor. Nick was a great advertisement for Levi's, but that was not enough to base a relationship on.

"Never mind," I said. "Why do you keep popping into

my life? And stop calling me crazy. I'm a perfectly normal human being. I've just had a rough couple of days."

"Uh-huh. Every time I look at you the first word that comes to mind is normal. You look worse than you did last night. And that's saying something. What happened to you?"

I shot him a look I reserved for students who were misbehaving and winced as he sat down at the end of the couch and put my feet in his lap.

"I fell out of a tree."

I ignored his burst of laughter and closed my eyes. I really hated it when he laughed. It changed his entire personality. It made him *almost* likeable.

"That would explain why you weren't wearing pants and why there was grass in your hair when you got in your car last night."

"I was wearing pants. There was just a big hole in them. You know what? Your words don't even matter to me anymore. I am bliss. I am calm. I am—"

"You're nuts."

I shot him a look meant to shrivel a lesser man, but he just kept smiling at me.

"I hate you."

"Well, that's good to know because the two of us are going to be spending a lot of time together. I need your help."

"What?" I sat up too quickly and a muscle cramp seized my thigh in a vicious hold. "Shit, crap, I hate you. Nothing ever goes right when you're around."

"I didn't think you'd take the news this well," Nick said, massaging the tightened muscle. He worked at it a few more minutes until I began to whimper in relief.

"Do you still hate me?" he whispered much too close to my ear.

There were places on my body that were warming at an alarming rate. This man made me crazy. I wanted to strangle him every time he opened his mouth, but whenever he touched me I wanted to jump his bones.

"I wanted to come by and apologize for scaring you last night." His breath was hot against my skin, and I shivered in reaction. All I had to do was move my head ever so slightly and our lips would touch.

"You—you're apologizing?" I asked, surprised. He didn't seem like the kind of man to apologize for anything. I was immediately suspicious, but forgot why when his lips started to feather the side of my neck.

"See how easy it's going to be for us to work together?" he asked, seductively. "I think it could be a pretty life-altering experience, don't you?"

My vision started to clear when I realized he was trying to make a point. Nick had ulterior motives. The rat bastard.

The knock on the door saved me from telling Nick exactly what kind of experience he was about to get from my knee to his balls.

"Ahh—saved by the proverbial bell." Nick put space between us but kept my feet in his lap.

"Come in," I yelled, before Nick could get up and answer it himself. He rolled his eyes at me, and I watched closely as he placed his hand on the gun at his hip.

"Have I interrupted something?" Kate asked, seeing Nick and I looking more comfortable than either one of us felt.

"No—"

"Yes—"

I gave Nick a disgusted look and tried to move away

from him, but my body wasn't in any shape to move anywhere, and all I could manage was a groan.

"Geez, you look like hell," Kate said.

"That seems to be the consensus," I said, irritated.

"I've stopped by to drop off a couple more cases, and I wanted to see if you had any luck with Gretchen Wilder. I have a meeting with Mr. Wilder tomorrow morning."

"The camera's on the table with the file," I said, going back to the splendor of the best foot rub I'd ever had.

"Wow, looks like you got an education," Kate said, scrolling through the pictures on the camera. "Mrs. Wilder's my idol."

"Yeah, mine too."

"So how'd you get the bruises? Did you get caught?" she asked.

"Nah, I fell out of the tree I used to look in the bedroom window. I didn't realize how long they'd been going at it and my legs fell asleep."

"Ahh—to be that young again," Kate said. "Ice it down and then go take a hot shower. I'd almost say you did it on purpose just so you could get out of your date tonight."

"What date?" Nick asked.

"Oh, shit! I forgot about the date. Look at me, Kate. I can *not* go out like this. I can barely stand." I put a little extra whine in my voice so she'd get the point.

"Look on the bright side. Maybe you two will hit it off and then you can spend the evening in bed."

"Yeah, because I always sleep with guys on the first date."

"True," Kate said, shaking her head sadly. "You're an inspiration to nuns everywhere."

Kate downloaded the pictures onto her computer and

gathered the files. "Make sure you're presentable by seven, Addison. I'll call your mother if I have to."

"Why does everyone hate me today? Can't you see I'm in pain?"

"Take some of that painkiller the dentist gave you when you had your wisdom teeth taken out. It's not like you'll be driving tonight."

"Great advice, Kate," Nick said. "It's always a good idea to go out with a complete stranger while you're drugged. What if he's a sex offender?"

"Fine, stay home and be pitiful all night. But I'm telling you, you can't let these things keep you down. You could be standing up your future husband tonight." Kate pulled open my front door with much less trouble than I always seemed to have and looked back at me.

"Don't forget the Officer's Gala is tomorrow night. Mike and I can pick you up if you want."

How big of a loser would that make me to be Kate and Mike's third wheel for a big party? So I did what any sensible girl would have done. I lied.

"There's no need to pick me up. I have a date." I winced inside as I heard the words, but they'd just slipped out somehow.

"Great. I can't wait to meet him," she said with a wicked smile.

I lay frozen on the couch, trying to come up with a solution for the mess I just made.

"You are so lying," Nick said.

"Shut up. I'll figure out something. If I hadn't told her I had a date she would have set me up with another stranger."

"She loves you and only has your best interest at heart."

"Which is about the worst thing you can say about anyone.

I'm perfectly comfortable going places without a man on my arm." This was actually a lie. Having a male escort to big events was like a security blanket to me, and going without one made me feel like I was walking into a room full of people naked.

"Why are you even going to the Officer's Gala?" Nick asked.

"I've gone every year since I was sixteen. My dad was a cop, and the gala always raises a lot of money. This will be the first year my mom doesn't go."

"Did your dad die in the line of duty?" Nick asked softly as he ran his hand down the length of my hair in a comforting gesture.

"No, he retired a few years back. He had a heart attack watching a Falcons game on the television last fall."

"That's pretty understandable considering how they played last season. I'm sorry you lost him."

"Me too. He was a good man. A good cop. Which is why I go to the gala and support the rest of you."

"Well, since we agree on that point, it only makes sense that we go together. I'll pick you up at seven-thirty. Now, do you have anything to eat around here?" he asked, dislodging me off his lap with a grunt and heading toward the kitchen.

"Excuse me. Who are you? It's like you've just invaded my life and now I can't get rid of you. That's the third time you've mentioned us working together, and I have to say I don't remember agreeing to anything of the sort. I'm not sure I even like you."

He just winked and went back to rummaging through my refrigerator.

"You can't stay," I said loudly. "I'm not in the mood for company." I heaved out a painful sigh and slowly got up off the couch. He wasn't going to ignore me in my own apartment.

"Hey, you didn't have to get up," he said as I leaned against the kitchen counter and tried to look intimidating.

"Oh, I think I did. You're sneaky, but I've got you figured out."

"Oh, do you?" he said with his heart-stopping smile again.

"Definitely. You've had too many sides since the first moment I've met you, ranging from serious cop to supreme asshole to the Boy Scout next door. Which one is the real Nick Dempsey, I wonder? The first words out of anyone's mouth when your name pops up is that you're a good cop. The compliments seem to stop there."

He was watching me with an unreadable face, the corners of his mouth set, waiting for me to go on.

"You need me for something," I said matter of factly. "You wouldn't bother with me otherwise."

He moved closer, like a hunter stalking his prey, and for the first time I really saw the quietly contained danger lurking within. My breath caught in my throat as he leaned in and put his face close to mine. Apparently the dark side was a huge turn on for me. Who knew?

"You're right," he whispered. "I do need you for something."

I could feel the hardness of his body pressed to mine and the heat that radiated from it, and I realized I was holding my breath.

I was still standing there turned on and confused when he backed away and grabbed his windbreaker.

"You did that on purpose," I said. "Tell me what you want and then get out. I don't have the time to play games with you, and more importantly I don't *want* to play games with you."

"You are such a liar," Nick said, giving me that

devastating smile. "Your refrigerator is emptier than mine. I'm not sure how that's possible." He seemed baffled for a moment but was back to his no-nonsense self in short order. "What I want from you is work related, but we can talk about it another time when you're not so—injured. I've got to get out of here. Don't forget the Officer's Gala tomorrow. Make sure you wear something sexy. Maybe no underwear."

I was pretty sure my mother wouldn't like Nick Dempsey.

"Oh, and Addison," Nick said, trapping me against the counter with his body again. "I might not have been completely honest earlier. I want something else from you too."

And then he kissed me. This was not a kiss meant to tease. This kiss was serious business, with tongue and everything. I remember thinking I should protest just a little so he wouldn't think I was easy, but then all the thoughts leaked out of my ears, and I found myself wrapping my arms around his neck and kissing him back. My head began to buzz and heat shot to all my favorite places.

Fortunately, Nick had more control than I did and he pulled back before I could embarrass myself by begging. He gave me a perfunctory kiss on the cheek and then he was out the door.

I learned two things from the whole experience. One: I've never had good sex. Two: I really wanted some.

I was tired, irritated, sore and really turned on, so I took Kate's advice and downed a Vicodin with the hopes it would put me out of my misery.

8

Friday

It was the last day of school.

Thank God.

And what made it even better was that there was only a half day of classes so the seniors could have plenty of time to get ready for graduation that night.

It was the second week of June, and summer lay over the state like a wet blanket that was suffocating the life out of everything. The weather was unpredictable, with severe storms raging one moment followed by heat waves that made citizens irritable and seniors die from heat stroke. The only thing worse than Georgia in June was Georgia in July and August.

When I was a teenager, I used to sit at my cramped school desk—one that somehow always managed to have gum on the underside so it stuck to my knees—and wait impatiently for the bell to ring at the end of the day.

As soon as I heard that glorious sound I'd grab my

backpack and rush out the door. I'd head directly to my job at The Drug Mart, where I sold a lot of condoms and greeting cards, and I'd wish like crazy that I could just hurry up and graduate so I could be a part of the real world.

Somehow, after four years of college, I'd ended up in the same place I started, sitting at a little larger desk and needing the bell to ring worse than a wino with the shakes and a booze shortage.

When the bell rang at twelve-thirty I grabbed my things and rushed into the hallway, taking five seconds to lock my classroom door. I turned around and ran right into Rose Marie Valentine.

"Oooomph," she said.

I watched her fall in slow motion onto her well-padded posterior. It wasn't pretty.

"Oh my gosh. Are you okay?" I asked, scrambling down beside her as quickly as I could with my sore knee. We probably looked like a Vaudeville act to the casual observer. I gathered her papers and purse and tried to heft her up by the elbow, but Rose Marie was a lot of woman. It was a two handed job and I was one short, so I dropped her things on the ground again and put more of my weight behind the effort.

"I'm fine. I'm fine," she said, her glasses skewed at an odd angle on her nose and her breath huffing and puffing like she'd just run the Boston Marathon.

"My goodness, you sure are in a hurry. You'd think this was the last day of school or something." She twittered at her own joke and adjusted her glasses. "Where are you off to?"

"I'm headed to the mall. I'm going to the Officer's Gala tonight with some friends and I need a new dress."

"Oh, really?" Rose Marie said, her eyes lighting up.

"That sounds so exciting. You have such an adventurous life. I just go home to my babies every day and do a lot of crossword puzzles. And then of course there's Days of Our Lives. It's like my second family."

I'd seen Rose Marie's babies. She had framed pictures of them all over her desk. She had two Great Danes that were the size of small horses and they each had their own bedroom in her small duplex.

"I wish my life was as exciting as yours. I don't even remember the last time I went to the mall."

Rose Marie's eyes got all misty and depressed and I felt as low as someone who had just kicked a puppy with a pointy-toed shoe. Not to mention the fact that I had just knocked her on her ass. Before I could stop myself, I heard the words coming out of my mouth.

"Why don't you come with me? It always helps to have a second opinion. But we have to hurry because I have exactly seven hours to make myself presentable."

Geez, I was such a sucker. Her face lit up, pink and round like Mrs. Claus.

"Why, that sounds like fun. And if we have time we can stop for lunch at that restaurant in the mall where each room is a different continent. I like to sit in the Australia room because the waiters are almost naked and they've got 'em all slicked up with oil."

I liked the restaurant for the same reason, so I nodded in agreement. "Fine, but if they try to put us in Antarctica I'm going to protest. There's nothing sexy about a pasty white guy in a parka."

"Amen, sister." Rose Marie practically bounced out of her faux leather mules her excitement was so palpable. "And maybe we could order a couple of those drinks with the fancy umbrellas and fruit. It could be a real girl's day out."

"Uh-huh."

Some day I was going to learn to keep my mouth shut.

"What do you think about this one?" I asked, as I paraded out of the dressing room in the twenty-second dress I'd tried on. Rose Marie was a fashion critic of epic proportions, which I considered odd for someone who looked like a dumpling wrapped in a tablecloth every time I saw her.

"Ooh, that one's good."

I kind of thought so myself and was already imagining what kind of shoes I could buy to go with the red strapless sheath. The hem even went past my knees, so it covered up the swollen parts and bruises. The shimmering red complimented my golden skin tone, and I knew it was just the thing to make Nick beg.

"Of course, that kind of dress might give your date the wrong idea," Rose Marie said with a little frown. "I don't know if you should advertise yourself like that."

I was past the point of caring what I was advertising. My feet hurt, my Extra Strength Tylenol was wearing off and I was one step away from telling Rose Marie exactly what she could do with her opinions on fashion. "I'm buying this dress," I said defiantly.

Rose Marie blinked up at me owlishly. "It's a beautiful dress. Of course, it'll look better with Spanx. That way you don't' have any unseemly lumps."

"Are you saying I have lumps?" I asked, my voice sounding suspiciously like a junkyard dog growling.

"No, no," she said, swallowing nervously. "Even the movie stars wear them. I read it in a magazine. It'll just make you more streamlined. Though it might be a hindrance if you're looking to get lucky." She pursed her lips and looked thoughtful. "There's nothing sexy about looking like your body's being squeezed out of a sausage casing."

My eyes got bigger the longer she talked and I realized I'd been out of the dating game far too long. Greg and I had been together two years, so I'd gotten comfortable not having to make too much of an effort.

"Sweet Mary," I said as imagines flitted through my mind of putting Nick's eye out with a girdle.

"Of course, you won't have to worry about it if you don't give in too easy."

"Right." I nodded my head in agreement and tried to look non-desperate. "Let's go buy some Spanx. It's like a modern day chastity belt."

Rose Marie hefted herself off the bench as I made my way back toward the fitting room. "Of course, you could always buy the crotchless kind just in case."

My eye twitched once before I closed myself in the dressing room. I really needed a margarita.

AFTER SPENDING A COUPLE OF HOURS IN ROSE MARIE'S company, I had the sinking feeling I knew why she spent most of her time with her dogs. She was the most socially inept person I'd ever come across. And I'd come across my share. Rose Marie made me look like a freaking diplomat.

I dragged her through the mall in search of killer shoes for the killer dress I'd just spent a fortune on. But the way I looked at it, a measly couple hundred bucks wasn't all that much in the grand scheme of the whole five thousand I was saving for. Skewed logic works in mysterious ways when you're desperate for sexy shoes.

I found the perfect strappy four-inch heels for slightly less than I paid for the dress and rationalized the cost somehow in my mind when I stood in line to pay for them, but I've since forgotten what my reasoning was.

Rose Marie was bouncing happily beside me as I handed over my credit card. She was obviously spending money vicariously. I was thinking I needed to skip the margarita and go straight to the hot fudge sundae. I didn't even have to feel guilty about it because I knew the Spanx would suck in the calories from the chocolate sauce.

"Excuse me," said a husky southern voice that was as thick as butter cream from behind me.

I'm not afraid to admit that I was a little scared to turn around. All I needed was an irate spouse who I'd recently caught cheating to shove a fist in my face. A broken nose wouldn't go well at all with my new dress.

I turned around and looked up into a pair of big blue eyes. Fanny Kimble had always been a beautiful woman, but I took a step back anyway. You never knew what a woman would do when her man was suspected of cheating. Even if I'd been decked out in my red dress with perfect hair and makeup, I couldn't hold a candle next to Fanny. Hell, Loretta Swanson would look like she'd just rolled out of the missionary barrel standing next to Fanny. Staring at Fanny Kimble was as close as I'd come in a long time to having a religious experience.

I heard a throat clear behind me and realized I was holding up the line, so I grabbed my new shoes and stepped out of the store with Fanny, Rose Marie trailing after me like a lost puppy.

"I'm sorry to catch you off guard like this," Fanny said. "But I've been trying to get the courage to speak to you, and this seemed to be my best chance."

Her hair shimmered like black diamonds under the mall track lighting and I couldn't help but notice how smooth her lipstick was. There were no creases or dead skin visible, and her eyebrows were perfectly arched and smoothed. She was six feet tall and I had to look up to see into her baby blues.

"If this is about the investigation, I believe you're supposed to speak with Kate. She's the boss."

"I know, and I will, but I just wanted to tell you personally that you can stop investigating John. I guess I had pre-wedding jitters and overreacted. He promised that I was the only one for him and that he loved me. There has to be unwavering trust between two people that are getting married, don't you think?"

I nodded, but I was pretty sure I wasn't the best person to ask. I had unwavering trust in my last fiancé and look where that got me.

"Thanks, Addison. I knew you'd understand. I think it'll be best for all of us if you just forget this whole mess. I'll make sure to compensate the agency for the time you put in." She walked in the opposite direction and every man in the vicinity stopped what he was doing and watched her exit.

"What's that look on your face?" Rose Marie asked.

"It's a look that means John Hyatt is scum. I'd bet my Z that he guilted her into making her think she was the one who was in the wrong. All that mumbo jumbo about unconditional trust. Which means he has something very big to hide. And until Kate gives me direct orders to stop working on the case, John Hyatt is going to be on my radar."

Depression and guilt over my monetary situation didn't set in until I was on my second margarita in the Australia room of the restaurant. The walls were made to look like rugged cliffs amidst the outback, and scraggly shrubs sprouted along the walls. A large fake snake was coiled behind Rose Marie's head and stared at me out of glass eyes, judging me every time I took a sip of margarita.

I'd sufficiently ogled our waiter—who was wearing nothing more than a pair of low-riding cargo shorts, a big-ass knife at his belt and a hat that sat crooked on his head. His chest was bulky with muscles and he was tanned all over. I would have been much more excited about the ogling if I hadn't taught him his freshman year of high school almost a decade ago.

"Wow, I'm just so amazed," Rose Marie said, looking around with wide eyes. "You live such an exciting life, buying sexy clothes and going to balls. You're just like a princess in a fairytale."

"Yep, that's me."

"I want to be just like you. Maybe we could do this again sometime."

The look on her face was so hopeful I didn't have the heart to tell her no way in hell was I going out in public with her again. So I just lied. Again.

I was mostly devout Methodist, but I was pretty sure I was going to have to do some kind of penance for all the lying I'd been doing lately. On the upside, practice did make perfect. I was about to order a third margarita when I glanced out into the busy mall from our window view table and saw a familiar face.

"Oh my," I said. I opened my shoulder bag and dug through the new files Kate had dropped off. "I'll be damned."

Eddie Pogue was a Whiskey Bayou resident and a dead beat. He was a few years older than me and he'd married someone a lot of years younger than me. Probably because a younger woman was easier for him to control.

He'd been in an auto accident nine months before. According to the file, Eddie was suing the insurance company for refusing to pay him when he put in a claim that he'd been unable to work due to injuries and mental trauma caused by the accident. My job was to disprove his claims of injury.

"What is it?" Rose Marie asked excitedly. "I heard in the post office the other day that you were a genuine private detective now. Is this a sting? Should we act covert?"

I looked at Rose Marie's lime green flamingo print blouse and matching broom skirt and sighed. Rose Marie was my cross to bear. I opened my mouth to tell her there was nothing we could do, figuring Eddie was probably not stupid enough to stop his act out in public. I was probably going to have to catch him around his house, mowing the lawn or beating his wife.

"Do you know who that is?" I asked Rose Marie as I pointed to Eddie.

Rose Marie had grown up in Whiskey Bayou the same as I had—only she'd graduated a few years before me.

"Sure, that's Eddie Pogue. Why's he using a walker?"

"Auto accident. How well do you know him?"

"We graduated together," she said, shoveling a nacho into her mouth. "He's a mean son-of-a-bitch. He was always too hoity-toity for the circles I ran with in high school. He was the no-neck jock, while I was Glee Club President."

Rose Marie said it matter-of-factly without resentment, so I didn't think much of it. The world was divided into two categories—the jocks and everybody else. Rose Marie and I were in the everybody else category.

"He liked to pull pranks on those of us that were unfortunate enough not to be him. He always thought they were funny, but he was really just cruel. He got that

Warwick girl in trouble a couple of years ago and married her. Everybody knows he knocks her around all the time."

I gave one more look at Rose Marie's flamingos and winced. "Come on," I said, grabbing my bag and throwing enough money on the table to cover both our meals. "I need to see what he's up to."

Rose Marie scurried after me, and I kept expecting her to slink behind columns and put her fingers up like a gun. I waved bye to the hostess when she gave us a strange look and kept my eyes on Eddie Pogue. He was headed toward the Starbucks at a brisk pace, his walker used like a battering ram to get through the crowd and into the line.

Perfect. I could grab a mocha latte to counteract the margaritas and get some pictures with my camera phone at the same time. Eddie wore a neck and knee brace to go along with his walker.

I inhaled the scent of coffee as we walked in the Starbucks, and we took our place in line a couple of people behind Eddie, and I silently judged him as he ordered a skinny mocha no-whip latte. The drink didn't fit with his baggy gangsta shorts and tank top, especially since he was rocking the middle-aged redneck look from the neck up.

Eddie took his latte and sat by himself at a table that overlooked the parking lot, managing to look pitiful as he sipped his coffee and we waited on ours.

Once we'd gotten our drinks, I directed Rose Marie to a corner table that gave me a direct line of sight to Eddie. Rose Marie's face was flushed red with excitement and her compact mirror was out so she could see what was going on behind her. I didn't have the heart to tell her that there was no way in hell Eddie hadn't noticed us.

Eddie exaggerated a limp as he tossed his drink in the trash and came over to our table.

"Hey there, Addison. Make sure you tell your mother hello for me." He ignored Rose Marie completely and walked off.

Damn small towns.

Catching Eddie Pogue was going to be difficult. Of course, every case I've had so far had left me maimed or addled, so having one that was only "difficult" sounded like a breath of fresh air.

When I was a junior in high school the quarterback of the varsity football team asked me to go to the prom. I, of course, being the naïve nerd that I was, thought he'd finally come to realize that smart girls could be fun, and I was going to represent the overlooked and underappreciated at James Madison High School.

So in preparation for the big event, I decided I needed a tan to show off my stunning white gown to its best potential. Never having tanned before, I didn't realize how necessary it was to wear the eye goggles when UV Rays are frying your body. I didn't want to have white eyelids on a tan face, so I didn't wear them and managed to sunburn my eyelids and damage my cornea, not to mention that I fried the rest of my poor body to pork rind quality. I couldn't see anything for almost two days after the incident.

This of course put a serious kink in the plans of Clint the quarterback, as his goal had been to bag the overlooked and underappreciated. To get his revenge on me for screwing up his plans of debauchery, he walked me into every doorway and table we came across. I finally realized what he was doing, so I sat down and listened to the music, my eyes so swollen I couldn't even see light, and called my dad to come pick me up.

There was a part of me that felt just like that sixteen-year-old kid with fried insides and blinders on every time I looked at Nick Dempsey, but I opened the door for him anyway.

"Wow."

A good vocabulary happened to be one of my strengths, but the minute I opened the door and saw him in a tux I was reduced to wow.

"Wow, yourself. Nice dress," he said, walking in and making himself at home while I held on to the doorknob for support with my mouth agape.

"If you keep looking at me like that, we're going to end up staying here and doing something that would probably be considered a mistake when we wake up tomorrow morning."

"Sorry," I mumbled.

Somehow the threat didn't seem all that scary. The man looked like he'd just come off the cover of GQ. His almost black hair was combed back, but there were still a few unruly strands that fell onto his forehead. The dark growth of beard on his face was freshly shaved, and he looked completely at home in a tuxedo, though I think I preferred him in worn jeans and t-shirts.

He started for me in a determined stride—I guess I'd been staring too long—and I could see the intent for wickedness clearly in his eyes.

"Let's go," I blurted out before he could get too close. I grabbed my purse and ran to the front door, ignoring his satisfied laugh. It was a damned good thing I'd remembered to put on my Spanx.

The Officer's Gala had been a tradition in Savannah for almost a hundred years. It began as a way to show support for our men and women in uniform and to recognize the best of the best. In recent years, it had become more of a political schmooze fest, but I'd always enjoyed going despite that fact. I went to support my friends now that my father was gone, because for some reason I liked hanging out with people who carry guns.

I sat in the passenger side of Nick's black truck while he gave his keys to the valet and came around to open my door. I twisted my hands nervously and picked invisible specks of lint off my dress. Tonight had potential for disaster written all over it, and with my luck disaster was bound to fall directly in my lap with minimal effort.

Nick held his hand out to me and I grasped hold of it tightly and planted my red spiked heel on the ground.

"You look beautiful," he said, kissing my hand, his eyes soft and seductive as he looked into mine.

My heart melted a little at the touch of his lips against my skin and my nerves settled.

"Thank you."

I've got to say, we looked stunning together, and I stood next to him proudly as more and more glances turned our way. I quashed down any feelings of jealousy at the women who looked at Nick with hungry glances. After all, he was with me for the night.

I spotted Kate and Mike right off and headed in their direction. Mike was a huge teddy bear of a man with dark red hair, so he was hard to miss in a crowd. His Irish roots made his cheeks red whenever he had anything alcoholic to drink and also made him seem completely out of place in a tuxedo.

Next to Mike's large form, Kate looked like a doll. She had managed to leave her ugly suits at home and put on a little black dress. She'd even bothered to put on makeup and jewelry.

"There you are," Kate said. "I was wondering if you'd

have the guts to show up, since I know you lied to me about having a date."

"I didn't lie. I came with Nick." Though I'd saw my tongue off before I told Kate that Nick had practically blackmailed me into going with him.

"Oh," Kate said and her smile was genuine. "I thought it would take a little longer for the two of you to hit it off. You can both be a little hard to get along with."

"You were trying to set us up?" I asked, appalled, and then a beat later, "I'm not hard to get along with."

"Well, of course I was trying to set you up. I wanted to find someone for you to replace Greg with. I didn't want you to be mopey, so I thought Nick would be a good choice for rebound sex."

"Thanks," I said, wincing.

The problem was I didn't want to have rebound sex with Nick. I wanted to have relationship sex with Nick. Now I could never be sure if it was one or the other.

"You look great tonight," I told her.

"Well, I figured if I didn't try at least a little in the dress up department you'd just bitch at me all night."

I thought about denying it, but she was probably right, so I kept my mouth shut.

"Speaking of Greg," Kate said. "I hate to have to tell you this, but they're assigned to our table. And before you ask, I've already tried to swap the seats out at another table, but no one else wants to sit with them either."

"What?" I asked horrified.

I was already looking for the exit, when I noticed Nick walking over to our table. I knew his full attention was on me because all the hair on the back of my neck stood up and my nipples wanted to turn in his direction like homing beacons.

"What's going on?" he asked, pulling my chair out for me.

"We have to leave," I said, grabbing my handbag.

"You can handle this, Addison," Kate said, pushing me down in my seat. "Just remember you can't hit Veronica unless she attacks first. I'd hate for you to get arrested. Of course, you do have friends with enough clout to get you off easy, and if we get a sympathetic judge you probably wouldn't have to serve any jail time."

Mike rolled his eyes at Kate. "Maybe you just need to have a drink and relax."

"A drink. That's a good idea," I said, the panic sending me close to hyperventilation. I grabbed Nick's arm in a death grip and stuck my head between my knees.

"Would someone please tell me what's going on?" Nick asked, looking at us both like we belonged in a looney bin.

"Addison's ex-fiancé and the other woman are sitting with us tonight," Kate whispered.

"Oh. So what's the big deal? We're all adults here," Nick said, obviously unfamiliar with what had transpired in the breakup process.

"Greg and the floozy got caught doing it in the limo on Addison's wedding day," Kate said, leaning as far around me as possible so Nick could hear the sordid story.

"Really?" Nick asked, the corners of his mouth quirked up in a smile that promised laughter.

"Don't you dare laugh," I said. "It's not the least bit funny."

"No, it's not," he said, continuing to smile. "Does that mean I'm your rebound?" He brushed his finger down the side of my cheek and sent heat straight down to my unmentionables.

I blushed red because I didn't really know how to

answer him. Was I interested in him only on the rebound? The tingles that coursed through my body told me I didn't want to be. I'd never felt those tingles before with anyone. I'm not the most experienced person in the world, so maybe the tingles only came when you were on the rebound. I'd have to ask someone who knew.

The good news was that the sexual pull of Nick's touch kept me from hyperventilating. The bad news was I still hadn't figured out how to get out of a situation that was bound to be uncomfortable.

The table got quiet when Greg and Veronica approached. Veronica was pulling Greg along behind her like a dog on a leash, a look of devilish excitement on her face when she saw where she was sitting. Her double D's barely held up a slinky column of shimmering silver that was slit up her side to show long tanned legs. I had no idea what that woman was teaching to a room full of teenagers, but it probably wasn't how to cook a roast turkey.

"Well hello, everyone," Veronica said, oozing honey and southern charm, all of which was as fake as her implants.

She made a point of shaking both men's hands and she lingered over Nick just a little too long for my taste. I think I started to growl because she backed up rather quickly, and Nick started to laugh.

"Easy, tiger," he whispered in my ear. "I'm not going anywhere."

Oddly enough, his words comforted me. Nick might have issues in etiquette, but there was something about him that said you could trust him. I relaxed in my chair and watched Greg take his seat next to Veronica.

Greg picked at invisible lint on his jacket and tapped his fingers nervously on the table. A light film of sweat coated his upper lip and forehead. Greg didn't look so good, and it took him several minutes before he met my eyes.

"Addison," he said, nodding his head. "You look lovely tonight."

I nodded a polite thank you and was extremely proud of myself. Civil was my middle name tonight. In fact, I wished I could have returned a compliment equally inane in value, but I couldn't lie. Next to Nick, Greg was wallpaper. Sure he was dressed up in his tuxedo and looked like the up and coming insurance salesman he was, but he was pale and boring next to Nick.

"I didn't think you'd be coming tonight, Greg," Kate said. Bless her soul for trying to keep the conversation away from me so I didn't say anything I'd regret later.

"I'm always looking for new clients," Greg said, a pinched smile in place.

This bit of news made me smile a big toothy grin because if Greg was out schmoozing for clients it meant Kate had been right and the gossip was true. Probably no one wanted to buy insurance from a known cheater.

I leaned over to Nick and whispered in his ear. "I think there's something wrong with Greg," I said, only marginally concerned.

"That's a no brainer. The man left you for a blow up doll. He's probably wishing he wasn't such a moron."

I grinned and kissed Nick on the cheek spontaneously. That was one of the sweetest things anyone had ever said to me.

"Thank you for the compliment, but that wasn't what I was talking about. Greg looks like he's about to keel over from a heart attack. Look how red his face is."

"I wouldn't be surprised," Nick said, taking a sip of beer. "It would make me nervous too if I was sitting in a room full of cops when I was wanted for police questioning."

"What?" I hissed in his ear. "You can't be serious. What happened?"

"It seems that you and Greg share a common hangout. The Foxy Lady is a popular place for Whiskey Bayou residents."

"Greg was at The Foxy Lady?" And then I thought about it for a minute and realized what that meant. "He saw me dance on stage?" I asked horrified.

"Yes and yes. I'll explain later. Just keep a smile on your face and pretend you don't know anything."

"I don't know anything."

"Perfect. And remind me later to give you some techniques on the art of stripping. I wouldn't mind you trying on that little leather number for me some night."

"In your dreams," I said, but I was smiling like he asked even though I wanted to move to Alaska.

We made it all the way through the first few courses in strained silence and awkward tension. Nick seemed to be the only who was oblivious to the undercurrents at the table, or at least he was a better actor than the rest of us.

I'd also managed to drink three glasses of wine before dessert was served, so I was at the point I didn't really care about undercurrents, though Veronica had yet to stop sending Nick sultry glances and massive flashes of cleavage.

The dancing and glad-handing had started, so Greg used it as an excuse to work the floor, shaking hands and smiling his phony smile. Both Nick and Mike were up and out of their seats as well, doing whatever it is men do when they have to wear a tuxedo in a crowded place with no sports available to watch.

So that left me, Veronica and Kate sitting cozy as little

clams at the table all by ourselves. I decided some kind of variation was in order to keep things interesting, so I asked for white wine with dessert instead of the red I'd been drinking.

"So I hear you've had to get another job because you're having financial troubles," Veronica stated, dropping the gloves as soon as the men were out of sight.

"John Hyatt's just full of information, isn't he?" I signaled to the waiter to fill up my glass.

"I guess it's a good thing you have a friend like Kate to give you a job because I heard you made a lousy stripper."

Kate and I both gasped aloud but for different reasons. Kate, because this was the first she'd heard of me being a stripper. Me, because my secret was out. Greg was the only person to blame. He had to have been the one who told her.

Veronica gave me her praying mantis smile and I knew I wasn't going to be able to stay on my best behavior. I sent a mental apology to Nick and Kate in hopes they understood and another out to my mother who was bound to be mortified once word got back to her.

I've mostly been the cause for every gray hair my mother has to color, so I figured she wouldn't be too surprised when she got the news. My mother was strong stock, and nobody had better criticize one of her children. Only she had the right to do that.

"I don't know what you're talking about," I fibbed. "Does Greg know you're sleeping with John Hyatt so you can get information on people's financial records?"

"Please," Veronica laughed. "I don't have to sleep with a man to get what I want. I have other ways. I'd say I'd give you a few tips, but I saw how you wrapped Mr. Butler around your finger."

"What does he have to do with anything? Let the man rest in peace for God's sake."

"You know, it wouldn't take long for a rumor to circulate about how you found his body. About how it was you who probably killed him in a jealous rage," she said with a snakelike smile.

Somehow, all three of us ended up in a standing position, Kate's hand resting lightly on my arm in case I thought of doing anything rash.

"You're a liar," I said, but the color had drained from my face. I knew it wouldn't take long at all for a rumor of that magnitude to get started and spread through the town.

"At least I didn't sleep with the principal to get my job," she said. "Do you think I wanted to teach Home Ec? I was more qualified to get your position, but it didn't seem to matter what I did to influence Mr. Butler. He only had eyes for you. Apparently he's drawn to women who have a body belonging to a middle-aged housewife. Tell me Addison, did Mr. Butler get tired of you just like Greg? Were you just another cast off? It's a pretty good motive for murder."

Veronica leaned toward me, spewing venom from her fangs, her huge breasts spilling out of her gown. I was still trying to figure out why she thought I had any kind of relationship with Mr. Butler, sexual or otherwise. We'd never said more than a dozen words to each other the entire time he'd worked at my school. And I was even more stunned by the fact Veronica thought she should have had my job. I was almost willing to trade her just so she could see the horrors she'd been missing out on. I wouldn't mind spending seven periods a day teaching kids how to crochet hot mats or change a diaper on a bag of flour.

"Look over there, even Nick's lost interest in the forty-five minutes he's had to spend in your company," she said, pointing toward the dance floor.

I shouldn't have looked. But Nick was supposed to be my lifeline for the night. He'd told me he wasn't going anywhere and I believed him. So I looked.

And there was Nick with his arms around some woman I had never seen before, dancing much too close for my comfort and laughing at whatever she'd just whispered in his ear. This was the last straw for me. If I was going to go down, I wasn't going without a fight.

"Bring it on, bitch," I said, looking straight at Veronica. "What's going to happen in ten years when the tits you're so proud of are hanging down to your knees and there's no one left to give blow jobs to that you haven't already serviced?"

I heard Kate stifle a laugh behind her hand. Veronica was sputtering and spittle was flying. No one messed with Addison Holmes. Well, sometimes they did, but not this time.

"Oh, yeah?" she said, eyes narrowing. "You're just a sexless wannabe that looks like a pathetic tramp in black leather and just plain pathetic the rest of the time. Maybe you should have stuck with your first instinct and stayed with your lesbian friend here. Oh, wait. You can't. Even the lesbian managed to find a husband somehow."

I was so furious I was shaking. The room was unusually quiet, and I glanced around to see a group of people raptly paying attention to what was going on between us. My gaze found Nick's across the room, but it was with indifference. He was nothing to me.

I was done with people who only made me look like a fool. I did a perfectly fine job of doing that on my own. I turned back to Veronica when Nick started towards me, hoping that I could make an exit and leave for home before he reached me.

"That's a fine specimen of man," Veronica said, her gaze also lingering on Nick. "You seem to be able to find the attractive men, but you don't seem to be able to keep them. Why is that, I wonder?"

Veronica's eyes gleamed like black marbles. Her satisfied smirk was more than I could bear. She knew she'd finally gotten to me, but her viper's tongue wasn't through inflicting damage. "I'm going to enjoy moving into that little house you've had your eye on. I think it's just perfect for newlyweds starting out. Maybe you'll have the money to buy it from us when we're ready to upgrade."

"That's my house," I said, eyes squinted and adrenaline pumping.

And before I knew it, my arm developed a mind of its own. In slow motion, wine flew from my glass and splashed all over the front of Veronica's silver gown, making the thin material even more indecent.

She took about five seconds to assess the damage and let out with a screech that would do a banshee proud.

"You cunt!" she yelled at the top of her lungs.

You could hear the collective gasp run through the entire ballroom. The C word was never used outside of bars or gaming halls and certainly not by a woman.

I never saw her coming. The next thing I knew I was on the ground with chocolate cake squished between us and her bony knees in my stomach. I screamed in pain and pulled her hair, bucking my body from underneath to try and dislodge her. I'm sure we made a sight, rolling around across the ballroom floor.

I scratched and clawed, and it was the only time in my life I'd been sorry for being a girl because that's exactly how

I fought. I heard fabric rip and got a face full of bare breasts. I did the only thing I could before being suffocated and poked her in the eyes just like I'd learned from *The Three Stooges*.

Greg loomed above us, trying desperately to break up the fight. He grabbed Veronica under the armpits and tried to lift her off me. I could tell he was thinking this episode was going to be hell on the insurance business. Veronica's head snapped back and flattened Greg's chiseled Roman nose and I started to laugh uncontrollably.

I finally levered myself up to my knees and was able to get a solid punch to Veronica's face. I had enough time to hear the satisfactory crunch of bone and cartilage before I felt a jolt on my ass and my brains scramble.

9

I CRACKED MY EYES OPEN AND LOOKED THROUGH HAZY vision to see Nick staring down at me, his face inches from my own.

"Am I dead?"

"Not yet," he said.

When I woke again, bright light was streaming through my bedroom curtains and every inch of my body ached. In fact, it had been so long since my body didn't ache I was getting used to the feeling.

My brain was fuzzy and I had a monster headache, so I carefully got out of bed and climbed into the shower. It was after I'd gotten in and turned on the water that I realized I hadn't had to take my clothes off. Someone had already done that for me.

Nick.

I began searching my memory for what could have possibly happened the night before. Surely I didn't have the only wild night of sex I'd ever experienced and then promptly forgotten it. I stuck my head under the hot spray and winced as the water hit the open scratches on my chest and arms.

Oh Yeah.

It was all starting to come back now. I'd made a fool of myself. Again. And Nick was lying scum, just like Greg. I was starting to see an unhealthy pattern develop and somehow I needed to change things. I vaguely remembered visions of Nick at some point during my unconsciousness, but that's where it ended.

I wrapped a white towel around my head and put on a soft cotton robe, since that would be the least painful to my wounds, and headed into the kitchen.

"You need to put some antiseptic on those scratches so they don't get infected. I put some on you last night, but you need to keep applying it."

I whirled around in surprise and clasped a hand to my throat at the sight of Nick sitting at my breakfast table with the newspaper in front of him and a bowl of cereal in his hands. His hair was still damp from his shower and his feet were bare and propped up on another chair.

"Thanks for the medical advice. Now get the hell out of my apartment," I said, turning my back on him to get a cup of coffee. I should have known he wouldn't listen.

He was silent as he moved close behind me. I don't know whether it was his sexy scent or the way I began to tingle as he approached, but I knew he was there. Still, I jumped when he placed his hand on my shoulder.

"Would you like to share why you're so angry with me, when in my opinion, it should be me that's angry with you? After all, it was my date that got into a knockdown drag out fight in the middle of the biggest social event of the year in front of my boss and all my co-workers."

He was trembling behind me, and I was almost afraid to turn around and face his anger. He did kind of have a point. But when I turned around it wasn't anger he was trembling from. His mouth was curved in a tight smile and he leaned against me trying to control the laughter.

"One thing you are definitely not is boring," he said, kissing me on the cheek and heading back to his cereal. "I like that in a woman."

I had a momentary lapse of why I was mad at him, but quickly got myself back together again.

"That doesn't change the fact that I still want you to leave."

"Why? We have work to do, and besides, I kind of like taking care of you."

"Yeah, you seemed to be taking pretty good care of your sexy dancing partner last night too."

He just smiled at the show of jealousy and continued to read the paper.

"Did you not hear anything that Veronica said to me last night?"

"I heard several choice phrases uttered last night, some of which were even said by you. Which one are you referring to?"

"All of them. Every word that she said to me was true, except the part where she accused me of seducing my principal and stealing her job. I don't know where she got those ideas," I said shaking my head in disbelief. "But she was right about one thing. I can't seem to keep a man's attention. I don't need another man like Greg in my life, even if you are just for rebound sex. I think my ego and self esteem have taken enough hits for the next sixty or seventy years. You're not worth it."

Tears stung the back of my eyes and I turned around to busy myself with breakfast.

"Of course I'm worth it," he said. "I'm one of the good guys. The woman I was dancing with was my partner for two years when I was on patrol. She's married with four kids and would be flattered to think you thought she was sexy."

"Oh." *Great, Addison. Real spiffy comeback.* "Well, Veronica was right about everything else." I wasn't about to let logic and truth interfere with my mood.

"Are you done with the pity party yet?" Nick asked. "You know what you look like. You're anything but average. Someone who could try moonlighting as a stripper doesn't really strike me as a person who's got problems with their ego or low self esteem."

I groaned. "I guess my secret's out?"

"Maybe not. You denied it, so it's your word against hers. I wouldn't worry about it. Besides, we'll find out soon enough who did murder Mr. Butler and none of what she said will matter."

"I don't suppose you want to enlighten me on why I woke up without clothes on."

"You were covered in chocolate cake." Nick grinned wickedly. "Though I had no idea what the hell you were wearing under that dress. I almost gave myself a bloody nose trying to get it off of you. I finally had to cut the damned thing off."

"Jesus, why me?"

"Don't worry. You redeemed yourself rather well." He folded the paper in his lap and his gaze skimmed down my body, making things tingle that had no business tingling at the moment. "I've got to be honest with you. I watched the tape of you squeezed into that sexy costume at The Foxy Lady, and I thought I'd gotten a good look at every curve of your body. But when I finally got that thing off you last night it was everything I could do not to wake you up and take advantage of you. There is most definitely nothing boring or plain about your body."

"Thank you for the creepy compliment. But I still want you to leave."

"Well, I happen to think you're lying."

He tossed the paper aside and stalked me until my back was to the wall. Blood rushed in my ears and my lungs burned with the effort to breathe.

"Where did you sleep last night?" I asked softly.

"I slept with you." He traced his finger down the side of my neck and then farther down to the knot that held my robe together, working it loose until it slipped free. My robe parted and I moaned as his finger circled my breast and then skimmed across my nipple. He leaned toward me until his lips were just a fraction away from my own. I watched with eyes wide open as he took my bottom lip between his teeth and bit gently.

My eyes rolled back in my head when his tongue soothed the sharp sting from his teeth.

"I want you," he whispered.

Yeah, the part that wanted me was pressed against my belly button. His fingers roamed lower and my brain began to function despite the new intimacy.

"Wait, this is too fast," I panted, pushing him away with both hands. I wrapped the robe back around me and tied the belt into a double knot.

"Okay, but maybe you could give me a timeline. I'd like to be inside you before I die of old age."

I had to close my eyes and gather my wits, because holy shit was I tempted to let him get his wish. "It's kind of embarrassing, considering all we've been through, but I've kind of decided that I don't want to have rebound sex with you."

"Good, because I don't want to have rebound sex with you either," he said.

"Oh." There was my prolific vocabulary again. I wanted to ask what exactly he meant. I couldn't tell by the look on his face because he'd banked the heat in his eyes and gotten his body back under control.

"You need to put some more cream on those scratches. They look pretty nasty, and I don't want them to get infected. There's no telling what kind of germs were under her fingernails."

"Oh, right," I said, still dazed and confused from jumping in and out of intimacy so fast. Not to mention the fact he'd just told me he didn't want to sleep with me.

I looked down at the scratches in question. They hurt worse than I wanted to admit, and I shuffled into the bathroom to get the antiseptic cream. I changed into a pair of heather gray jersey shorts and a soft white tank top. When I came out of the bedroom Nick was reading the paper again.

"Is anything else injured?" he asked.

"Just my pride. She weighs a lot more than she looks."

"Yeah, but you got in a couple of pretty good punches before you got stunned. She'll have at least one black eye, and her nose was bleeding like a faucet. Very unattractive."

"You're just trying to make me feel better," I said, smiling. "Hey, what do you mean before I was stunned? Are you saying somebody tasered me?"

"Hey, don't look at me like that. I didn't do it. It was the only way anyone could get in between the two of you to stop the fight. You were cemented together with chocolate icing and you had a death grip on her hair."

Nick shuddered at the memory.

"I got knocked on my ass twice trying to get to you. One of the beat cops pulled a taser out of her purse and got you both."

"I guess that would explain the memory loss."

"Sweetheart, be lucky you don't remember. It's something people are going to be talking about for years."

I grabbed a cup from the cupboard and filled it with coffee. Nick had left the sugar and cream out, so I put both into my steaming mug and then put them away in the proper places. He at least had the decency to rinse out his cereal bowl and put it upside down in the drain pan. I gulped the coffee standing up and the cobwebs started to clear from my mind. There was something different about my kitchen, but I couldn't put my finger on it. Then it hit me. The cream and sugar. The cereal. I had food.

"Where'd the cereal come from?" I asked. I still hadn't had time to go to the grocery store since starting the job for Kate. I just hoped Nick hadn't gone begging for food from my neighbors. I'm sure my mother had had enough phone calls about me in the last twenty-four hours.

"I went early this morning and got a few essentials," Nick said, not looking up from his reading.

I opened the fridge and the pantry to see what Nick considered essential. "Two loaves of bread, whole milk, macaroni and cheese, pork rinds, beef jerky, beer, potato chips and Frosted Flakes. It's good to see you eat such a well-balanced diet."

"You didn't think I kept such a manly physique by eating a bunch of fruits and vegetables, did you?"

"Hmmm," I said, getting my own bowl of cereal. "You have some explaining to do about a few things."

"Like what?"

"Well, for starters you said you needed my help on Mr. Butler's murder and then you don't tell me anything about it. And then last night you drop the bomb that Greg was there at The Foxy Lady at the time of Mr. Butler's death. Care to explain?"

"Eventually. But first I want to know about these." He upended a big manila envelope full of photos on the table. They all had one thing in common. I was in every photo.

"Where did you get those?" I asked. The spit in my mouth had dried up so the question came out as a croak.

"They were taped to your door when I got back from the grocery store this morning."

I flipped through the photos. There were pictures of me leaving yoga class and in the teacher's parking lot. There was one of me leaving my mom's after a Sunday dinner and another of me having dinner with Kate and Mike at a restaurant in Savannah. I tried to look at them dispassionately, but inside I was sick.

"Is this the first time someone has left photos?" Nick asked.

I winced inside because I knew he wasn't going to be happy with my answer. "Not exactly," I said.

I shuffled through my bag until I found the photo that had been taped to my car, and I handed it to Nick. "I also received a phone call," I said and punched the play button on my answering machine.

Nick listened to the entire message without saying a word, but his face darkened and took on the appearance of a thundercloud.

"Jesus Christ, Addison. Did it ever occur to you that

whoever left that message could be a killer? And now he's stalking you."

"When you say it that way it sounds a lot worse than what I'd worked out in my mind. I just figured it was some kind of prank." I chewed on my bottom lip as I thought it through. "Mr. Butler took this photo with his camera phone while I was on stage. I saw him do it. But someone left it taped to my windshield after Mr. Butler's murder. If Greg was at The Foxy Lady, do you think he could be Mr. Butler's killer and the one who left the photograph?"

Nick looked through all the photos and I could tell he was thinking things through in that methodical cop way he had. "I wouldn't rule it out," he said.

Nick picked up a black duffle bag and riffled through it. He pulled out an envelope lined with bubble wrap and pulled out a disc. "I've got the surveillance tapes from The Foxy Lady I'd like you to look at. You seem to be the only link between The Foxy Lady and Bernard Butler and Greg, and maybe you can spot something I can't. I'm desperate at this point."

"Oh, thanks a lot. I'm so glad you resort to my help in times of desperation. I'm not completely incompetent you know. I'm even thinking of getting a real P.I. license."

"God help us all," Nick said with a smile. "Make sure you take out personal protection insurance. You haven't had the best track record since you started this job."

"I don't have to take this from you. You're the one that needs my help. And to show you what a team player I am, I'm willing to make you a deal."

"I can't wait to hear this."

"I'll help you on your case if you'll help me on one of mine. It'll be an even trade."

"You think it's an even trade for me to help you with

amateur detective work while you help me with a murder investigation? You're out of your mind."

"Unless you're afraid that I'll be of more help to you than you will be to me. I guess it would look pretty bad for a detective to get shown up by a history teacher."

"Ha! You're as transparent as glass, Addison. You don't think that *you* can solve your case by yourself, whereas I know I can solve mine, it just might take a little longer without your help."

I wasn't willing to admit that he was right, so I stared him down with a look that any poker player would be proud of.

"I'll tell you what," he said. "I'll help you out. But—I have a couple of stipulations."

I rolled my eyes. "I've already told you I don't want to have sex with you, so you can steer clear of that idea."

"No, you told me you didn't want to have rebound sex with me. I, however, would like a date with you. With the chance of non-rebound sex to be followed closely after."

"That's blackmail," I said, outraged.

"Take it or leave it," he said, the grin on his face challenging. "Your nipples are hard, so I have to think that the idea of spending a night with me isn't completely repulsive."

"It's cold in here," I said, crossing my arms over my chest.

"Liar."

"Fine, it's a deal." I took the surveillance DVD from his hand and headed over to my 52" television.

"Everything about you is such a contradiction." He sat back on the couch with the remote in his hand and I took the spot beside him. "You have all this sweet electronic equipment, fancy furniture and a sexy car. Why the hell do you live in this dump?"

"The rent is cheap, which allows me to be able to almost afford all the sweet stuff. Tell me what you want me to look for."

Nick punched play and the screen split into six boxes, all labeled with which security camera they came from. Nick brought up camera one so it filled the whole screen.

"We've got your ex who arrived alone just after noon. He made himself comfortable in a booth and ordered a drink. He looked back and forth impatiently between his watch and the door for almost half an hour."

Nick fast-forwarded a few seconds. "Then we have an unknown woman who showed up at a quarter till one. None of the cameras got a shot of her face. She walked past the bouncer at the door with minimal fuss since she was wearing a table napkin for a skirt and her attributes were shown to their full advantage. She kept her head down all the way to the booth and slid in next to your ex."

"So Veronica meets Greg at a strip club for a little hanky panky and she's dressed like a slut. What else is new?"

"Look carefully at the video. That doesn't look like the woman I saw last night."

I looked at the shadowed photo carefully. "This woman has smaller breasts than Veronica," I said automatically. And then I gasped because that meant Greg was cheating on Veronica just like he'd cheated on me. "That sorry bastard. At least I can get rid of the guilt that it's something I did that made him cheat. Apparently he's just a horn dog."

Nick smiled and kept fast-forwarding. "Do you recognize her?"

I looked closely, but without seeing her face it was hard

to be sure. "No, sorry. She just looks kind of generic. She could be a prostitute or someone that Greg met at an insurance convention. Why don't you ask Greg who she is?"

"We'd love to, but Greg conveniently went out of town last Sunday and didn't get back until just before the gala last night. Veronica told us he flew out Sunday morning to a convention in New York, but when we checked the airlines we couldn't find him on a flight."

"Maybe he took the week off to spend with his new honey."

"Maybe. Or maybe he was running but had to come back to Whiskey Bayou to tie up a few loose ends. He does have a business here and a few remaining clients. Either way, we'll find out," he said. "As you can see, the booth was almost in complete shadow, and they got down to business pretty quickly. None of the floor security could see exactly what the woman was doing, but the security guy manning the cameras got an eyeful."

"Holy crap. She was doing that to him in public?" I asked. I wasn't sure I was completely comfortable watching what basically amounted to porn with Nick. "Okay, maybe you can fast forward some."

"Chicken." Nick squeezed the back of my neck, and he hit a button so another view came up on screen. "At the same time Greg was getting serviced by the unknown woman, we have your principal getting a lap dance. The girl doing the service had her name legally changed to Destiny Dollar when she turned eighteen two months ago."

I watched Destiny writhe and shake around Mr. Butler and wondered how he was able to pay attention to what was going on on stage with all the flesh and feathers in front of him.

Nick paused the disc. "This is where Butler notices you on stage," he said with laughter in his voice.

"This is so embarrassing," I said under my breath. I was grateful Nick didn't bring up the stage camera. I knew he'd seen it, but I was perfectly content not to relive the event.

Nick fast-forwarded some more and paused once again. "You've left the stage and Destiny can tell she's lost Butler's interest, so she takes his money and moves on to another customer. Butler stumbles out of his chair and heads for the bathroom, just past Greg's table, where Greg's sitting by himself again. They don't notice each other, or at least pretend not to. But look here," Nick said pausing the disc again. "Butler comes out of the hallway where the restrooms are like a bat out of hell. Or like he's seen something he's not supposed to. Then he books it out of the front door to the parking lot. Greg looks at his watch again and throws money down on the table before he leaves, the mystery woman is nowhere to be found, and Girard Dupres slips out the back door to the alley. Bernard Butler is killed within the next few minutes and none of these people are accounted for."

"Couldn't it have been a stranger passing through that killed Mr. Butler?" It was easier for me to believe that a stranger killed him than someone I'd slept with for a year.

"We're not ruling out the possibility," Nick said, cautiously.

"How does Girard Dupres fit into this?"

"Dupres has been under surveillance for running guns and money through The Foxy Lady. If he went outside to do business and Butler saw something he wasn't supposed to, Dupres or his clients wouldn't hesitate to kill him. They've done it before."

"So you're telling me I was engaged to a potential

murderer and I went to work for an illegal arms dealer," I said as the blood drained from my face.

"Pretty much," Nick said unfazed. "You've got lousy instincts, but cheer up. I'm a good guy. You've made a step in the right direction by deciding to not have rebound sex with me."

"Don't remind me," I said, feeling slightly ill. I remembered something else that had been bothering me. "What do you know about Robbie Butler?"

"After that scene he made at his brother's funeral mass I'd say there's a few pieces of silverware missing out of his drawer. He's obviously angry at a woman he thought his brother was seeing, but we didn't find any evidence Bernard Butler was in any type of relationship. Why?"

"I think maybe I was the woman he was talking about."

"So you're the Jezebel that led Butler to his death?" Nick laughed so hard I thought he'd fall out of his chair.

"You don't have to be insulting," I huffed. "I could be the kind of woman that leads men astray if I wanted to."

I was saved from defending my sexual prowess by the ringing of the phone. Then I remembered that there was someone out there who liked to leave scary messages and take pictures of me without my knowledge.

Or it could be my mother on the line. I couldn't decide which person I'd rather talk to.

"Answer the phone, Addison. If it's the same guy as before, we'll deal with it. This is my job."

I picked up the phone with the care of someone holding a bomb that was about to detonate. "Hello?"

"Addison Holmes?" a man asked.

"This is Addison."

"Oh, thank heavens. This is Victor Mooney."

I could hear his rapid breathing and wondered what he was doing.

"I have information for you regarding what we talked about. I don't want to tell you over the phone because I think someone has been listening in on my calls. I've made a few inquiries that might have made someone angry."

"Are you all right?" I asked concerned that I'd involved Mr. Mooney in something that I shouldn't have.

"I'm just a bit winded. I ran from my car to a pay phone so I could call you. Meet me at The Blessed Sacrament Catholic Church in half an hour. I've even got pictures," he said, sounding excited. "I've been giving some thought to getting my P.I. license ever since you came to talk to me. I haven't had this much fun in years."

"I'll meet you there, Mr. Mooney. Be careful," I said, but he'd already hung up.

We arrived at the Blessed Sacrament Catholic Church with five minutes to spare. The rain had started again but was just a miserable drizzle instead of a torrential downpour. I'd changed out of the soft cotton tank and shorts into a short denim skirt and a stretchy pink top, which might not have been completely appropriate clothing for church, but none of the fabric touched my numerous scratches or bruises, so God would just have to understand.

"Have you ever noticed how creepy churches are when they're empty?" Nick asked.

"No. Not until you mentioned it."

The gothic style cathedral was a cornerstone in Whiskey Bayou. Its flying buttresses and stoic arches were intimidating enough to make even the worst sinners walk with a soft step past its doors. I kept expecting bats to swoop down, so I let Nick walk in front of me.

The church was empty as we made our way inside, and

the little creaks and groans of the building settling around us gave me the willies as we walked down the nave to the altar. My voice echoed through the empty room as I called out for Mr. Mooney.

"Maybe he changed his mind," Nick said.

"He said he thought someone had been listening to his phone calls. You don't think something happened to him, do you?"

We walked up the aisles and headed to the north balcony just to make sure he wasn't there.

"Nah. He could have gotten caught in traffic for all you know. You women always worry over nothing." Nick put his hands on his hips and his windbreaker shifted so I could see his gun.

"You're wearing a gun in church," I whispered, looking around to make sure there was no chance of getting struck by lightning.

"Honey, the only time I don't wear a gun is when I'm in bed or in the shower. You'll have an opportunity to see for yourself before too much longer."

Nick winked at me and I got a mental image of him wet and naked holding his gun. The euphemism wasn't so subtle that I didn't catch on. My body temperature spiked as Nick walked away with a whistle. It was a good thing I wasn't Catholic because I'd have to confess to having impure thoughts in a church.

"Where are you going?" I asked, jogging to catch up to his long stride.

"I'm going to check out the crypt and the graveyard and then I'm going to take you home and get you back in those tiny shorts you were wearing earlier."

"I didn't put them on to entice you," I said, exasperated. "I put them on because they were comfortable."

"I can promise you the fit of my jeans became decidedly uncomfortable as soon as you put them on. I've always considered myself a leg man."

"Should we stop by a Kentucky Fried Chicken on our way home?"

"You're a laugh a minute, Addison." Nick opened the heavy door that led into the crypt and would eventually lead to the cemetery behind the church.

"Surely he's not going to be in there," I said, backing up a little. "Why don't you check there, and I'll go around and meet you in the cemetery?"

"What's the big deal? Surely you're not afraid to be around dead people."

"Of course not," I said, insulted. The truth was I was terrified of being enclosed in a large cement room with dead people. Closed in. Underground. Surrounded by stone and concrete.

"You're a history teacher," he went on. "You should look at this as a way to study this cathedral's past. You could learn something important."

"Uh-huh," I said as we made our way through rows of sarcophagi and plaques. "Remind me to tell you about the time I took a bunch of students on a field trip to the catacombs in Rome. You'll understand why I have a problem with this."

I had a death grip on Nick's hand and jumped when I heard a squeak somewhere ahead of us.

"Relax, honey." Nick pulled me close and rubbed his hands up and down my chilled arms to give me some warmth. "Buildings this old make a lot of noise shifting. Especially this far south where the ground can turn into a marsh at any time.

I nodded my head yes, but my eyes were saying no, no,

no. I needed to get the hell out of here because I was a minute or so away from hyperventilating and fainting at Nick's feet.

"Addison, look at me," he demanded as I started to wheeze.

I looked up and he held my head still between his hands until I focused on his eyes. They were impossibly blue and filled with understanding, humor and lust.

"I'm not going to let anything happen to you. You'll always be safe with me."

Nick decided to take things into his own hands. Suddenly his mouth was on mine and his tongue was becoming much too familiar with my tonsils—not that I was complaining. And to give him credit, it was impossible for my teeth to chatter with his tongue in my mouth.

"What are you doing?" I asked, pulling back.

"What does it look like I'm doing? Don't worry, I'll still take you on that date we talked about."

"Okay. Good. Whatever. Just kiss me again."

Nick hitched me up so I could wrap my legs around his waist, and I moaned as he pressed his hardness against my aching loins. My skirt rucked up around my waist, and I could feel my panties getting wet. I moved against him until he was hitting my sweet spot over and over again and I was moments away from the orgasm of a lifetime.

"Christ, you make me insane," Nick said as he licked into my mouth. He carried me to a wide stone bench that sat in the middle of the aisle and sat down so I straddled his lap.

I pushed Nick's windbreaker off his shoulders and shuddered as he found the front hook to my bra and made fast work of removing it. My shirt was twisted up around my neck and all I cared about was feeling Nick's skin next to mine. I pulled his shirt up and pressed my naked breast to his chest, and both of us groaned at the contact.

"Hurry, hurry," I panted.

He tore his mouth away from mine and fought with the scrap of lace that covered my most intimate parts.

"To hell with it," he said and tore them from my body.

I fought with his belt buckle and had just gotten it loose when I looked up and saw a statue of a saint staring straight at us.

"Ohmigod, stop. We have to stop," I said, pushing him back with both hands and jumping off his lap.

"Are you crazy? You can't just say stop. What's wrong with you?"

"We're in a church," I whispered. "I can not have sex in a church. My mother would kill me."

"I won't tell her," he said. "I swear. Now get back over here."

"No, aren't you listening? We're in a church. And all of these saints are staring at us," I said horrified.

"Are you Catholic?" Nick asked.

"No."

"Then it doesn't count. I think I read that somewhere. And technically we're not in a church. We're in a crypt. There's a difference."

"So now we're not only being disrespectful to God, but to dead people too. Great. We're going to hell."

"I promise if you'll come back over here I'll make it worth the trip," he begged.

I looked over Nick's hard body and was sorely tempted. He was laid out on the stone bench like an offering, his chest naked and the bulge behind his zipper swollen to the point that it looked painful. His eyes were clouded with lust and his breath was labored. He looked good enough to eat, and I groaned as I argued my wants against my morals.

I didn't have to make a decision because footsteps echoed and a door slammed, and I was so freaked out that someone had just witnessed me commit a mortal sin that I pulled my skirt down and was attempting to get my shirt untangled when a gunshot rang out.

Nick was off the bench in a split second, his weapon drawn and the lust in his eyes replaced by a look of such intense hardness that I took a step back in fear. He ran towards the sound of the shot, through the door leading to the cemetery, and left me standing by myself in the middle of a bunch of dead guys.

"Nick!" I screamed and took off after him. I couldn't decide if I was angry with him for leaving me alone or angry that he'd run full speed ahead toward the sound of gunfire.

I burst through the crypt door into the graveyard. The rain was back to torrential downpour status and the dark clouds made it hard to see. I couldn't see Nick, but my adrenaline and fear wouldn't let me do anything but run full speed ahead. My foot caught on a headstone and I went flying. It was fortunate that it was raining because landing on mud was a lot softer than landing on hard-packed dirt. I sprawled in an ungraceful heap on the graves of Dr. and Mrs. Stanley Took and grimaced as I noticed I'd uprooted the flowers that someone had so carefully planted.

"Nick!" I called out again.

I sat in the mud and rain in silence and waited to hear Nick's voice or footsteps or another gunshot. My teeth chattered, there was mud in places best left unmentioned, and I was close to tears with fear that something bad had happened to Nick.

"Addison!"

I heard Nick's bellow and breathed a sigh of relief. He wasn't dead and I wasn't alone. Things were suddenly looking up.

I followed the sound of his voice, playing an impromptu game of Marco Polo, until I saw his shadow next to the wrought iron fence that surrounded the cemetery. His gun was still drawn and he was talking on his cell phone requesting an ambulance and back up.

I looked down at his feet and saw the reason. Victor Mooney was lying face down in the mud, the blossoming blood from a gunshot seeping from his back.

"Oh my God," I said as I took a step back.

Nick hung up the phone and glared at me. "I know you have a hard time thinking before you act, but next time you hear gunshots don't run full speed ahead into the line of fire until I give you the all clear."

"You left me by myself in a room full of dead guys," I screamed at him. "And besides, you ran full speed ahead into the line of fire."

"I'm a cop. I have a gun. That's what I'm supposed to do," he yelled back. "I can't believe this. You've made me so crazy that I'm yelling in a graveyard."

"You feel bad about yelling in a graveyard after you just tried to have sex with me in a church?" I screeched.

Nick closed his eyes and was obviously counting to ten many times over. "Listen to me, Addison. As soon as backup arrives I'm going to have an officer escort you to your car, and then I want you to drive straight to Kate's. Nowhere else. Do you understand?"

"I'm not going to Kate's looking like this," I said. "Why can't I go home?"

"Because you've been receiving photographs and threatening phone calls and a man you were supposed to meet is lying dead at your feet. Call me crazy, but I think you might be in a little bit of danger, and I don't feel comfortable sending you home while I'm occupied with a homicide just to have some whacko waiting for you once you open the door. Just do what I ask for once."

"Fine." I squished my way over to a bench so I could wait for my babysitter to arrive.

I sat in my car with a white-knuckled grip on the steering wheel and watched the rain pound against the windshield. I was soaked to the skin, my skirt was ripped, and blood seeped from both knees. There were scratches on my arms and neck, and my face was blotchy and red from crying. Along with the external wounds, I'd lost a good deal of my sensibilities, most of my faith in mankind, and all of my underwear somewhere between a graveyard and a church parking lot.

I hadn't yet found the courage to get out of the car and go into the McClean Detective Agency. I was working my way up to it, but the last time I'd tried to open the door it started to hail and hurricane force winds slammed my door shut. Not to mention the fact that the mud in my crevices was drying at an alarming rate and I might be stuck in this position forever.

I guess I'd been sitting out front too long because I could see several faces inside peeping out the windows at me, and my cell phone rang in the seat beside me.

"Are you coming in or are you just going to sit out there looking pitiful all day?" Kate asked.

"I haven't decided yet. I'm not allowed to go home, but I'm not sure I have the energy to come inside and explain."

"Nick already called and explained, so if you come in I'll give you some clean clothes and the use of our shower with minimal questions."

I sighed into the phone. "That's the second best proposition I've had all day."

I disconnected and put on my raincoat just so it would hide the fact that I wasn't wearing a bra. I slogged my way up to the entrance and pushed against the glass doors.

Lucy Kim came from behind her desk with a stack of gray warm-ups and a bar of soap. Her legs scissored quickly on black spiked heels as she headed in my direction. Her face was expressionless and her lips were freshly painted red. If the mud hadn't stuck my shoes to the floor I would have backed up because she looked like she wanted to kill someone. Probably me for dripping on the carpet.

She walked past me without saying a word and stopped in front of a white door with an old-fashioned knob. She held the door open and stared at me with black eyes so intense that I wouldn't have been the least bit surprised if they shot lasers or set things on fire.

I dripped my way over and took the clothes from her. She gave me a firm push with the tip of her finger and slammed the door behind me.

"It was nice talking to you too," I yelled through the door.

The bathroom was spacious and old fashioned. It was obviously for employee use as there were little cubbies that lined one wall with names taped to them. I stood on the cold tile and peeled the clothes from my body and then put them in the trash. They were a lost cause—much like my life.

I enjoyed a luxurious half hour under the hot spray and borrowed shampoo from a woman named Susan. I was pretty sure she wouldn't mind. I dried off and dug around in the cabinets until I found a first aid kit. The skin on my palms and knees was rubbed raw from my fall and my arms had scratches on them, so I rubbed on some antibacterial cream so I wouldn't get graveyard germs.

I put on the sweats and decided I was getting much too comfortable going places without underwear. I tried not to think about how I ended up without it, or when Nick was going to try to make me go without it again.

I tidied the bathroom and walked in my sock feet down to Kate's office, feeling like a new woman.

"I was about to come down and make sure you hadn't drowned," Kate said as I plopped face down on the couch in her office.

"It took a while considering some of the places I had mud."

"You've also got a nasty case of whisker burn on your neck. I don't suppose you want to explain that?" Kate asked.

"Let's just say things got complicated before we stumbled over the body."

"You'd better hope your mother never finds out you had sex in a church."

"We didn't have sex," I growled.

"Which would explain why you're in such a good mood."

"No, I'm pretty sure sexual frustration is the least of my problems. I'd say the biggest one is that I keep finding dead bodies."

"You don't think the murders are related, do you?"

"I don't know. Mr. Butler didn't have anything to do with me, but I feel responsible for Mr. Mooney. I guess I should confess that I asked Mr. Mooney to snoop around and keep track of who was going in and out of the Hyatt mansion. And now he's dead. He said he had information for me, so I'm thinking whatever it was made someone nervous enough to kill him."

Kate closed her eyes and looked like she was counting.

"Is there anything else you need to tell me?" she finally asked.

I thought back through the last week and grimaced. There was probably a lot I needed to tell Kate, but none of it would make her feel better, so I decided to keep quiet and shook my head no.

"Well, this is out of our hands now, Addison. It's up to the police to find out who killed Mr. Mooney and if his death had anything to do with your principal's. I guess it's just our luck that Fanny Kimble withdrew her offer for us to investigate John Hyatt. We'll let the police do their jobs and you can go back to your normal surveillance routine. At least you should be able to stay out of trouble without stumbling across any more bodies."

I sat and stared at Kate in shock. She'd gone back to reading the papers on her desk. "Kate, I feel responsible for Mr. Mooney's death. I'm not just going to stop investigating things because you or Fanny Kimble says so. I've got a stake in this, and I'm going to see it through."

"Addison, listen to me," Kate said deliberately enunciating each word, a sure sign she was about to lose her temper. "If you want to work for me then you will do what I say. Period. I'm worried about you, and this is not something you need to stick your nose into. Lord knows, somebody has to keep you out of trouble."

I was about to interrupt when she held up a hand to silence me.

"I also have a business to worry about. A business with a good reputation. If you can't follow my rules then I will fire you."

My mouth opened and closed like a guppy. "You'd really fire me?" I asked, incredulously.

"In a heartbeat if it meant saving either your life or my business. Do we have an agreement?"

I looked at Kate closely, but she wasn't bluffing. She really would fire me.

"Fine," I said. "But I can't promise that I can stay out of it completely. Nick's already told me he thinks I'm somehow caught in the middle of this mess. All I can do is wait and see if he's right."

"As long as you're not actively seeking trouble out. Now tell me about these pictures you've been getting."

"Geez, does Nick tell you everything? What a blabbermouth."

"He's telling me things that I should have heard from you. I don't like to hear about my employees being stalked, not to mention my best friend."

"I don't know. My gut tells me it's probably Veronica. It wouldn't be the first time she's stooped to such a juvenile level. And the things she said at the Officer's Gala keep replaying in my mind. She really thinks that I've screwed her over, and she's out for revenge."

"Let me do some checking for you. If it's Veronica I can find out, and believe me when I tell you I can put the fear of God into her."

"Thanks," I said, grateful. "It'll be nice to have one less thing to worry about."

"Just don't let your guard down," she warned. "I feel better that Nick told you to stay with me until he can take over. You can come hang out at my house until he gets done with the preliminary investigation. He'll follow you back home and make sure your apartment is safe. But it could be a little while because he said he was having trouble with Whiskey Bayou's sheriff."

"What's the problem?" I asked.

"Jurisdiction. Nick just called in a Crime Scene Team from Savannah and overrode him in that patient way he has. The sheriff wasn't too happy to have the city boys on his turf."

"Can't blame him. It makes me uncomfortable to have Nick on my turf all the time."

10

BANG, BANG, BANG.

I groaned as I heard the pounding on the front door and rolled over to look at the clock. It was just past seven in the morning, and I knew if I was awake I'd have to break down and go to church. I wouldn't be able to use the "I overslept" excuse.

I pulled the pillow over my head and hoped whoever it was would go away.

Bang, Bang, Bang.

I heard the scrape of the lock and sat up in bed. The only person who had a key to my apartment was my mother.

"Rise and shine, sleeping beauty," a familiar voice bellowed out. "We've got things to do."

Before I could pull the sheets up to hide the fact that I didn't sleep in pajamas—mostly because I didn't have air conditioning—Nick opened the door to my bedroom and shut it behind him.

"Well, well," he said, his gaze so heated I was lucky my sheets didn't catch on fire. "It looks like the early bird catches the worms after all."

"Do you know what time it is?" I asked him, pulling the sheet higher. "How did you get into my apartment?"

"I picked the lock."

"I assume you have a reason for breaking and entering at this hour. Or maybe I just need to call the cops and have you arrested for trespassing. You're probably not on the sheriff's list of favorite people right now."

Nick groaned and backed off. "You'd probably do it too," he said with his hands up in a sign of defeat. "I came by to check up on you and noticed someone left you a gift under your door last night."

Nick held up a plain brown envelope sealed with enough packing tape that it could have survived a swim in the Atlantic Ocean.

I pulled the sheet loose from my bed and tied it around me sarong style. "Let me see that," I said, holding out my hand.

"Unh-uh. Make yourself decent, and we'll take a look." He pushed me back and shut the bedroom door in my face.

I threw on a pair of black shorts and a white halter-top and was back out in the living room before he had time to get a pot of coffee going. I'd had it with whoever was leaving me these little gifts. I was pissed and ready to kick ass. I made a mental note to check into taking karate the same time I checked into getting my P.I. license.

I sat at the little table in my kitchen and waited until Nick brought me a cup of coffee and sat down across from me before holding out my hand for the envelope.

"Why does this keep happening?"

"I had officers scheduled to drive by your apartment

every hour last night, so someone dropped these off sometime after I followed you home and in between drive-bys. As to why it keeps happening, I have no idea, but I'm getting close. I can feel it."

I went to the kitchen and grabbed a knife from the drawer and worked at the top flap, but my hands were shaking so badly from anger and fear that Nick carefully took the knife from me.

"Let me do it," he said gently.

He slit the envelope open, dumped a short stack of photos onto the table and then put the envelope in a freezer size Zip-Loc baggie.

"Great, more pictures," I said. "Why do I feel like this is something bigger than an old high school rivalry? Surely Veronica doesn't hate me this much."

"You never know what's going on inside of other people or how they've been affected by the events in their lives. But don't be naïve in thinking Veronica should be the only suspect on your list. Surely you've managed to piss off more than one person in your life," he said with a quick grin.

"I'll have you know I'm a perfectly nice person. Most of the time," I mumbled under my breath.

"I want you to look at each photo carefully," he said, pulling a small notebook and pen out of his jacket pocket. "Are they recent?"

I picked up the first picture and tried to look at my image dispassionately. I was having dinner with Kate at the Good Luck Café. We'd been in a booth next to a window, and the picture had been taken from outside a good distance away. "We have dinner like this a couple of times a month," I said, shaking my head. "This could have been taken last year or in the last two weeks."

"Look closely, Addison. Look at your hairstyle and the

kind of clothes your wearing. Do you think it's possible it was last year?"

I did as he asked and tried to focus on the details. My hair looked the same as it did now, which meant it was a recent photograph. At this time last year I'd had blond highlights in my hair and it had been several inches shorter. "Okay," I said, exhaling in relief that I hadn't been stalked and clueless for more than a year. "This is recent. Within the last couple of months I'd say."

I grabbed the rest of the photos and looked at them all. Me at the dry cleaners. Me at a high school basketball game. Me at the park with my mother. All recent. I was sure of it. "These are, too," I said.

"Were they all taken before or after you found Bernard Butler's body?" Nick asked. I started to open my mouth and ask why, but he interrupted. "Think about it carefully," he said.

"Before," I finally said. "Why is that important?"

My question went unanswered. Nick was in full cop mode, and there was nothing I could do to get him to share his thoughts with me.

"I can't believe someone would do this," I said.

"Not just someone, Addison, but more than likely the murderer."

"I keep thinking about Robbie Butler and his reaction to me during his brother's funeral. There's no way I misread those looks he was giving me. He hates me for some reason, and he certainly knows his way around the church."

I was also thinking about the first photograph I'd received. The one my principal had taken of me on stage at The Foxy Lady. Could Robbie Butler have killed his own brother? I looked out the window and noticed the sun was shining for once, but it didn't make me feel better.

"You've read my mind," Nick said. "Robbie Butler is definitely a person of interest in this investigation. But you need to let me handle this. I want you to go stay with Kate."

For the first time since we'd opened the package I noticed the fine tremors of anger radiating from Nick's body. There was nothing in the world that would make me miss Nick confronting Robbie Butler.

"I don't think so," I said and grabbed my bag.

"Fine, but let me do the talking."

I wasn't going to argue. I was more than happy to let someone more competent than I was be in charge.

Robbie Butler lived in a town home just south of the historic district in downtown Savannah. Each building housed two units. Red geraniums were planted along the sidewalk that led to Robbie's front door and huge elm trees lined the street. Nick parked his truck at the curb and I hopped out with all the enthusiasm of Marie Antoinette heading towards the guillotine.

"Nice place," I said, knowing the rent in this area was astronomical.

"Yeah, the youngest Butler is an investment banker. The other unit in his building was occupied by his oldest brother."

"Mr. Butler lived here? My principal?" I asked, surprised. "Maybe I need to check into becoming a principal."

The curtains in the front room fluttered and I knew we'd been spotted. Nick rang the doorbell and rapped on the door twice, and when Robbie Butler answered the door I had a hard time connecting the image I'd seen at the funeral to the one standing in front of me. He was dressed in torn jeans and a t-shirt that looked like he'd been sleeping in it. Days old stains littered the front of his shirt—ketchup, whole grain mustard, pickle relish and grape jelly. It must have been a hell of a sandwich. My lip curled involuntarily at the yellow stains under his armpits, and my eyes watered at the stench emanating off his body. His eyes were red-rimmed, his face gaunt, and he hadn't seen a razor since the funeral. The only thing that was recognizable was the belligerent hostility etched on his face.

"Robbie Butler?" Nick asked.

"Yeah. What do you want?" He addressed his question to me, and it was obvious he still thought of me as the woman who caused his brother to die.

"I'm Detective Dempsey with the Savannah PD. I've been investigating your brother's death."

"His murder, you mean," Robbie interjected.

"Yes. I need to ask you a few questions."

"I've already talked to the police. The person you need to question is standing right beside you, but it's pretty obvious she's wormed her way into your bed too."

I could feel myself turning red. What was it that made people think that Nick and I were already sleeping together?

"We can do this here or I can take you down to the station," Nick said. "It's up to you."

We waited patiently while Robbie made up his mind. He finally stepped back. "Fine, but make it quick. I've got things to do today."

He left us standing in the entryway while he sat down in his recliner and flipped on the T.V. Nick walked around, past crumpled beer cans and empty pizza boxes, looking at family photographs and other things lying around. I'd never been in an investment banker's home, but I couldn't imagine that most of them looked like this one on the inside.

I stayed back at the door out of Robbie's sight in hopes it would make him a little more cooperative.

"Can you tell me your whereabouts for yesterday morning between ten and eleven o'clock in the morning?" Nick finally asked.

"I was here," Robbie said, his eyes never leaving the T.V. "I haven't been out of the house since the funeral."

"Huh, that's strange because someone has been leaving photographs of Ms. Holmes here taped to her door and she's been getting some threatening phone calls. You wouldn't happen to know anything about that, would you?"

"Nope. I don't know what you're talking about."

He was either a really good poker player or he was telling the truth. Then I noticed his white knuckled grip on the T.V. remote.

"So it's just a coincidence that one of her neighbors saw you in the building late at night twice this past week."

This was the first I'd heard of this. I guess Nick had meant it when he said he'd take care of things.

Robbie finally turned his head and looked at Nick. "If she's getting photographs and phone calls it's probably because she deserves them. It wasn't me. Do I need to call my lawyer?"

"Only if you think you need to," Nick answered. "You see, Robbie, I have enough on suspicion to bring you in for formal questioning. We have neighbors who can describe you, and you don't have an alibi during the time of a murder. It all seems pretty suspicious to me."

"What the hell are you talking about?" Robbie asked. "What murder?" He finally turned off the television and gave Nick his full attention.

"Let me tell you what I think, Robbie." Nick's voice was

as soft and smooth as ever. It reminded me of the first time we'd met, when he'd questioned me in the same patient way. "I think you're fixated on Ms. Holmes. I don't know why and I don't care, but stalking can be a felony in the state of Georgia. I think you've been following her and photographing her, and yesterday you followed her to the Catholic church where your brother's funeral was held and took some pictures of Ms. Holmes doing some very private things in the crypt. Were you planning on blackmailing her?" Nick didn't give Robbie a chance to answer, but instead went in for the kill. "And then do you know what I think, Robbie? I think you stumbled across someone who caught you in the act, and you shot him in cold blood. How does that sound to you? Pretty accurate?"

Robbie whirled around and faced me, a look of absolute horror on his face. "You were having sex in a church?" he asked.

"I was not having sex!" I yelled. "Why doesn't anyone believe me? And besides, I wasn't in the church. I was in the crypt."

Robbie crossed himself. "I'll never understand what Bernie saw in you. He loved you, and you flaunted yourself in front of other men. It drove him crazy the way men always flocked to you."

"Are you sure you're talking about me?" I asked. "Because I think I'd remember if men were flocking. Usually the men in my life flock to other women. It seems to be a theme."

"It's not funny. He's dead because of you. You lured him to that place and someone killed him. Probably another of your jealous boyfriends." Robbie was openly crying now, and I felt a little sorry for him.

"I'm sorry. I don't know where you got the impression

that Mr. Butler and I were anything more than acquaintances, but that's really all we were. It was as big a surprise to see him at The Foxy Lady as it was for him to see me."

"I don't believe you." Robbie crumpled to a heap in his chair and sobbed. "It was all in his diary. He had details of all the things you did sexually. He had dozens and dozens of pictures of you. How could you say you weren't close? He was in love with you."

Nick took over at that point because I was trying to deal with the fact that my principal had been stalking me for months and I'd never caught on. How could I be that clueless?

"And so you found your brother's diary and the pictures of Ms. Holmes and you sent them to her because you blamed her for your brother's death."

"Yes," he said, barely audible. "I wanted her to see what she looked like through another's eyes. How she should be ashamed for the way she acts and dresses."

"And did you kill a man in cold blood because of your own obsession with Ms. Holmes?"

"No, no, I swear," Robbie said. He got up and paced the floor, agitated. "And I didn't make any phone calls either. I taped one photograph to her car window and I left a manila envelope full of pictures at her apartment a couple of times. Those were all of them. I don't have any more. And maybe I followed her around some, but it was just so I could prove that she really was responsible for Bernie's death. I'll take a lie detector or do whatever, but I swear I didn't kill anyone."

Nick looked at me, and I looked at the pitiful man that was back to sobbing in his recliner. I knew Nick was waiting for me to decide how I wanted to proceed. I didn't really want to press charges against someone who was obviously having a difficult time dealing with the death of a loved one.

"I won't press charges against you if you can promise that you'll leave me alone," I finally told him.

"I told you I already gave you all the pictures. As far as I'm concerned I never want to see you again."

"As far as the murder goes," Nick said. "I suggest you find someone who can verify you were at home yesterday. I don't suppose you still have your brother's diary, do you?"

Robbie shook his head. "I burned it in the grill on my patio. I couldn't take the chance that anyone else would see it."

"Convenient," Nick said. "I don't suppose you'd mind if I took a look at your grill."

"I don't care. Just leave me alone," Robbie said.

"Mr. Butler," Nick said, his voice serious and expression grave. He waited until Robbie looked him in the eye before speaking. "It might be a good idea to contact that attorney after all."

Nick put his hand in the small of my back and led me out a set of French doors that opened onto a large deck in the back yard. The deck stretched across the length of both brothers' houses, combining the two properties. They also shared a large swimming pool and an enormous stainless steel grill.

Nick pulled a pair of latex gloves from his pocket, slipped them on and lifted the grill lid. I stepped back as he pulled the grates out, one by one, and ash floated into the air.

"Is it in there?" I asked.

"There's something in here." He sifted through the ashes and held up a tiny piece of black leather inscribed with gold. "Bernard Ulysses Butler," Nick read. "This must be what's left of the famous diary."

"God, I hope so." I watched as Nick bagged the tiny piece of leather and a handful of ashes from the bottom of the grill. We left through the side gate, which was fine with me since I had no desire to ever run into Robbie Butler again.

"So what do you think?" I asked as we got back in his truck.

"I think he's probably telling the truth, but I'm going to put a couple of plainclothes officers on surveillance out here. I don't want him to leave town."

Nick called in and requested the police surveillance on his cell phone.

"Come on, Jezebel," Nick said. "I'll buy you lunch and then I'll help you out with that case you were having trouble with. I've got nothing better to do on my day off."

"Gee, thanks. As long as you realize this doesn't count as a date."

We grabbed lunch at a Mexican restaurant before heading back to Whiskey Bayou. I was uncomfortably full of enchiladas and queso, and I knew it had been a mistake to take part in the all you can eat buffet. I was going to have to do a few sit ups once I could get my pants buttoned again.

"Tell me about this case you need help with," Nick said.

"It's not that I'm having trouble with it," I said primly. "It's just that I'm not exactly sure how to go about catching him in the act."

"Is this another adulterer?" Nick asked.

"Insurance fraud. Eddie Pogue is his name. A real jackass." I filled him in on the rest of the file while he drove.

I was a little uncomfortable in the silence that stretched between us. It was weird to sit next to a man that had seen me naked but left me unfulfilled. Of course, that pretty much described my entire relationship with Greg, but my brain kept telling me I hadn't known Nick long enough to keep making reckless decisions. My body, however, was saying "Go For It."

I sighed loudly and looked out the window as we turned onto Magnolia Street.

"What was that sigh for? What's wrong?"

"Nothing."

"Oookay. You know, I have to say I don't really believe you. I've been married before, and in my experience, when a woman says there's nothing wrong it means you're in deep shit."

"You've been married before?" I asked, my voice only a tiny bit shrill at the news.

"Of course I've been married before. I'm thirty-two years old. Do you think I just hatched a week ago when we met for the first time? Besides, I'm a cop. We all get married at some point. It's just staying married that seems to be the problem with most of us."

I was surprised to find I was a little bit jealous of that nameless woman who had shared a life with Nick. My gloom intensified and I sighed again.

"Look, if you're going to be all depressing I'm not going to help you out. I bet I know something we could do that will perk you up," he said with a wink.

"I think that's what's depressing me, so no thanks." I turned and faced him in defeat. "Did you love your wife?" I asked.

"Hell, Addison. Is this going to be one of *those* conversations?"

I rolled my eyes and sighed again. "You're right of

course. We barely know each other, and we certainly don't have anything going on between us."

"Like hell we don't," Nick said between gritted teeth. "I was married for about six months eleven years ago right after I got out of the Army. It was a mistake all around, and no hearts were broken. Is that good enough for you?"

"I told you, you don't have to explain. I'm not looking for a relationship at the moment, so you can get that panicked look out of your eyes. And besides, you and I would never suit. The passion would never last and we'd end up killing each other. No, I couldn't care less about your past. I'm just re-evaluating my life."

Nick slammed the car into park and I could tell he'd like nothing more than to lean across the seat and throttle me. I gripped the door handle, preparing to escape, when he grabbed my arms, hauled me across the seat and kissed me.

"You drive me crazy," he said, depositing me back in my seat. "But you'll have to re-evaluate some other time because we're here."

I was still a little bemused by the kiss when I noticed that we were parked in an alleyway about a block away from Eddie Pogue's address.

"Why are we so far away?"

"Because it'll look more believable to the neighbors if people just see a nice looking couple out for a Sunday stroll. We don't want to tip him off."

"Oh, good idea."

"I get one every now and then," Nick said sarcastically. "You won't need your camera today. We're just going to canvass the area and see if we can get a clear shot into his house. We'll come back another time and try to get it on film."

I thought the plan through and felt better about catching Eddie Pogue than I had about anyone else. This was going to be smooth sailing. All I needed was a mentor. I'd hyped myself up pretty good until I realized what Nick was doing.

"Holy shit, Nick, we're not going into the O.K. Corral. I thought we were just doing surveillance."

I watched as he strapped on his shoulder holster and put a backup piece in the lower part of his back. Man, I was getting hot just watching him. I shuddered to think what would happen if I actually got to see him in uniform.

"The first rule is to blend in. The second rule is to be prepared."

"Wait a minute. These are different from the rules Kate gave me. Is there a book I can buy with all this information?"

Nick smiled and grabbed my hand. "Come on, we're just a happy couple strolling hand in hand down the street."

"Get real. No one would ever believe we're a happy couple."

"What'll be hard about it? Just look at me like I'm a god and drool a little like you usually do."

I gave him the finger and made a mental note to myself to stop trying to picture him naked. He was obviously very adept at reading the female mind.

"Let's go," he said.

I followed at a less than enthusiastic pace, considering I was still full of Mexican food.

The alley was little more than gravel, and an eclectic mix of houses lined each side. There was a run down trailer on the corner, a ranch-style house next door and a two-story Colonial at the end of the block. This was truly a neighborhood for everyone. The good thing was that tall trees and overgrown shrubs ran the length of both sides of the alley, so there were plenty of good hiding places.

We stopped behind a modest, one story brick home with a good size back yard. A chain linked fence closed in the yard and an overgrown garden sat unattended in the middle of the lot. There was a detached garage at the back of the house and the skeleton of a storage building being constructed sat next to it. There were no cars in the garage.

"Can you believe this?" I said outraged. "How is it that John Hyatt will give a putz like Eddie Pogue a home loan, but he insists on giving me nothing but trouble?"

"Probably Eddie Pogue didn't have to overcome Veronica Wade," Nick said. "All right, time to act lovey-dovey."

"Umm—what exactly am I supposed to—"

The breath was knocked out of me as Nick backed me against the fence. He kissed me like he was searching for the lost city of Atlantis and all I could do was open my mouth in surprise and try to keep oxygen flowing to my brain.

"Move slightly to your left," he said, biting my earlobe. I could hear the click of the camera on his iPhone as he got off several shots of the back of the house. "I don't see him anywhere on the premises, but he's left all of his tools out, so it's likely he won't be gone long. We'll have to come back so we can catch him in the act."

The jerk was working. The kiss had no effect on him at all, and I was a pitiful puddle at his feet. I shifted slightly and made sure my foot connected with his shin in the process.

"Ouch, dammit, what the hell was that for?" he said, slipping his phone into his back pocket.

"I don't like being used as a distraction."

"Geez, what's the big deal? It's not like you didn't like it."

Men. The fact that I liked it was beside the point, though I wasn't going to ever admit it out loud.

"Let's just get out of here. I'll have better luck catching Eddie Pogue when you're not here to stick your tongue down my throat."

11

MONDAY

I SMELLED THE FRESH AROMA OF COFFEE BEFORE I noticed the alarm blaring in my ear. I looked at the time and didn't care that I was running a few minutes behind. School was out and all I had left was one lousy teacher workday. What were they going to do? Fire me?

I threw on some jeans, a T-shirt and my Nike Shox because I had to get my room packed up for the summer. I pulled my hair back in a ponytail and cursed the bangs I'd thought were such a great idea.

I'd gotten my books packed away and most of the things off the wall by ten o'clock, and I was ready to say to hell with it and not bother with the rest. Rose Marie came in just as I'd decided to sneak out for the day. My eyes crossed at the zebra print top she was wearing, so I busied myself by stacking boxes on a dolly to wheel out to my car.

"Hey, I heard what happened at the Officer's Gala between you and Veronica," she said loudly.

"Everyone's heard about what happened at the Officer's Gala. I got a call from Rudy Bauer at the Gazette asking if I had any comments to contribute to the article that would be in Thursday's paper. All I could tell him was that Veronica's tits were fake and she wasn't a natural blonde, but he told me he already knew all that."

I thought about the surprise on Veronica's face as I ripped out a chunk of her bleached hair. I couldn't keep the grin off my face.

"She's not here today," Rose Marie said. "Word has it that you ruptured one of her implants while y'all were rolling around on the floor."

I gasped in surprise, pulling my arm close to my body to protect my own breasts in an involuntary movement.

"Ouch. I didn't realize," I whispered, horrified. "I got tasered before I could assess the damage for either one of us."

I got a mental impression of Veronica walking around town with a deflated boob and started to giggle. Rose Marie wasn't far behind me, and before long we were both doubled over with tears running down our face.

"We shouldn't be laughing about this," I wheezed, trying to catch my breath. "It must have been horribly painful," I said, trying to stifle another fit of giggles.

Tears of mirth rolled down my face and Rose Marie looked like a jolly cherub, pink and round.

"I think this is karma," she said. "It's okay to laugh when other people's karma comes around to bite them in the ass. In fact, it'll make your karma bad if you don't laugh."

I couldn't really argue with her logic so I let another roll of laughter peal out before getting myself under control.

We both deflated like a balloon with a hole in it and I sat down in my desk chair. Veronica was in the hospital, which meant she couldn't have killed Mr. Mooney. But that didn't let her off the hook for Mr. Butler's murder in my opinion. Nick did say both murders looked like different people had committed them, even though he was certain they were related in some way.

"I came by to ask you for a favor," Rose Marie said.

"What do you need?" I had my fingers crossed that she didn't need me to feed her dogs. The last time I'd had the honor I'd ended up with a hole in the back of my favorite pair of jeans and dog slobber in places best left unmentioned.

"A friend of mine is starting a new business. She gives those home parties, you know, and she's giving one tonight to show some new products her company has just marketed. I told her I'd get as many people as possible to show up since this is her first one. She's a little nervous. There are a few other teachers going too, so you'll know some people there. It would really mean a lot if you'd come."

"Sure, that sounds like fun." And I actually meant it. A night out with the girls was just what I needed.

"Great, here's the invitation, and the address is on it. I'll see you there."

It was turning out to be a great day. Veronica Wade's boob exploded, and I'd get to buy some new Tupperware. And it's not like buying Tupperware was splurging. It was economical and something I'd need to store all the Welcome to the Neighborhood casseroles and cakes I envisioned my new neighbors bringing me. Life was good.

I heard the first strains of the 1812 Overture and fished my cell phone out of the bottom of my purse while avoiding a head-on collision at the same time.

"Damn, I'm good."

I'd stopped by the agency and traded the Z for Kate's

boring beige Taurus. I was on my way to Eddie Pogue's house for an impromptu visit, and I was doing it without Nick.

"Hello," I said into the receiver as I parked the Taurus down the street from Eddie's house.

"How was your day, sweetheart?" Nick asked on the other end of the line.

I could hear the smile in his voice and pictured him sitting at his desk with his feet propped up, the phone tucked between his shoulder and ear as he accomplished ten things at once.

"Just fine, honey buns," I said sweetly. "Veronica Wade's tit deflated and I'm going to a Tupperware party tonight."

"Sounds like a full day. Let's talk about murder."

"You know, sometimes a girl likes to talk about things other than work. Sometimes a girl likes to have a little courtship."

"Do you want to have dinner tomorrow night?"

"Sure."

"Now can we talk about murder?" he asked.

"Sorry. My plate's a little full at the moment."

"You wouldn't be going after Eddie Pogue right now, would you?"

The man would have made a fortune as one of those psychics on television. "Nope, not me," I lied and hung up. Sometimes a girl had to take drastic measures.

I parked in front of the big Colonial down the street from Eddie's and decided I'd go from the front this time. The street was quiet since it was a Monday and it was the middle of the day. These were working class people that had to pay for car loans, dance lessons and time-share packages.

I looped the camera around my neck and shoved open the door of the Taurus. I didn't bother locking it because I figured Kate would be better off if someone stole it.

The only sounds I heard as I approached Eddie's house were birds chirping and the blare of Montel Williams from someone's T.V. I hid behind a crepe myrtle that was exploding with pink blooms and peeped around until I could see the front of Eddie's house. The lawn was freshly mowed and someone had left an expensive looking lawn mower and weed whacker lying on the grass. There was no sight of Eddie, so I walked up his sidewalk as bold as you please and looked in the open window.

I got a glimpse of a spotless kitchen and figured Eddie's wife was the responsible party. She was probably at work like Eddie should have been, but Eddie was in front of the T.V. involved in the woes of hermaphrodites in love and using his Bowflex. He was shirtless and in a pair of loose athletic shorts and there was no sign of a neck brace or the walker. Eddie Pogue looked like he was in the prime of his life, and he was busted.

I snapped several pictures before I forgot that I was standing in a flowerbed. I looked down at the smushed flowers beneath my feet and scooted back, but my heel hit the brick ledge that lined the beds. I sprawled onto my backside and couldn't muffle the curse as my posterior took a hard knock.

I looked up as the front door opened and Eddie Pogue stood in the doorway.

"Addison Holmes, what the hell are you doing here?"

And then he saw the camera slung around my neck. His face turned red and veins started popping out all over his body. I crab walked backward until I thought I had a chance of getting my feet under me.

"Give me that camera," he said and started to head in my direction.

"Can't do that, Eddie. It doesn't belong to me." I stood slowly, put my hands up in an offering of peace and gave him my best pals smile.

"Give me that goddamn camera or I'm going to take it from you," he said. His voice was menacing and I automatically took a step back.

"Give it to me," he screamed and charged straight at me.

I didn't stop to try and reason with him. I took off as fast as my gimpy knee and aching ass would allow. I heard the sound of a motor starting and I looked back over my shoulder as Eddie held the weed whacker over his head like an extra on *Nightmare on Elm Street*.

I stopped to take photographs just to clinch Eddie's guilt and then realized he wasn't about to start trimming his lawn again. He took off at a dead sprint wielding the weed whacker in front of him like a sword. He was headed straight for me.

"You're crazy!" I screamed and put everything I had into getting to Kate's car. The camera was flopping around my neck and banging me in the ribs. The sound of spinning blades was getting closer, but I didn't bother looking back. If I was going to get decapitated I didn't want to see it.

I frantically searched my pockets and remembered I'd left the keys in the car. I yanked the door open on the Taurus, slid into the grimy seat and locked the doors just in time to hear the blades make a *thwap, thwap, thwap* sound on the bumper.

I took a couple of more pictures before I turned the key in the ignition, only for reasons unknown to me, the Taurus decided to sputter into nothingness. I had a crazed maniac after me and the car wouldn't start.

"Come on, come on," I said. My hands were shaking and I pushed down the pedal to see if I could get the ignition to catch. Eddie had moved to the front of the car and was bashing the windshield and the side mirrors with all his Bowflex strength.

"Finally!"

The engine caught and I pushed the gas pedal to the floor. I left Eddie Pogue standing in the street waving his weed whacker like a madman.

I parked Kate's Taurus at the back of her building and went inside to swap keys. She was in a meeting (thank goodness), and so the only person in the office was Lucy. When I got back to my car I called and left a message on Kate's voicemail.

"Ummm, Kate? This is Addison. I just wanted to let you know I'm sorry about the Taurus, but it wasn't my fault. I'm sure insurance will cover all the damages, and probably you can find another Taurus that was just as ugly as that one on the Internet."

I hung up. I needed to find Nick and tell him the list of people who could possibly be after me had increased by one. I'd learned my lesson about keeping secrets about my enemies, and probably Eddie Pogue wouldn't be sending me an engraved invitation to his incarceration when all was said and done.

On the drive to Nick's precinct, I realized something crucial. I didn't even know the man's cell phone number. I knew nothing about him at all, not where he lived or even if he was living with someone. Or, God, what if he had children? The only thing I knew about Nick Dempsey was the shape of his tonsils, that his chest hairs felt great rubbing against my breasts and that he'd been married once before.

Nick's precinct was in the heart of Savannah's historic

district, and the building looked nothing like a place that held criminals and overworked cops within its walls. It was pretty, with shade trees and soft red brick.

I took stock of my appearance and grimaced. I looked like I'd just been chased down the street by a madman wielding a weed whacker. My hair was disheveled, my eyes still looked slightly dazed and there were grass stains on the back of my pants. I was pretty sure the cops inside had other things to do besides worry about what I looked like, so I grabbed my purse and climbed the stairs to the front entrance.

It might be hard to tell that this was a police station from the outside, but the inside was exactly how I remembered from my childhood—horrible pea soup colored walls, metal desks lined straight as soldiers, and frazzled cops who looked years older than they actually were.

I let the sweet smell of nostalgia rush over me, and then I held my breath because cop shops always smelled like BO, urine and burned coffee. I bypassed the harassed looking woman at the front desk and looked around to see if I could find Nick. And boy did I find him.

He looked to be in the middle of a heated discussion with one of the other plainclothes officers. His brow was furrowed and his dark hair hung slightly over his forehead. He was dressed like the other detectives, a sport coat and tie knotted loosely at his throat. The only difference was that he looked good. Too good for my peace of mind. His hands were at his hips and his shoulder holster was visible. And then that heated gaze pointed in my direction and I didn't know whether to run for cover or rip my clothes off.

He left the man he was talking to in mid-sentence and headed in my direction.

"Are you okay?" he asked. "You look like you've been in some kind of accident."

"Eddie Pogue," I said by way of explanation. "Did I come at a bad time? That guy you were talking to sure looked angry."

"No, it's not a bad time. He's just mad because he lost a bet on the game last night."

We stared at each other for several seconds, me knowing he'd just lied and Nick probably wondering if I was going to make a big deal about it. I decided to let it rest. It was too early to argue, so I blurted out something else instead.

"Do you have children?"

"Is this one of those trick questions that women ask?"

"It's a yes or no question, you jackass."

"Then, no. I don't have kids. I told you I was only married for six months, and I didn't even get sex out of it the last three. But I wouldn't mind trying to make a few if you were up for it. I've got about twenty minutes to spare," he said looking at his watch.

I shook my head no, so he led me to a metal desk in the middle of the room stacked with file folders and paper cups and pulled a yellow plastic chair up close for me to sit in.

"I've never understood how you guys can work in all the chaos," I said, looking around.

"That's right, I'd forgotten your dad was a cop. Not everyone can live with one, that's for sure. Especially when they don't know if you'll be coming back."

"Well, that's just stupid. I was never anything but proud of my dad. He was a damn good cop. We never worried about him because it's what he loved to do, and I bet it pissed him off something fierce that he died in front of the T.V. instead of in the line of duty. You can't take that away from someone when it's that entrenched in their blood. That would be cruel."

"My ex-wife didn't think so. She thought I was selfish for not at least trying to be something else."

"Well, I guess it's a good thing you divorced her then."

"I didn't divorce her. She divorced me, and then promptly went and married an orthodontic surgeon in Atlanta. I consider myself lucky."

I had to wonder if Nick still had feelings for the woman who had left him. Had he had closure? He seemed kind of sad about the whole thing. So of course I had to open my big mouth.

"Are you sure you don't still love her?"

"Hell, no. I don't think I ever really did. It was just one of those things you do when you're too young and stupid to know any better. We had great sex and thought it would sustain a marriage. So what's this about Eddie Pogue?" he asked, all business.

For some reason, I didn't particularly feel like sharing any more.

"Have you found out anything about Mr. Mooney's murder?" I asked, hoping to change the subject.

"I've got a lot of theories and a lot of suspicions, but so far everything is leading to a dead end. We still haven't been able to find your ex and question him. He took off while you and Veronica were distracting the rest of us at the gala. Nobody's seen him since. Veronica's still in the hospital, and Girard Dupres had a solid alibi since he was arrested Friday night for hiring a minor to dance at his club. And your pal Robbie Butler was at home all evening as far as the officers I had posted out front could tell."

"What about John Hyatt?"

"We questioned everyone in Victor Mooney's

neighborhood after he was murdered, including John Hyatt. He and his estate manager were going over guest lists and details for some party that is held at the bank every year for the bigwigs. Loretta Swanson corroborated his story when we finally tracked her down. Neither of them noticed anything suspicious about Mr. Mooney's behavior."

"Maybe they're lying for each other," I suggested. "John Hyatt has a fiancé, but he seems to spend a lot of time with his estate manager just to have a platonic relationship. And Loretta Swanson doesn't seem like the type of woman to be platonic. She practically oozes sex."

"You've got that right," Nick said with a dreamy smile.

I kicked him in the shin and felt better.

"Sheathe your claws, woman. For some reason I'm attracted to accident prone ex-strippers who have a jealous streak."

"Whatever. I bet you say that to all the girls."

He smiled but I could see the frustration and worry behind his eyes.

"My gut tells me the two murders are related, but the evidence suggests there are different killers. We've got no DNA and so far we haven't gotten any hits from the fingerprints found on the envelope. You're the only thing that links both of them, Addison."

"So what are you saying?"

"I'm saying be careful. And let me know if you get any other surprises."

"I'm not sure I can take any more surprises. My biggest fear at this point is I'll damage my body even more than it already is. I haven't been able to make it to my yoga classes in almost two weeks because I've been too sore."

Nick's eyes glazed over at the mention of my yoga

classes, and I could tell he already had grand plans for our upcoming date.

"Do I need to leave you alone with your fantasies?" I asked.

"Nah, you'll be privy to them soon enough. Just make sure you don't injure yourself anymore between now and tomorrow. I wouldn't want you to miss out on my great idea."

"What great idea is that?"

"The one where we're both naked and your ankles are up by your ears."

My insides heated to the temperature of molten lava, and I could hear my heart pounding in my ears. The picture that Nick painted was awesome in my mind. It was too bad I'd have to disappoint him, because I didn't think there was any way possible for my ankles to reach my ears with all of my swollen and bruised body parts. It probably wouldn't be a bad idea for me to spend some time soaking in a hot tub though.

I'd fallen asleep as soon as I'd gotten home from seeing Nick, and when I woke up I was running late for the Tupperware party at Rose Marie's friend's house.

I jumped in the shower and tried to tame my hair, but it was still in shock from being chased with a weed whacker. I pulled on the first thing I could find in my closet and barely had time to put on lip gloss and slip on some sandals when I heard the knock at the door.

I glanced at the clock on my way to the door and put a little jog in my step. My tongue caught in my throat when I opened the door and saw Nick leaning with one arm against the frame and holding a six-pack of Corona in the other. His hair was tousled from a long day at work and the dark stubble on his face was way past a five o'clock shadow.

His blue eyes held heat and desire and something I didn't even want to think about because I knew it would be dangerous.

"If you don't stop looking at me like that, you won't make it to your party tonight and we definitely won't make it to the restaurant I've made reservations at tomorrow night."

"Oh, man," I said, licking my lips. That was an impressive threat. One I wasn't sure I didn't want to take him up on.

"Wh—what are you doing here?" Great. The man had me reduced to a stuttering fool.

"I'm here to watch the game," he said, backing me slowly into my apartment. He slammed the door shut with his boot, and I gulped in reaction. "It's the playoffs, you know."

"Of course I know. I have it set to TiVo. And besides, I've already told you I'm going to be out tonight."

"You like basketball?" he asked, surprised.

"Of course I like basketball. Who doesn't like basketball?"

"What about baseball? Do you like baseball?"

I gave him a look like he belonged in the special class. "Baseball is king. All other sports dim in comparison."

"Oh my God. I'm going to have to marry you."

"Not until you take me to dinner first. What kind of woman do you think I am?"

"One that I want very, very badly," he said, backing me into the wall. He took my bottom lip between his teeth and bit gently. I moaned in response and tried to think of what it was I was supposed to be doing.

"Wait a minute," I said pushing him back. "What are you really doing here?"

"Let's just say I want to be here in case you have any uninvited guests."

"You could have just asked, you know, instead of trying to muddle me with the whole seduction thing."

"The seduction thing was just a side benefit for both of us," he said reaching for me again.

"Oh, no you don't. I've got to get out of here. I'm going to be late."

I pushed him back with all my might, with only a small hope that he'd be more persistent in taking things further, that way I could blame him for missing the party.

"Have a good time," he said, already heading to the living room and flipping the TV on.

All I could do was grab my purse and walk out the door. I'd completely forgotten why I was going to tell him he couldn't be there while I was gone. But I'd sure as hell give him a piece of my mind when I got back and my brain was in working order again.

Much to my surprise, I'd been able to save up a good chunk of money since I started working for Kate, and I hardly felt guilty at all for planning to splurge on the Tupperware. A few more weeks of falling out of trees and being chased with sharp objects and I'd have all the money I needed for the rest of the down payment. Hopefully, I'd still be alive to enjoy the fruits of my labor.

I pulled in right behind Rose Marie's bright yellow Volkswagen Beetle and hopped out of the car. Rose Marie shoehorned her way out of the Beetle, and I was left standing with my mouth hanging open and my eyes on the verge of exploding at the cacophony of colors that came barreling out of the tiny car.

Rose Marie was wrapped in a swirling sarong of every color in the rainbow and she'd wedged her size eight feet into size six hot pink mules. The fashion gods were probably in a coma. I wished I could join them.

"Wow, Rose Marie. You sure do look—summery," I said, lamely. I looked down at my own short khaki skirt from The Gap and my white sleeveless top and felt way under dressed.

"Thank you. It's new," she said, her face beaming.

We made our way up to the door of the ranch style house. The sun was still bright though it was almost seven o'clock.

"I'm surprised you actually came tonight," Rose Marie said out of the blue. "I've always thought you seemed kind of prudish. No offense," she hastened quickly.

I was confused. What did buying Tupperware have to do with being a prude? And, dammit, I'm not a prude. Would a prude dance topless at The Foxy Lady? I think not. I almost broke down and told her about it when I remembered it was probably not a good idea to let that knowledge circulate around town.

"I'm not a prude," I said defensively. "And what does that have to do with buying Tupperware?"

Rose Marie gasped. "This isn't a Tupperware party, Addison. I thought you would have gone to the website on your invitation."

A ball of dread gathered in the pit of my stomach, and I asked the only question that mattered. "What kind of party is this?"

"It's a passion party," Rose Marie said, her cheeks pink in delight.

By then it was too late. I couldn't run screaming to my car. The front door was opened and I was ushered into a spacious living room already crowded with women. Candles were lit and wine and cheese were set out. It didn't look like a den of iniquity so I went further into the room. I stopped next to Rose Marie as a woman approached us.

"Welcome, ladies," she said, handing both of us a Q-tip. "Please go into the restroom and apply this gel to your clits. As soon as you're finished, we'll start the party."

The woman walked off without another word and I was left standing there alone, my mouth hanging open and my face red as a lobster.

Rose Marie had already gone into the restroom to apply the gel, and I took a closer look at the little swab that was bound to make for an interesting evening.

Rose Marie came out of the bathroom, her face flushed pink and excited, so I had no choice but to go in and do the deed. Would people know if I just threw it away? Was there some kind of invisible sign that would tell everyone that I was too chicken to put a little gel on my privates? Well, I wasn't going to be called a coward in front of a bunch of strangers, so I squinted my eyes closed and got the job done.

After I finished, I realized I had just put something on my body, and I had absolutely no idea what it was. What if it gave me cancer or made me blind? I didn't think well under pressure, but obviously I needed to keep my wits about me the rest of the night.

I walked back into the living room, face red because obviously everyone in the room knew exactly what I'd just done. I could see their knowing glances and hidden smiles. I stiffened my spine, grabbed a large glass of wine off the table, and sat on the sofa next to Rose Marie.

"Isn't this just great?" she whispered.

"Peachy," I said, knocking back the whole glass before I lost my nerve and ran out the door.

"Welcome ladies. My name is Donna Limpkin, and I

want to thank my good friend Rose Marie Valentine for bringing so many new faces for me to show my products to."

Yeah, thanks, Rose Marie.

"You're all here today to see that passion lies within each and every one of you, and there is absolutely nothing to be embarrassed about when discussing the sensuality that each one of us contains inside—sometimes repressed, sometimes aggressive. Women are marvelous creatures that hold so much power when it comes to sex, and I hope each of you will leave here today a little more knowledgeable, a little more intrigued and a lot more powerful. Let's get started."

I wasn't repressed. I could do anything any of the other women in the room could do, and I bet I could do it better. I took the wine bottle as it was passed around once again and filled up my glass.

I watched Donna Limpkin pull a bottle out of her bag and smirked. With a name like Limpkin she'd better be a hell of a salesman to convince a bunch of women that her products worked. I was feeling warm and tingly all over and decided I should take it a little slower on the wine.

"This remarkable little gel I hold in my hand is what I had each of you place on your genitalia when you first came in. Enough time has passed that each of you should be able to feel a heated tingling through your bodies, and some of you might even feel slightly aroused."

I looked around the room in horror because she was right. I did feel turned on and there wasn't a man in sight. My body was heating from the inside out and I found I wanted to wiggle around on my seat a little too much. The worst part of it was that I was sitting in a room full of women who were all experiencing the same thing. Why was

I the only one who felt this was an awkward situation to be in?

My mind turned into a hazy blur as I consumed more wine, and I watched as the woman pulled an endless amount of toys out of her oversized suitcase—the suitcase of sex as I was starting to refer to it. Handcuffs and feathers, lotions and leather whips, not to mention things that my brain wouldn't even let me whisper.

My favorite apparatus was "the swing," and I was just tipsy enough to think about buying it. I was finally able to put a name to the apparatus Gretchen Wilder had been using, and boy did I want one.

When Donna told me that she'd give me a twenty percent discount off the two hundred dollar sales price I was sold. Apparently, I could install it above my bed with a standard hook, and when I needed to take it down I could replace it with a fern to keep people from asking what the hook above my bed was for. It was a brilliant plan, only it was all ruined by one of the other teachers asking me how things were going with finding a new place to live. It was like a bucket of cold water being poured on my head, and I realized spending two hundred dollars for an apparatus I didn't currently have a partner for—Nick and I weren't quite at the swinging monkey sex stage of our relationship— would not be the most fiscally responsible thing to do.

Donna and I both huffed at the loss of the sale, so I bought a battery operated toy called the Mr. Incredible to make up for it. No one needed a man if they owned one of those suckers.

We all toddled out the door a little after nine, bags full of goodies and door prizes loaded into our arms. I was just tipsy enough to tell myself that if I went by Dairy Queen and got a double fudge sundae to dilute the alcohol, I should be able to make it home okay. I gave Rose Marie a cheerful hug and didn't protest at all as she took my keys and shoved me in the front seat of her canary yellow Beetle.

I heard the television blaring in my apartment when I got to the door, my arms full of bags.

Nick opened the door before I could remember that Rose Marie had taken my keys and forgotten to give them back. I fell forward, as I'd been leaning my head against the door. He caught me in a crashing heap that sent both of us to the floor, and I took advantage of my position by tangling my fingers in his hair and planting my lips onto his.

"Mmmm," I said, nipping at his bottom lip. "You taste good."

The gel from the party was still tingling its way through my body. I gasped as he put his hands on my hips and pulled me close enough to tell that Mr. Incredible didn't hold a candle to Nick Dempsey.

"Have I ever told you that I take yoga classes three times a week? I'm very flexible," I slurred.

"Dear God in Heaven," Nick said, crushing his mouth back to mine. "You taste like chocolate fudge and Raspberry Schnapps. I think it's a combination I'm not going to be able to take advantage of tonight." He peeled me off his delectable body, and hefted me up under the arms to get me to my feet. I gave him the dopey grin of the pleasantly drunk.

"Are you drunk?"

"Nope," I said, giggling. "I went to Dairy Queen and got a chocolate sundae to dilute the alcohol. I'm good to go."

"How did you get home?" he asked, finally getting around to shutting the front door.

I could see the tic in his jaw working and just wanted to bite it. He was so sexy when he was angry.

"I rode in a yellow bug. It was very small. How else would I get here?" I headed into the living room to fall on the couch. The game was still on, and I settled in to watch, blissfully unaware of the predatory male who was still staring after me.

"You rode home in a yellow bug? Are you high? What kind of party was this?"

I laughed until tears rolled down my face. "Can you go get my car for me? I parked it on the street, but I don't remember which one."

"Sure, I'll put a BOLO out for a red Z somewhere in the state of Georgia. We should be able to find it in no time."

"You're the best," I said, giving him a lusty wink.

Nick looked resigned and shook his head at me, but I could see the threat of a smile lurking in the corner. He picked up the large bag I'd dropped near the door and looked inside, making his way into the living room.

"Umm, Addison, I hate to break this to you, but this is not Tupperware."

He held up the Mr. Incredible between two fingers, his eyes glittering with laughter. "You want to tell me what kind of party you went to?"

He tossed the device onto the coffee table, and I watched the Mr. Incredible bounce off the table twice and land on the floor. I stifled a giggle on one of the couch pillows.

"It was a passion party, and it was wonderful," I said, stretching out on the couch. "I'm a very passionate person, I'll have you know. I took a test that told me so. I got a perfect score."

Nick rolled his eyes and kept looking through the bag. "You didn't have to take a test to know that you're passionate, babe. I could have told you that if you'd asked."

The banked desire in his eyes was enough to rekindle the gel I'd slathered on earlier, not to mention that one look at Nick was enough to send my natural hormones into orgasmic bliss. He upended the bag on the table, and I finally got a look at everything I'd purchased that night. It looked like I'd bought the entire catalog.

"I think I got a little carried away," I said, looking at all the toys and creams. I groaned as he laid down next to me on the couch, the feel of his hard body next to mine making me want like nothing I ever had before.

Nick put his leg between mine and brought us together slowly, kissing his way up my neck, around to my ear and finally finding my mouth.

"God, you feel good," I said, straining closer. "I've heard it takes a person two years to get past the point where they can have a relationship without it being considered a rebound. Two years feels like a pretty long time right now."

I curled my leg around his hip and we both groaned as our bodies aligned perfectly. My nails bit into his shoulders and I hissed out a breath as his hand came between us and palmed my breast.

"Oh, baby. You have no idea how good I feel." He whispered the words against my lips and I all but melted beneath him. "But I can promise you're going to find out a hell of a lot sooner than two years." He kissed his way along my jaw to my ear and bit down on my earlobe, scrambling the remaining brain cells I had.

"Oh, God," I said. And then I passed out.

12

TUESDAY

I WOKE UP ALONE ON THE COUCH, THE HAZE OF SLEEP still clouding my vision, and the beat of a thousand tiny men marching through my skull. I leaned up gingerly and noticed the throw that covered me, and I looked to the table where dozens of sexual aids sat staring at me. If Nick wasn't scared off by those maybe he *was* the man for me.

The clock on the wall said it was almost noon, and panic gripped my belly before I remembered school was out. Thunder rumbled outside and I could tell by the water level in the buckets I had sitting around that it had been raining awhile. Storm clouds roiled menacingly, almost black, and lightning crackled through the sky like fiery whips.

A raging thunderstorm seemed an appropriate backdrop for someone who had a monumental hangover. But rain or no rain, I had a hot date in less than seven hours to prepare for, and it was time to put on my big girl panties.

I scooped all the sex toys back into the sack and shoved them in the far recesses of my closet. I took four aspirin, showered, and threw on a camouflage green short skirt and olive green tank top that matched my complexion. I felt almost normal by the time I opened my fridge and saw it full of the things that Nick had bought the other morning. I grabbed a Diet Coke and a bag of pretzels and went in search of the phone to call Kate.

I'd gone through all but one of the surveillance cases Kate had passed my way and decided to see if she had a few more. I hadn't started the surveillance on Harry Manilow because I hadn't had a chance to get back to Savannah, and I still had John Hyatt and Fanny Kimble on the backburner, though unofficially since I'd kind of promised Kate I'd drop the case.

I had to keep working because I still needed the money for my house just in case Veronica got saline poisoning and couldn't follow up on her threat to buy it out from under me. As far as the other threats went, Nick assured me the police would be driving by to check on me, so I felt relatively safe there would be someone nearby if I ran into trouble.

Before I reached the phone, I noticed the blinking red light on my machine. I had six missed calls. I hit the voicemail button and munched on pretzels while I waited.

"This is Mark Mathers at Whiskey Bayou Bank and Trust. I'm the Vice-President for Mortgage Operations. I need you to call me back regarding your loan for the property at 522 Hutton Street."

He hung up and I took a drink of Coke. I remembered hearing the phone ring several times the day before and winced in regret as I'd shrugged off the calls as unimportant. But at least the bank was calling me. Maybe things were going to work out after all. The next message started and I ate another pretzel.

"This is Mark Mathers again at Whiskey Bayou Bank and Trust. I still haven't heard back from you regarding your loan application. I'm sorry to inform you that we've decided to opt out of our contract with you concerning the property on Hutton Street. Another buyer has met the full requirements for purchasing at this time, and as it states in your contract we have the option of going with a more qualified buyer. Your initial down payment has been deposited back into your account. Please contact me if you have any questions."

The pretzels in my mouth suddenly took on the consistency of sawdust, so I took another drink to clear the taste. The pretzels turned to paste in my mouth and I started to cry, big heaving sobs that would eventually give me hiccups and swollen eyes.

"Well, so much for everything working out," I said, hiccupping as I tried to hold back a fresh batch of tears. "Stupid contract. Stupid bank."

I dropped down to the floor in a little ball and cried my heart out. Maybe if I were lucky some poor sap would find me dead on the floor after I'd choked to death from a wad of pretzel dough stuck in my throat. I'd be the Mama Cass of Whiskey Bayou, except without the soundtrack.

Everything I'd been working for all this time was for nothing. I'd degraded myself in front of strangers and stumbled over dead bodies in the pursuit of my dreams, but it all came down to nothing. It was a devastating realization. And pathetic.

The wet plop on my forehead that had nothing to do with tears was the last straw. I looked up at the ceiling from my position on the floor and saw the new water spot and moisture gathering at its center.

I was going to do something drastic. I knew this because I had the same feeling in my gut now as I did the morning I answered the ad in the paper for The Foxy Lady. I was going to find somewhere better to live than that stupid house on Hutton Street.

I grabbed my bag and didn't bother with an umbrella or galoshes. I waded out to the parking lot and shook my fist at the sky, as the heavens seemed to open and pour more water onto Whiskey Bayou. The water was halfway up my tires and I wondered not for the first time why I couldn't have been more practical and gotten a Jeep or a monster truck to navigate washed out country roads.

"I don't get this wet in the shower," I mumbled. I searched in my bag for my keys, but couldn't find them. It was then I realized Nick had somehow found out where I'd left my car the night before and brought it to me. I opened the door and saw the keys on the floorboard along with a note.

Interesting friends you have. She asked if I would be willing to sleep with you—Nick

I could only assume the friend he was talking about was Rose Marie, since she was the person who'd confiscated my keys. I tried to look at her comment to Nick in a positive light. Rose Marie probably wanted me to be happy and wasn't thinking she'd made me look pathetic and desperate. I wasn't going to worry about it. I had a new purpose in life.

I climbed into the car and took off my shoes, tossing them in the floorboard on the passenger side. I breathed a sigh of relief as the Z started with no problem and I rammed it into reverse. I looked behind me and pressed the gas pedal, slogging my way out of the parking lot and towards downtown Whiskey Bayou. Visibility was almost zero and I was fortunate there were no other cars on the road as I sped down Main Street with rage boiling in my blood. It seemed I had a little pent up resentment from the bank's phone call after all.

I noticed something on the side of the road and slowed down a little. I was pretty sure it was some kind of large animal, but I couldn't see well enough to be sure. The only thing I did know was that it wasn't in good shape. I was trying to decide if I should stop and try to squeeze it into the Z or call animal control when it ran into the street right in front of me.

I slammed on the brakes and the Z hydroplaned, turning at an odd angle as it skated along the street. It was everything I could do to maintain control of the wheel. The car hit something solid and my teeth smacked together and my head jerked back and hit the headrest as impact was made.

"Oh, God," I said. The front of my car steamed and the hood was slightly buckled. Whatever I'd hit had been big enough to do major damage. I was crying as I got out of the car, positive I was going to see Lassie under my tires.

Instead I saw a pair of Kenneth Cole shoes peeking out from under the car a la Wicked Witch of the East. Spots danced in front of my eyes until I thought I'd gone blind with shock.

I knew those shoes.

I'd bought them for an anniversary present less than a year before.

"So I guess you know why you couldn't get in touch with Greg," I told Nick less than half an hour later.

After flattening Greg, I'd run screaming back to the car to grab my cell phone and call 911, and then I'd promptly thrown up in the gutter on the side of the street. Nick found me huddled on the sidewalk in the pouring rain, rocking myself back and forth and crying. I was on the edge of hysterical leaning toward straitjacket crazy. Nick had taken one look at my chattering teeth and shoved my head between my knees before wrapping me in a blanket and putting me in the back of a squad car.

It's not everyday a woman gets to run over her cheating ex-fiancé, but I have to say the reality isn't nearly as exciting as the scenarios I'd made up in my mind.

An officer I'd never seen before got into the back of the car with me and took out a tiny notebook. "Ms. Holmes?" the officer said. "I'm Officer Ruiz. I need to ask you a few questions."

I turned to Officer Ruiz and nodded my head. My movements felt sluggish and I wasn't sure I was capable of speaking at all.

"Do you recognize the victim?" Ruiz asked.

"Y-- es," I stammered. "His name is Greg Nelson. He lives here in Whiskey Bayou."

"I see," Ruiz said. "Tell me what happened from the moment you saw him."

"I was just driving." I looked past Ruiz's face and out the window so I didn't have to face his scrutiny. "I thought it was a dog running down the sidewalk, and I wondered why it would be out in this weather and not looking for some place dry to take shelter. Then all of a sudden it ran right out in front of me. I slammed on the brakes, but it was too late. And it wasn't a dog after all," I sobbed.

"Take your time Ms. Holmes," Ruiz said, handing me a small packet of tissues. "You said you thought the victim was an animal. Can you think of something specific that made you think that?"

LILIANA HART

I thought for a minute and tried to replay the scene in my mind. "I guess it was the way he was hunched over toward the ground. And he wasn't exactly running. It was more of a fast shuffle. I remember thinking the animal was hurt because of the way it was moving."

"Did you see which direction he was running from?"

"I could barely see anything at all. I was almost right on him by the time he was visible. It looked like he was heading into town, same as I was, but then he just turned and ran right out in front of me."

"Did he look confused or disoriented?"

"I can't say. I never saw his face. I'd still thought he was a dog even after I hit him. I didn't realize who he was until after I got out."

"Did you have a personal relationship with the victim?" Ruiz asked.

The question and tone of voice caught my attention and I looked Ruiz in the eyes. The calculating look was there and I could practically see the wheels turning in his brain. "Yes," I answered. "He was my fiancé up until just a few months ago."

Ruiz grunted, closed his notepad and left me in the back of the squad car alone.

Nick stayed out of the questioning officer's way because he had a conflict of interest, meaning he didn't think it was right for him to question a woman in an official capacity when he was trying to get her into bed. After Ruiz asked his questions, Nick bundled me into his truck and drove back to my apartment.

I knew he had work to do, but I needed the human contact, and I was terrified the moment I got alone I would lose something of myself that only Nick was able to fulfill. There had been too much death. A person could only take so much before breaking, and Nick was my anchor.

I'd hardly said a word since Greg's body had been zipped in one of those black bags and carted away to the medical examiner's office. What sent me into shocked silence was the tow truck that had pulled up and taken my Z away. They told me my car was an item of suspicion in the investigation and they would have to impound it for the time being.

Nick had been staring at me like he was afraid I was going to shave my head and take up Russian roulette. It was creeping me out. I took a sip of the hot toddy he'd forced on me, and it calmed me down immensely. "Why would Greg do that?" I asked. "Just run out in front of a car that way?"

"I don't know, but Greg's involvement in this mess has been suspicious from the beginning. Maybe he decided it was easiest to end it all."

"Maybe, but it's just hard to believe. Something wasn't right about the whole scene. I can't believe he'd deliberately do something like that."

"People do things they normally wouldn't when faced with prison terms."

"So you think it was Greg who killed Mr. Butler?"

"No, I know Greg didn't kill Mr. Butler. But he wasn't completely innocent either."

"If you know Greg didn't kill Mr. Butler, then that means you must know who did," I said surprised. "Why didn't you tell me? Why aren't you arresting them? Get off your ass and get to it. I don't need a babysitter if that's what's holding you back."

"I'm waiting for the proof before I can make an arrest. The bad guys always make a mistake, Addison, and that's what I'm waiting for."

"Well, who is it?"

"I can't talk about it. This is a small town, and I don't want to give him the opportunity to make my job harder."

"Are you saying you think I'm going to take the information you give me and run around telling everybody who the killer is?" I asked. Blood rushed to my ears and I could only hear the sound of my heart beating in anger. "What kind of person do you think I am?"

"A civilian," Nick said patiently. "This is my investigation and you're already too involved. I don't want you to get hurt."

"Your investigation," I said, understanding. "I'm right in the middle of this mess and you don't want to involve me in your investigation. You're threatened because if you tell me what your suspicions are I might catch the murderer before you do. It's because he and I have some sort of twisted connection."

"You're out of your mind. You think you're Magnum P.I. since you started working for Kate, but you have no clue how dangerous the situation you're in is. I'll handle this, Addison. I don't want you interfering. I want your word."

"I don't think so. These are people from my town that are being targeted, and I feel like it's my fault. Their deaths are weighing me down until I feel like I'm going to suffocate. This isn't about you doing your job. It's about your protective instincts as a man. I'm just as capable of drawing the killer out as you are. And that's exactly what I'm going to do."

We were both standing at this point, tension and anger radiating off both of us in waves.

"If you know something or are planning some harebrained idea you need to tell me. I'm the investigating officer on this case and you do not want to be charged with obstruction. You are a high school history teacher. Do you see how there's one of us that needs to be kept in the loop, and it isn't you?"

"What a horrible thing to say. I've helped you with this investigation from the beginning. You came to me asking for help. I have as big a stake in it as anyone. Bigger as far as I'm concerned."

"I've got plainclothes officers in place doing round the clock surveillance. You snooping around and stirring up trouble is not going to help me." His voice had increased in volume the longer he talked.

"You're yelling at me," I said, surprised.

"I'm not yelling. I never yell," he said doing just that.

"I bet I can find out who the killer is before you. What do you say to that?"

"You're turning this into a competition?"

"If you want to be crass about it, then yes."

"I can't believe this. Why couldn't I have found a nice girl somewhere who just wanted to make a nice quiet life with me and keep me warm at night?"

"Nobody could make a nice quiet life with you. You're completely unreasonable. As far as keeping you warm at night, it sounds like you're wasting your time with me. What you need is a lapdog."

Nick growled low in his throat and for a second I feared I'd pushed him too far. "What does the winner of this farce get?" Nick finally asked.

"Ohmigod," I said and burst into tears. "I can't believe I'm arguing with you like this is some stupid competition after I just killed Greg." Nick wrapped his arms around me. "I'm s...s...sorry. I c...c...can't h...h...help it." I snuffled and snorted and soaked his shirt while he held me tight and let me cry it out.

"It was an accident, Addison. And from the looks of him, it seems like somebody did a number on him before he ran in front of your car. From what you said in your statement it looks like Greg was definitely running away from something. We'll find out for sure once we get the ME's report back."

I cried harder. "It's okay," he whispered. "You've had a lot to deal with over the last two weeks. I'd be worried about you if you weren't having this kind of reaction."

Greg's death had hit me harder than I'd thought. He'd been out of my life for months and I'd only wished bad things on him. It looked like my wishes had come true, and guilt was eating at me from the inside out.

I wiped my eyes on a towel he gave me and backed away. "Thanks," I said mortally embarrassed. This was not a good way to start a relationship—extreme adrenaline rushes followed by bouts of lust followed by the bizarre, the surreal and finally the desolate.

"I've got some things to do to follow up on the case, so I need to take off for a few hours." He ran his fingers through his hair in a frustrated gesture. "I've got two dead bodies that are somehow linked and a third I have a sinking feeling about. Something about Greg doesn't sit right with my gut. The first victim was stabbed multiple times with a damned pocketknife and the second was killed with a freaking .22. The ME is putting a rush on Greg's autopsy, so I'll have a report before the end of the day. I'll call you as soon as I know anything conclusive.

"Oh, well, you probably need to get started," I said even more depressed.

"I called your mom earlier. She's going to come over and stay with you until I can get back. I don't want you to be alone right now."

"You called my mom?" The tension headache from the day's events came back in full force.

"Of course I called your mom. You can't stay here by yourself, and I can't spare an officer to guard you full time. I need every man I've got on duty."

"But my mother? Couldn't you have called Kate? Haven't I been through enough for one day?"

Nick rolled his eyes. "You're overreacting. Don't forget we're having dinner tonight. And don't argue with me about it. You need to get away from here for a little while and wind down. And I need it, too. It's no wonder you're upset. I would be too if I lived in this pile of rubble."

"You'll regret bringing my mother into this. Just wait until she starts interrogating you. My mom has a tendency to leave people a little rattled. Or maybe the word I'm looking for is confused."

"Why, because she asked me if I was single and if I liked children? Or maybe because she wanted to know my medical history and asked point blank if I'd ever had an STD."

I groaned and ducked my head. If I wasn't the reason Nick should be running for the hills then surely my mother was.

"I especially liked it when she asked if I was only looking to 'dally' with you," he said grinning.

"What did you tell her?"

"I told her I wanted to get you naked as soon as possible and then she invited me to Sunday dinner. We're supposed to bring a dessert by the way."

Nick smiled over his shoulder at my open-mouthed expression before shutting the door behind him. I was not ready to bring Nick home to eat dinner with my family. Nobody had bothered to ask me if my intentions were honorable. I was having some pretty naughty thoughts about "dallying" myself.

I heard the rumble of my mom's Dodge before it turned into the parking lot. It was a big boat of a car, and my mother looked like a child sitting behind the wheel.

I'd showered and changed into dry clothes, and I was currently looking for something to wear out to dinner that portrayed grief and lust both at the same time. There weren't a lot of outfits in the world that could combine the two so I just decided to go casual.

My mom unlocked my front door and came in with bags slung over both arms.

"What's all this?" I asked.

"I've brought you a few necessities," she said, pushing me towards the couch until I was laying flat on my back. "That nice young man mentioned you're without a car, so I brought mine for you to use until you get yours back. I'll call and have a neighbor come pick me up when I'm finished here. I stopped by Peach Tree Bakery and bought an ice cream cake. I've got a twelve-pack of Corona, my manicure kit and Sleepless in Seattle."

"That's so sweet." My eyes started to well with tears again. I'm not much of a crier normally, but I seemed to be leaking tears at an alarming rate. Maybe it was hormones. I was thinking I probably needed to drink quite a bit of that Corona so I wouldn't get dehydrated.

"I also brought the video from when you graduated high school," she said, and I started to cry harder. "I was so proud of you. I got great footage of your valedictory speech. Maybe we should watch that first."

I could think of about a million things I'd rather do instead, but I just nodded my head noncommittally.

"Of course, it was also a bitter-sweet moment because I

realized how old I'd gotten without even noticing. Then before I knew it I was afraid to wear a bikini in public anymore and my pubic hair started to turn gray. Let me tell you, that's a real eye opener."

I always had such nice, tender moments with my mother. I decided this moment needed the gift of silence.

"Now there will be no more crying today," my mother said briskly. "I've got just the thing you need." She whipped a large cucumber out of her handbag.

I was pretty much speechless.

"Do you always carry produce in your handbag?"

"Only when necessary. Now lie back and let me put some slices on your eyes."

"Oh. Slices on my eyes. Good idea."

"Of course slices on your eyes. What else would I be doing with it?"

I had no idea, but it was probably best if I turned my brain off and stopped thinking of the possibilities.

Amazingly enough, the cucumbers worked like a charm and my face lost the puffy redness that too much crying always brings. I'm not one of those pretty criers anyway, so the fact that I looked less like Quasimodo and more like my original self was a step in the right direction.

I'd gotten my mother to leave before Nick showed up so he wouldn't have to go through the inquisition twice in one day. I heard my front door open and paused. A combination of adrenaline, fear and ice cream cake roiled in my belly. I'd left the door unlocked and I hoped to God it was Nick letting himself in instead of the murderer.

I didn't have a gun or a knife, and the towel rod on the wall had fallen off long ago, so I didn't have anything I could hit him with either. I took stock of the cabinet and pulled out a can of hairspray in hopes I could blind him long enough to escape.

I heard the muttered curses and relaxed. It was just Nick, and he was irritated about something. I put away the hairspray and continued to put the finishing touches on my makeup.

"Don't you ever lock your doors, woman?" Nick bellowed from the other side of the bathroom door. "There's a murderer out there."

Considering Nick had yelled the statement and I was locked in the bathroom, everybody in the whole building now knew I sometimes forgot to lock the door. It's not like there was a lot of traffic on the fourth floor of a condemned building.

When I came out Nick was lounged back in a chair and watching ESPN highlights. I'd pulled on a comfortable cotton sundress in bright yellow and sandals, but when Nick turned and looked at me the desire in his eyes made me feel like I was wearing something sinful.

Of course, I'd picked the sundress because I hadn't been able to get my other skirt buttoned after I'd finished off a good portion of the ice cream cake. It was a good thing I'd eaten those cucumber slices to offset the calories.

"I really don't feel like going out," I said. I'd hoped he'd changed his mind about the whole thing. I didn't feel like facing a crowd of people, some of which would be rude enough to ask what it had been like to run over my ex-fiancé.

"The last thing you need is to sit in this depressing apartment and wallow."

"But I want to talk to you about what happened this afternoon. About Greg. What did the ME say?"

Greg sighed. "The ME said Greg had been poisoned. The discoloration of the lips and the slight smell when she opened the stomach makes her think it was arsenic. She said it would take a while to get the results of the Marsh test and make sure, but she was almost positive it was the cause of death."

"What?" I asked. "But I thought I was the cause of death."

"Arsenic is a poison that can be found in almost every household in one form or another." Nick ran his fingers through his hair in a frustrated gesture. "Which means we're going to have a hell of a time narrowing down the source. The ME said whoever gave Greg the dosage didn't give him enough to kill him right away. He could have ingested the poison and been deathly ill for up to two days before dying. Stomach cramps, nausea, chills, fever. It's not a pleasant way to go. He would have been in and out of consciousness. Someone was holding him against his will and he managed to escape, despite the poison working its way through his body. The ME said Greg was in the last stages when he ran in front of your car. She can't be sure if the organ damage and the hemorrhaging he suffered were due to the poison or your car, so she's going with the poison. Which means I have myself another homicide that ties into all this. I told you my gut didn't feel right about Greg's death."

"That's terrible." What Nick had described sounded like the worst kind of torture and I wouldn't wish that on my worst enemy. Not even Veronica. "Poor Greg."

"I'll find out who did it, Addison. It's my job." He squeezed my shoulder and pushed me toward the door. "Now we're done talking about murder for the rest of the night. We're going to relax and get to know each other."

That was something to think about. If we didn't talk about murder, what else would we talk about?

To say that dinner was a disaster was an understatement of epic proportions.

"I've never been here before," I said, inanely. "I hear the food's very good."

"Mmmhhhmmm," Nick said, noncommittally.

We both looked around, our eyes on anything but each other, trying to think of something to say that would get us through what looked like an impossibly long meal.

He'd taken us to the The Waterfront, a seafood place between Savannah and South Carolina, and we'd been led to a table that overlooked the lake. The whole scene should have been very romantic, but we'd managed to make it the most awkward dinner ever. On the positive side, I hadn't run into a single person I knew.

There was one point during the meal where I leaned over a little too far, and I was sure Nick got a glimpse down the front of my dress. His eyes glazed over and his features softened, and I thought, *Oh, boy. Here it comes. Here's the Nick Dempsey I've come to know.* But then the magic was interrupted by the waiter refilling my water glass, and I was left with nothing but a shortness of breath and a need for extra dessert.

We left the restaurant in silence. I think the word "date" had become an obstacle as soon as it was mentioned. We were doing just fine without mentioning any kind of potential relationship.

I turned in my seat as Nick drove us back to my apartment, admiring the strength of his profile and trying frantically to figure out a way to get us back on at least "friendly" terms. I could only think of one thing to say.

"Nick, I don't think we should date anymore."

He turned and looked at me, his face solemn. "I think you may be right."

We attacked each other as soon as we reached my front door. If I hadn't gotten my key in the door in another thirty seconds, Nick would have taken me where we stood, and that would have been perfectly all right with me. Nick slammed the door shut with his foot and pushed me against the wall, his hands everywhere at once and his lips fused to my own.

"God, I want you," Nick panted as his lips made their way down to the valley between my breasts.

I wasn't capable of rational conversation, so I pulled off his shirt and ran my hands over his torso. I didn't protest at all as the straps from my sundress slipped over my shoulders and the bodice fell below my breasts. All I cared about was having a Nick induced orgasm.

When the heat of his mouth found my nipple, my knees gave out and Nick had to press me harder against the wall so I wouldn't fall in a gooey puddle to the floor. I worked his belt free and unbuttoned his pants so I could feel what I needed inside me with my hands.

"Please—please," I begged.

I protested when Nick kept my hands from stroking his shaft.

"Stop, baby, I won't last, and I need to be inside you right now."

I agreed whole-heartedly, so I wrapped one leg around his waist. He had my dress pushed up far enough to see that the expense of an underwear of the month club membership was well worthwhile. I was in the perfect position to feel a strange and erotic sensation coming from the front of his pants.

"Nick, your pocket's vibrating," I said, biting his earlobe

and running my fingers through his hair. God, I loved his hair, thick and just long enough to tangle my fingers in.

"You haven't seen anything yet, baby. It can do a lot more than that."

"No, I mean, it's really vibrating."

Nick stopped his hand from taking the journey the rest of the way up my thigh, and I moaned in frustration when the tip of his fingers just skimmed the edge of my panties. He detoured away from giving me ecstasy to reach into his pocket.

He leaned his forehead against my own, his breath shaky while he checked the display, and I could feel the struggle within to get himself under control as he listened to whoever was speaking on the other end. I was surprised the phone didn't disintegrate as tight as he was holding it.

"Shit," he yelled, leaving my half naked body against the wall and throwing the phone hard enough to leave a dent in my wall.

So much for control.

13

WEDNESDAY

"Fuuuuuuuuucccccccccccckkkkkkkkk!"

In the grand scheme of things I thought I handled the new disaster in my life fairly well. I woke up vaguely depressed, mostly because I was alone and the people around me seemed to be dropping like flies, but I think part of it was the fact that my eyes were swollen almost completely shut. Apparently, I had some kind of allergic reaction to cucumber. Who knew?

So I did what everybody does when they're faced with sickness or something else equally horrible. I called my mother.

I reached for the phone on my nightstand and congratulated myself for buying the kind with the large buttons, so at least now I could feel out her number. When my mother answered I had a sudden urge to cry. Just the sound of her voice, vaguely questioning and oddly comforting made me yearn for something I couldn't explain.

The only thing that kept me from crying was that I didn't know where the tears would go since my eyes were swollen shut. Would it make my eyelids explode from the tear buildup? It wasn't something I wanted to find out first hand.

"Addison, is that you? Stop blowing your nose into the phone. I can't understand what you're saying."

"I'b gob a lurbic abtion," I said and cried harder.

"What was that? Are you sick?"

"Yeb."

"I'll be right there."

I hung up and waited for her to arrive. I laid spread eagle in bed and traced invisible maps through my mind of my mom's route to my apartment. My thoughts eventually veered back to the night before and what would have happened if Nick hadn't been called in to work. He gave me a hard kiss on his way out the door and promised he'd be back. I hoped it wouldn't be any time soon, considering this newest predicament.

I heard the key turn in the lock on the door and whimpered a little, knowing my mother would be able to fix everything in no time at all. I tilted my head and listened closely as my mother made her way to the bedroom. I'd never noticed before how distinctive her walk was.

"Mom?"

"I'm here, sweetheart. I dropped off a few groceries in the refrigerator. I know you don't take the time to eat a balanced meal now that you're living on your own."

I refrained from reminding her that I'd been living on my own for ten years now and hadn't died of malnutrition yet.

"Dear God! What happened to your eyes?" she asked, dropping something on the floor and sitting beside me on the bed.

"Is it really that bad?"

She hesitated too long before she lied, so I knew it must be pretty bad indeed.

"No, it's not bad at all. We'll just get some cold compresses on them and I'll give Dr. Jones a call to see if he has any suggestions."

Mom didn't wait around to see if I was going to ask her to tell me what I looked like. And of course, that's exactly what I was going to ask her. She practically ran to the kitchen to use the phone before I could tell her to use the one on the nightstand.

When she came back in she told me she was holding a bag of ice and the Aloe Vera plant I kept on my windowsill and not to be surprised by the cold.

"See, we'll have you fixed up in no time," she said, taking her place beside me again.

"So, what do they look like?" I was trying to envision the expression on my mother's face as she described my newly deformed face. I could practically hear the corners of her mouth pinch tight and her eyes squint in concentration.

"Do you remember that time you fried your eyeballs in the tanning bed?"

"Yes," I said, dreading what was coming next.

"This is worse. How in the world did you do this anyway?"

"It was the cucumber."

"Oh, no," my mother said, horrified. "I had no idea you were allergic to cucumbers. You've always loved cucumbers."

Not really, but I wasn't going to break my mother's heart by telling her that. "It seemed to work so well. All the swelling was gone by the time Nick came by last night."

She began rubbing the Aloe on my itchy lids and the

cool, soothing balm was like an answered prayer. "And how is Nick?"

"He's good. And still hanging around despite the fact you gave him the third degree."

"He seemed very excited about getting a home-cooked meal. Not everybody is as blessed as you are to have a mother who likes to cook. I'll make meatloaf. Everyone loves my meatloaf."

"Hmmmmm," I said for lack of anything better.

The truth is my mom's meatloaf has the consistency of an Acme brick, and it's still one of her best dishes.

"We've got to get the swelling down," I said. "I have work to do tonight, and I'm sort of on a deadline."

I thought about the murders and how Nick was keeping information from me. I needed to pay a visit to John Hyatt. This time in a professional capacity instead of as a hysterical wanna-be homeowner. There was something fishy about the Hyatt situation. I needed to find out for sure what his relationship was with Loretta Swanson and if she was lying for him to give him an alibi. There was no reason for Victor Mooney to be dead unless he'd seen something he wasn't supposed to. Since he was supposed to be watching John and Loretta, it made sense that the secrets should lie with them. Not to mention there was still something about Loretta that I didn't trust.

"I don't know if I like you working in all these dangerous situations."

"It's not dangerous, mom. All I do is take pictures."

I didn't bother to tell her I was more of a danger to myself than any criminal could be. I told her about Nick's suspicion that Mr. Butler's death at The Foxy Lady was somehow related to Mr. Mooney and now Greg.

"Poor Greg," she said. "But I don't understand what you

have to do with Bernard Butler's death. You've never even been to that place where they found his body."

"Maybe it's because we worked together." It was a lot easier to lie when you weren't able to look anyone in the eye. There was no reason for her to know about the new job on my resume or the fact that my principal was a stalker. "Mr. Mooney called me and wanted to meet before he died, and someone poisoned Greg. I've got to be connected somehow."

"This is just awful. I can't believe something like this is happening in Whiskey Bayou. We have to do something to stop it."

"There's nothing *we* can do about it, Mom," I said. A little niggling of worry was making itself present in the depths of my bosom. I knew that tone in my mother's voice. "The police are doing their jobs, and I'm trying to help them out in a limited capacity."

I didn't bother to mention the promise I'd made to Kate or the fact that Nick wanted me to stay out of police business. I was skating on thin ice as it was. My mom would go ballistic if she found out I was skirting around the police and starting an investigation of my own.

"You can't go anywhere in your condition. You need someone to drive you around. I can do that for you. I'll be your sidekick."

I prayed for the cucumber infection to enter my bloodstream and take me quickly, but no such luck.

"Now get some sleep. When you wake up adventures will still be waiting. We'll be just like Batman and Robin," she said.

Lucy and Ethel was probably a more accurate assessment.

I woke a few hours later to cold cream being slathered

221

on my eyes. Amazingly enough, when your eyes are swollen shut you have no other alternative but to eventually fall asleep.

"Dr. Jones dropped this by for the reaction," my mother said. "He said it should make the swelling go down."

I was secretly relieved she had stayed while I slept and hadn't left me alone to stumble my way to the bathroom or the kitchen.

"And I've made you a little something to eat. I hope you don't mind."

I nearly fell off the bed when I realized I could open my eyes the smallest bit. A flood of something I won't even begin to try to describe ran down my cheeks, and I had a slight moment of panic when I still couldn't see, thinking that my eyeballs had dissolved.

"And to think a little cucumber did this," my mother said. "You'd think it'd do the same thing to your insides. Maybe it'd be best if you didn't eat them any more."

I couldn't have agreed more. I laid back in bed with little to do but sleep.

When I woke up again I could hear my mother rustling around in my closet. I could open my eyes a little farther this time and even managed to see what was going on, though things were still a little blurry.

"What are you doing?" I asked.

"I'm getting our things ready. It's getting dark outside and we'll need to leave soon if we want to find a good place for a stakeout."

I groaned and flopped back on the bed. I felt like hammered dog shit, and now I had to go sleuthing with my menopausal mother. What else could the fates throw at me to make my life miserable?

"I've got our things all laid out," she said excitedly.

"This is going to be so much fun. It's been ages since we've been on a mother-daughter outing. The last one was when we took that camping trip to Allatoona Lake. You got poison ivy and a second-degree sunburn. That was a memorable trip."

No kidding.

"What things did you get ready?"

"Our outfits, of course. We don't want anyone to recognize us."

I looked at the outfit on the chair and started laughing hysterically. Tears rolled out of my sore eyeballs, but it couldn't be helped. My mother had dug a black trench coat out of the back of my closet that I never wore anymore because it was missing the buttons. She'd laid a black fedora over it I recognized as my father's.

"Where'd you get Dad's hat?"

"I ran home and got it while Dr. Jones was here. Isn't this exciting?"

"Uh huh." It was then I actually got a good look at my mother. She was dressed in head to toe black—a skintight black cat suit with bell-bottom legs, ballet slippers and giant hoop earrings. But the kicker was the Do-rag tied around her head. She looked like a slutty pirate.

"It's ninety-five degrees outside. I can't wear a trench coat. And you can't wear that outfit. You're a mother for goodness sakes."

"Columbo always wore a trench coat, no matter what the weather was like. And it was wearing outfits like this that made me a mother in the first place. Don't be such a prude, Addison."

"Hmmm," I said. She was right. Columbo always wore a trench coat, and *he* never looked out of place. And I guess my mom had the right to dress however she wanted, no matter how much I hated it. I could only hope our disguises worked because I couldn't bear to give everyone in town more to talk about.

Since my car was still at the impound we were left with the Dodge for transportation.

"Where are you going?" I asked when I noticed her heading into Savannah.

"All this planning has made me hungry, and I don't want to eat in Whiskey Bayou. Those people ask too many questions, and I assume you want to keep our after hours activities a secret."

My stomach growled at the mention of food. The last time I'd eaten was with Nick the night before. And mom was right about the people in Whiskey Bayou asking questions. There was nothing normal about either of us in our current state.

My mom pulled through a Burger King drive-thru and placed our orders, and the guy at the register only looked slightly appalled at the two of us. His bland reaction did wonders to ease my self-esteem issues.

"I can't believe John Hyatt could be cheating on Fanny. First Greg, now John. I don't know what the world is coming to. Men need to learn how to keep their flies zipped if you want my opinion. John Hyatt and his family are practically legend in this town. Whiskey Bayou would be a ghost town if his family hadn't used their own money to support the businesses during Prohibition and the Depression. And then the train depot stopped running and all those jobs were cut. The man is practically a saint. And now this. An adulterer."

The thought had crossed my mind more than once of what the ramifications would be if I brought down a pillar of the community. Would I lose my job? Would they take my picture down from the wall in the Good Luck Café from the time when I ate all those hot dogs and won a free T-shirt? The consequences were too unbearable to think about.

We pulled into a parking space and ate our burgers. A knock on the window had both of us jumping in our seats. A middle-aged man with a comb-over and thick glasses looked at us and blinked like an owl as he caught a good look at us. My mom rolled down her window slowly.

"Sorry to disturb you," the man said. "But I found this on the ground next to your door." He handed my mom a five-dollar bill, said goodbye and ran to a blue Honda Civic before she could tell him thank you.

"Holy shit," I said, cramming our wrappers back in the bag. "That's Harry Manilow getting into that car. He's one of my cases."

"Harry Manilow? I just love his songs. Especially *Mandy*. Is he cheating on his wife?"

"You're talking about Barry Manilow, mom."

"Oh, well, who's Harry? Are they related?"

I decided not to roll my still sensitive eyes to save myself the headache. Also because I had kind of been wondering the same thing myself.

"He's one of the cases that Kate gave me to check on. Look, he's getting in the car with that woman in the passenger seat. And I'm pretty sure that's not his wife."

"Are you sure that's a woman? I don't think I've ever seen a woman with forearms that hairy."

"I think so." My eyesight was still fuzzy so I couldn't be sure, but mom was right. That was one hairy woman. "Maybe she has a hormone imbalance, or maybe he's just into kinky sex."

My mom gasped at this declaration, but I could tell she was silently thinking the possibility over.

"Step on it. We need to follow them."

She took me at my word and floored the Dodge across two lanes of traffic before settling in behind Harry and his furry companion. I dug around in my bag for his file, but I still couldn't see well enough to read.

"They're taking the Forreston exit," my mother whispered.

No one wanted to be caught in Forreston. It wasn't exactly the south's version of Compton, but it was still a place mothers warned their children never to go.

"I think we should turn around and go back," she said nervously. "We've already dedicated ourselves to John Hyatt tonight. I think Harry Manilow and the Sasquatch should wait until another day."

"We'll be fine. Just keep going. There's still plenty of daylight. I just need to get a couple of photographs."

I perched on the edge of my seat, the vinyl seam pressing a dent into my thighs and knuckles sore from my grip on the Nikon. Adrenaline coursed through me. My heart raced. I even noticed a shortness of breath. For what? Chasing cars with my mother? Trying to catch people having sex?

Jeez. What a loser.

"What are you mumbling about, Addison?"

"Nothing. I was just thinking. Look, they're turning in up there. Slow down a little so they don't spot us."

"I don't think they're going to notice us one bit," my mother said.

She was right.

"You'd think they'd wait until they could at least check

into the hotel instead of going at it in the parking lot like teenagers," she said, shaking her head in disbelief.

I took a stream of one picture after the other, thanking God I couldn't see all that well.

I couldn't begin to describe how uncomfortable it was to sit with my mom in a car and watch two strangers hump like rabbits. My mother was paying apt attention to every detail like there'd be a quiz over it someday, and I kept expecting her to ask for a bucket of popcorn.

"All right. Let's get out of here."

I looked over when the car didn't start moving.

"Hello?—Mom?"

"I'm ready," she sung out, just a little too cheerful. "My word, this is an exciting job. And just think, the night's not over yet."

We drove back into Whiskey Bayou and turned onto John Hyatt's street. Lights were ablaze inside the mansion, and it seemed like a waste of electricity just for one person. Mom drove to the end of the street and turned around in the cul-de-sac.

"Look there," I said, pointing to a dark blue sedan parked on the side of the road.

"Why are those men just sitting there?"

"I bet those are the plainclothes officers Nick has doing surveillance. Since Mr. Mooney lived in this neighborhood it makes sense they'd keep a close eye on things while the investigation is still ongoing."

If I were to bet money I'd say that Girard Dupres and Robbie Butler were also still being watched very closely. And there was probably someone else keeping a watch over Veronica just in case she decided to take her deflated boob and run. Nick was covering all his bases, which meant he'd lied when he'd said he had an idea of who was responsible for the murders. He had a bunch of dead ends that led to a whole bunch of nothing.

"This street's a little crowded for what I have in mind. Why don't you drive to the park and we'll walk back up to the house? That way we can stay hidden in the trees behind the house," I suggested.

"Ooh. Good idea. You're a natural at this, baby."

"Do you really think so? I've been thinking about getting my Private Investigator's license and a permit to carry. I always feel left out when I go to dinner with Kate and Mike, plus I do seem to have a natural affinity for this type of work."

"And you have summers and Christmas break free because of the school schedule," she added. "You could do such a service to the community in those short amounts of time."

My mother turned off the headlights and drove slowly through the park to the same place I'd tried to observe John Hyatt's house from before. I got out of the car slowly and felt my way around to the hood. It was pitch black and when my eyes did start to adjust everything was still blurry.

"Just let me gather some things and we'll head off," my mother said. "I packed us some snacks and caffeine just in case we needed the stimulation. I didn't know how long this was going to take, and I didn't want to be stranded out here without anything to eat. I even brought toilet paper in case we have to answer the call of nature."

I looked at the bulging picnic basket my mom held in her arms and knew we could've been stranded out here for the next two weeks and still had plenty of food.

"I hate to say it, but I'm going to have to leave the hat and coat in the car" I said. "It's too hot to go walking around in anything less than a bathing suit. I'm sweating like a pig."

"You're right," my mother agreed. "Your face is all flushed. Do you think Columbo would be disappointed?"

Columbo would be laughing his ass off, but I didn't want to hurt her feelings. "Nah, a good private investigator knows how to adjust to any situation." I didn't know if this was true or not, but it seemed to perk my mother up considerably.

"You're going to have to lead me around," I said. "I still can't see. I'll just hold on to the back of your unitard."

"It's a bodysuit. It was very fashionable when I was younger," she said huffily. "Look, I can see the lights up ahead from John's house."

"Well, I can't see diddly squat," I said, irritated. "Slow down." I'd managed to trip over a log and run into a tree before deciding I needed to follow a lot closer if I was going to make it the rest of the way in one piece.

"Sorry," she said, slowing her step a little.

We made a small camp of sorts about ten feet from the wrought iron fence that surrounded the Hyatt property. When I say small camp, I mean that my mother opened her backpack and laid down a camouflage blanket that my dad used the one time in his life he'd decided to go hunting.

"It's not a picnic, mom."

"I know, but there's no need to rough it when we have every available comfort at our fingertips."

"Just grab the camera and that notebook over there. You're going to have to document every detail for Nick's records. This camera is great for long-range shots, so you should have no trouble getting the evidence we need. Okay?"

"Gotcha. I can do this. Maybe I'll get my Private Investigator's license as well. This is fun."

I remembered that Victor Mooney had said that very thing to me just before he'd died.

"Can you see anything?" I asked to change the subject. My vision was limited and all I could see were the bright lights that poured out of the back windows of the Hyatt estate.

"Lord, would you look at all those windows. Could you imagine having to clean them?"

"Mom, focus! Can you see anything through the windows?"

The sound of her gasp brought me to full alert.

"What? What's happening?" I hated not being able to see. I was missing all the good stuff.

"There's a blond woman in one of those silk Kimonos."

"That must be Loretta Swanson. She shouldn't be here this late. Something must definitely be going on between the two of them. Make sure you're writing everything down in the notebook I gave you."

"Right," she said, doing just that.

"Do you see anyone else?"

"There's a man sitting in a chair, but his back is to me. But I don't think it's John Hyatt. This man has too much hair, and it's not as dark. It's kind of a dishwater blond."

"Are they upstairs or downstairs?"

"Downstairs, right in the living room. I think she should be a little more circumspect about entertaining gentlemen in her robe. I don't think it sends the right signals."

I had a feeling that my mother and Rose Marie would get along famously.

"Can you see in the upstairs rooms? Is John Hyatt up there?"

"Just a minute. Let me get out the binoculars."

I watched in nervous silence as my mom filled pages in

the little notebook I'd given her and snapped pictures like a pro.

"Come on, mom. Don't leave me hanging. What's going on?"

"Let's just say that the blond and her guest are getting very familiar with each other."

"Do you recognize him?"

"There's something familiar about him, but I just can't put my finger on it. Maybe something will click once he takes the rest of his clothes off."

"Mom!"

"When did you turn into such a prude, Addison? I raised you better than that." She clucked her tongue and turned back to spying in the windows. "Oh. My. God."

"What? What happened? Shit, I hate not being able to see anything."

"Take my advice when I tell you to be glad for small blessings in disguise."

"Has John Hyatt come into the picture?"

"Most definitely," my mother said, snapping pictures.

"Well, what are they doing?" I was up off the ground now, my face pressed between two of the iron bars that kept us out. I still couldn't see anything other than blurred shapes no matter how hard I strained to see.

"Let's just say you're going to be very surprised when you get a load of these photos. I could sell these to the National Enquirer and become a millionaire."

I waited for another twenty minutes in impatient silence, hating the fact that I was being left out of the loop on such great gossip. My mom closed the notebook, took one last photo and packed up our supplies. She grabbed me by the arm and practically ran with me to the car.

"Let's get out of here," she said, sliding behind the wheel. "I think I need to take a cold shower."

I was full of questions on the short drive back to my apartment, but my mom kept her mouth shut and sped through the town's two traffic lights like the cops were on her tail. She squealed to a stop in front of my apartment stairs, blocking the entrance and taking up two handicap parking spaces.

"This is terrible. Just terrible," she muttered as she slammed her door shut and circled the car to help me inside. I knew she was agitated because she'd left the car running. I leaned over and groped for the keys and turned off the ignition before she hauled me out of the car. She pulled me behind her up the steps like I had full sight capabilities.

I didn't.

If I held something very close to my face I could make out the larger details, and I could see large shapes and tell where light was coming from. But that was it.

My shins banged against each step, but my mother couldn't hear my shouts of pain because of all the muttering she was doing. When we got to the fourth floor, she forged ahead, leaving me to find my own way down the hall while she unlocked my door. Left to my own devices, I wrenched my left shoulder when it slammed into a door jam, and my forehead managed to make contact with a wall sconce.

By the time my mom led me into my living room, I couldn't have cared less about what scandalous thing she saw at the Hyatt mansion. I just wanted an ice pack and a soak in the tub, but I settled for lying on the couch. She called one of her neighbors to come get her, and I grunted as she sat at the other end and put my bruised legs across her lap.

"How could you put me in this position?" my mother asked.

"Hey, you were the one who wanted to be just like Columbo. Don't blame me for this. You're just upset because you know you can't be the first to spread the news around."

"It's my duty to the community," she said primly.

It was true. My mom's ability to ferret out juicy information was right up there with those guys in the military who were experts on torture techniques. I'd put her in a terrible position. She had a reputation to uphold.

"Maybe it's not as big of a deal as you're making it out to be. Why don't you tell me what you saw?"

"I can't bear to speak the words." She bent down and pulled the camera out of the bag at her feet. "You can see for yourself."

"I'm not going to be able to see." I was like a little girl ready to throw a tantrum. I really wanted to see what was on that camera.

She turned on the camera and handed it to me. If I closed my left eye things became a little clearer, but after I caught a glimpse of what was on the screen I was afraid I would be permanently blind. I wheezed in a breath and saw my life flash before my eyes.

"Who would believe me if I told them?" my mom asked.

"Well, we do have the pictures, but you're right. This town is not ready for John Hyatt's secrets. We'd have to move out of state."

"That's not such bad news for you. You've been evicted."

"Thanks for reminding me," I said. "I'd almost forgotten."

14

I OPENED MY EYES THE NEXT MORNING WITH CLARITY, something I was hoping for but not expecting, considering the way my life was going.

It was still shy of eight o'clock. I jumped in the shower and scrubbed quickly so I could look at the pictures my mom had taken the night before one more time. This time with clearer vision. Maybe I'd made a mistake in what I'd seen. I sure to God hoped so.

I jumped out of the shower and wrapped a thick towel around me. I left my hair dripping wet and headed to the computer. I had just opened up my laptop and plugged in the camera when I heard the knock on the door.

"Oh, great."

I closed the laptop and hid the camera because I had a sneaking suspicion who it was. When I looked through the peephole Nick winked back at me, so I didn't really have a choice to do anything but open the door.

"I can't really talk right now. I'm kind of indisposed," I said through the crack of the door.

"I like it when you're indisposed. Let me in," he said, slowly pushing on the door and crowding his way inside.

"Mmmm, you look delicious," he said, pushing me back.

I felt like Little Red Riding Hood right before the wolf tried to eat her.

"Um—Nick, I really don't have time for this today."

"It won't take long, baby. It'll be just enough to take the edge off until tonight. I promise you'll like it."

We were playing tug of war with the towel tied around my breast, and I knew I had to pull out the big guns.

"As much as I appreciate the romance of your proposal, I have to decline. I've made a breakthrough in the case, and I have things to do."

Those were the magic words, because the sexy I-want-to-eat-you-alive Nick disappeared and was replaced by Nick the cop. His eyes went hard and focused and the line of his mouth straightened.

"Wow," I said. "I'll have to use that more often."

"What kind of breakthrough?"

"I can't give you the specifics," I said. "You're the competition."

He grabbed my wrist in a tight grip and I was so surprised I let go of the fledgling towel. Being naked for the first time (or the first time I was conscious) in front of a man was a big step in any relationship, but I have to say this wasn't how I pictured the moment. The look in Nick's eyes was enough to scare me spitless. I had a feeling I'd gone a little too far this time, but I didn't have any choice but to brazen it out.

"This isn't a game, Addison. People are dead and you're playing Nancy Drew. The killer is getting careless. I don't want him to be careless with you. It's only logical that you're the next target. If you've found something out I want to know."

"I don't know what I've found out," I said shakily, pulling my arm free.

I picked up the towel and wrapped it around me, and then curled myself in the overstuffed chair in my living room. Chills racked my body and goosebumps pimpled my flesh with the enormity of what I knew about John Hyatt. I had good reason to be afraid and Nick was right to worry.

"Just give me a little more time, Nick, and I swear I'll tell you everything I know. Did it ever occur to you that I might be worried about you during this whole mess?"

"Why? I'm not the one who keeps finding dead bodies. I'm just trying to find a murderer."

"Except that when we were at the graveyard you ran toward danger like some macho caveman trying to protect the little woman. You didn't know what you were running to, but that didn't stop you. And I know it's your job, but I have a job to do too, and I take it very seriously. I can't help it if one of my cases accidentally overlaps with one of yours. You can't stop me from doing this," I said, a lot more bravely than I felt.

Nick's jaw was clenched together so tightly I thought he was bound to get a cramp, and the veins in his neck and forehead were bulging dangerously.

"You have until noon to get your act together before I pull the plug. Don't think for one second that I won't put you in a cell for your own protection."

He gave me one last glittering look and walked out of my apartment. I had to wonder if it was for the last time.

A few minutes later I sat in front of my computer screen. The images on screen were different than what I remembered. They were much, much worse than anything I'd thought I'd seen the night before. When I heard the 1812 Overture warbling from inside my handbag, my reflexes were too slow to answer it in time.

Someone pounded on my door but I couldn't get my shocked body to move from the chair. When Kate opened the door and let herself in, I looked at her with the glazed expression of someone who had just gotten her hand caught in the cookie jar. I was going to have to do some fast footwork to keep my job.

"You will never believe what I just heard," Kate said by way of greeting.

I stayed silent, but she kept up her end of the conversation and didn't notice my odd behavior. I had no idea what she was saying.

"Are you okay, Addison? What are you downloading from the camera?" she asked shifting her attention. "Have you finished the cases I gave you?"

"You could say that," I said, tossing her the file on Harry Manilow so I could pull the screen saver up on the computer. "We've been friends a long time. Right, Kate?"

She uhhmmed as she continued to read the file.

"So let's say I had something really important to tell you. Something that could change our friendship. Would you want me to tell you?"

Kate finally looked up from the file. "What have you done, Addison?"

"Just answer the question. We'd always be friends, no matter what. Right?"

"Right. Unless you decided you were attracted to my husband. Then I'd have to shoot you."

"Well that goes without saying," I said, stalling. "And what if I invoked the friendship rule?" Neither of us had ever called on the friendship rule before, but it had been put in place when we were in junior high just in case. The friendship rule claimed that anything could be said within a five-minute period, and anything said during those five minutes would have no consequences. The words would be forgotten as soon as the time was over and neither party would walk away mad.

"This must be pretty serious," Kate said. "Should I sit down?"

"Just say whether or not you agree for me to invoke the rule."

"All right. The rule is in effect. What have you got?"

I tossed her the notebook with a blow-by-blow account of the night before.

"I didn't know you were writing romance novels," she said. "What's the big deal?"

"Just read it."

Loretta propped her leg on the table so the robe she wore gaped seductively. She rolled the sheer stockings on her legs down slowly, teasing the man who sat captivated across from her with glimpses of the unknown. A passionate embrace, a wet kiss, and the two lovers fell to the floor with thoughts only of each other.

"I can't read what comes next. Your handwriting is terrible."

"It's my mother's writing. And she wrote down the actual events of what took place while we were snooping around John Hyatt's house last night." I squinted my eyes shut and waited for the angry questions to start, but Kate stayed silent. When I opened my eyes I could tell she was angry by the white knuckled grip she had on the notebook, but her face was as calm as ever.

"You've got three minutes left," Kate said.

"I need to ask you to keep the things you're about to see to yourself. I don't want you to take the information to Nick."

"I can't promise that if it has to do with his investigation. I could lose my license for interfering in a police investigation. Not even the friendship rule can usurp that."

"But it's not really like that. I've already talked to Nick and asked him for just a few more hours to get all the information together. He's given me until noon, and I'm just asking you to do the same. I'll take this stuff to him myself after that. It's just a few hours, and I need to prove that I can do this myself."

Kate looked at the ceiling and closed her eyes. I was a pain in the ass, and I was going to have to make things up to her somehow.

"Why do you feel like you have something to prove, Addison? This isn't like you at all."

"I just feel responsible, that's all. Mr. Butler was at the wrong place at the wrong time, and it's pretty obvious after looking at these photos that he saw too much. But Mr. Mooney was a sweet old man who was having the time of his life playing some hard-boiled detective. And he's dead because I asked him to keep watch over John Hyatt and anything that was going on in the house."

I looked at Kate pleadingly. "I still don't know how I feel about Greg's death, or how his murder is even related to the others. He was at The Foxy Lady, and he knew the other victims. It doesn't make sense. But just because he's dead doesn't mean that I can stop hating what he's done. And I guess I feel guilty for that. Shouldn't I have more compassion for the dead?"

"The only reason you should have any compassion for Greg is because he's hauling coal in hell right now. The man used you and obviously gave you this annoying complex you've overtaken to blame yourself for everything. Not to mention how he screwed up the potential for any future relationships."

"You're right, but somebody in John Hyatt's house is a killer, and I need to prove it."

"What do you mean somebody?" Kate asked.

I moved the mouse so the images on the screen appeared.

"Is that Loretta Swanson? No wonder Fanny Kimble is nervous that John's cheating on her. Who's that man in the chair?"

"I guess that's where the surprise comes in," I said.

I flipped to the next photo, and Kate sat down hard on the floor. "Ohmigod!"

Kate had her head between her knees and was sucking in air through her teeth, so I jumped up and grabbed her a beer from the refrigerator. It was still early in the morning, but if you took away the alcohol beer was probably a pretty nutritious breakfast.

I placed the bottle in her limp hand and closed her fingers around it. Kate took a long swallow and made herself get off the floor. She took the notebook my mom had written in and shoved it in her bag.

"I'll give you until noon and not a minute more. As soon as this is over I want all of those photographs. My agency is going to have nothing to do with any of this. I'll honor the friendship rule, which is lucky for you because I should fire your ass for getting us into this, but you're handling this on your own. No one in my office has any knowledge of what you're doing."

I heaved out a sigh of relief. It was more than I could have hoped for.

"I'm sorry, Kate."

"Your five minutes is over. We can't talk about it anymore."

After the door shut softly behind her I blinked my eyes rapidly to keep the tears from falling. Kate was a good friend.

The beginnings of a plan started to form in my mind once I'd called the bank and found out John Hyatt was sick at home with a cold.

I had enough proof to ruin careers and reputations, but I didn't have proof of murder. I was going to have to go into the lion's den and find it myself.

I pulled the Dodge up in front of John Hyatt's mansion. Immediately my cell phone rang. I looked at the caller I.D. to confirm my suspicions. It was Nick, probably wondering what I was doing. I didn't answer because I wasn't quite sure what I was doing either.

I didn't know who was going to answer the front door after I rang the bell, but whoever it was would determine how I proceeded.

John Hyatt answered the door in pressed khakis and a golf shirt. He looked anything but sick, but as soon as he saw my face he turned an interesting shade of green and tried to shut the door in my face. I stuck my foot in the door and winced as my toes got crushed. Obviously, I should have forgone the flip-flops and worn steel-toed boots.

"I didn't have anything to do with your loan being turned down," he stammered out. "And I won't have you coming here and threatening me."

I was a little surprised by his fear. I didn't think our last conversation had resulted in anything but me blowing hot air.

"I'm not here to talk about the house," I assured him.

241

"Good, because I thought for sure you'd want to try and buy it again since Veronica Wade decided to withdraw her offer."

"Wait, Veronica withdrew her offer?"

"I thought you knew. After Greg—" he said, trailing off awkwardly. "But someone else snapped it up before I could contact you and let you know it was available. Honest."

"It's all right," I said. I mentally shook off the news and tried to remember why I'd come. "Really, that's not why I've come to see you, Mr. Hyatt. Would you mind if I came in for a few minutes? This is very important."

He stepped back reluctantly and let me through the front door.

I walked into a white marbled entryway that looked cold to the touch, and followed him in to the large living area that I was familiar with from the pictures taken from the night before.

"Please have a seat," he said gesturing to the sofa.

I looked at the couch and the chair sitting beside it and thought of all the things that had been done on it the night before.

"No, thank you," I said cheerily. "I don't want to take up much of your time."

He looked at me with a mixture of impatience and displeasure and nodded his head. "I'm very busy, Ms. Holmes. I'm working out of my home office today and have many things to do."

Like foreclosing on widows or having kinky sex on your desk? I wanted to ask.

"Is your estate manager here by chance?" I asked.

"No, Loretta took the day off to see to some personal business."

242

"Good, because I think she's been killing people." My subtlety even amazed me at times.

John Hyatt's mouth opened and closed like a fish. "That's preposterous. Why would you come into my home and make accusations against a woman who has worked for me for seven years? I think you need to leave now."

Sweat beaded at the top of his lip and on his brow.

"Please listen to me, Mr. Hyatt," I begged. "I'm scared for my own life. Please."

I brought a couple of tears to my eyes and tried my best to look distraught. I could see his worry ebb and a calculating look come into his eye. John Hyatt wasn't nearly as good of an actor as I was.

"Yes, I can see that you're quite serious. Let me get you some water, and then I want you to sit down and tell me why you think Loretta could commit murder."

He hustled off to the kitchen and came back with a glass of water that was sloshing over the edge of the glass. "Sit down, sit down," he said pushing me into the infamous chair from the night before and shoving the glass into my hands. "Tell me what happened."

I grimaced as my behind touched the upholstery of the chair, but hopefully it came across as fear instead of disgust. I had to make a decision of how much truth to tell and which lies he'd believe.

"You know that I took a job at the McClean Detective Agency to earn extra money," I said, looking at him for confirmation. I wanted him to feel like he had the upper hand. "Well, before I worked for Kate, I took a job at The Foxy Lady."

"Oh, my," he said. If I hadn't been looking for it, I would have thought he was genuinely surprised. "Isn't that where your principal was killed?"

"Exactly." I beamed at him like he was one of my brightest students. "I came by your house last week to talk to you about my home loan, and I met Loretta. I knew I'd seen her somewhere before, but I couldn't remember where. There's something about the way she moves," I said absently.

John Hyatt squinted his eyes like he was trying to read between the lines and see what I was really saying, but I smiled at him guilelessly and his expression smoothed out.

"So when the police showed me the surveillance tapes and asked if I recognized anyone, I was able to point her out."

In reality, I hadn't realized that the woman on the surveillance tapes was Loretta until I'd seen the photographs of her last night and the pieces of the puzzle started to fit together.

"And she wasn't there alone." I tried to look desperate and devastated and figured I was pulling it off when he took a hanky out of his pocket and gave it to me to dry my tears. "I'm embarrassed to say this, but she was with Greg Nelson."

"Your ex-fiancé?"

"Yes, yes. So you can see why this is such an embarrassment. Don't you understand what this means?"

John Hyatt shook his head slowly.

"It means that my principal caught them there together doing things that could ruin both of them in a small town like this one, and so when he got up to leave Loretta followed him and killed him in the parking lot."

John was looking at me like a child and shaking his head. "Addison, that is hardly conclusive evidence of murder. It could just as easily have been Greg."

"But now he's dead too." I decided now was where I

should start to lie a little. "When I identified Loretta as your estate manager the police put her under surveillance. They asked Mr. Mooney next door to keep an eye out for anything suspicious. I happened to be with the detective in charge when Mr. Mooney called him and said he had important information, but Mr. Mooney was killed before we could speak to him. It's obvious Loretta didn't want him telling her secrets. I can only imagine what it was he wanted to share."

John Hyatt looked a little green around the gills. He was staring off into the unknown and I could see sweat stains under the arms of his expensive golf shirt.

"And what about Greg Nelson?" he asked softly. "What's your theory on his murder?"

"Well it's pretty obvious to me that she killed Greg because he knew too much. He was poisoned, you know," I said conspiratorially. "And everybody knows that poison is a woman's murder weapon. If Loretta was threatened because Greg was going to turn her in it would be the perfect motive for killing him. Of course, she kind of botched that job, because she didn't give him enough and he managed to escape from wherever she was keeping him. The police probably never would have figured it out otherwise. I guess it was just her bad luck."

I choked back a sob that was for real this time and stood up. "I'm sorry. Would you mind if I used your restroom to put myself back together? This has been so difficult for me." I dropped my head down and my shoulders shook as I poured on the drama.

"Yes, of course, right this way," he said robotically. John Hyatt's mind was obviously elsewhere. He showed me through a long corridor that led to a large guest suite on the first floor. It was on the backside of the house and had its own French doors that led out to a private patio and hot tub. He showed me where the bathroom door was and left me alone.

I closed and locked the door behind him and turned on the water in the faucet. I needed to get upstairs to the master bedroom, and I had no idea how I was going to do it.

I left the water running and left the bathroom, closing the door behind me. The guest suite was spacious and private, but I was afraid John would come back and check on me if I didn't get out of there soon. I opened the French doors quietly and slipped out. I used a large shrub as cover while I looked for a way to get to the second floor. My answer came when I noticed the vine covered trellis that attached to the second floor balcony. And if I wasn't mistaken that balcony led to the master suite.

I looked down at my flip-flops, kicked them off and was glad I'd at least had the good sense to wear shorts instead of a skirt. I started the slow climb to the top and had an epiphany that I wasn't as young as I'd used to be.

I put my foot through another rung and heard the distinct crack of wood snapping just before the bottom half of the trellis crumbled to kindling twenty feet below. I was hanging by both hands and my feet were flailing in the air.

"Oh, shit." Upper body strength had never been my strong point. My life hung in the balance for a couple of minutes before I realized how much it would hurt to fall, so I pulled with all my might until I was able to hitch a leg over the balcony rail.

I laid on the hard floor gasping for breath and knew I didn't have a lot of time left to do what I'd come for, so I rolled over and pushed myself to my feet.

I hit a stroke of luck when I found the balcony doors were unlocked. I slipped in as quietly as my heaving chest would allow and into an ornate and fussy room in shades of blue. John Hyatt was a man of many facets.

I searched under the bed and through a closet full of navy blue and charcoal gray suits. Ties were color coordinated on a tie rack and shoes were lined at the bottom of the closet. The overly fussy bedroom didn't match the obsessiveness of the closet.

I riffled through dresser drawers and looked in the medicine cabinet in the adjacent bathroom. There was nothing of interest anywhere. Then I noticed the sliding door that was in the corner of the bathroom and painted the same color as the wall. And then I saw it was locked.

I pulled as hard as I could but the door wouldn't budge. I dug through the bathroom cabinets looking for anything that could pry the door open. I found a metal pick like the ones they use at the dentist office to scrape away plaque. It would have to do.

I slipped the tool in the silver lock like they do on the television and moved it around. I had no experience picking locks, but I figured they would teach me that in my private investigator's training.

I crouched down on the floor and jiggled for everything I was worth. It was while I was on my knees that I noticed the small key on the floor behind the toilet. I picked it up gingerly because there was never anything good that happened around a man's toilet.

I stopped to listen and only heard the sound of my pulse beating rapidly, so I slipped it in the lock and winced as the sound of the tumblers seemed to echo through the room.

I slid the door open and felt for a light switch along the wall. I pressed a button and lights flickered on, one row after another until a closet the size of a bedroom appeared. In it were rows and rows of women's clothes and shoes.

And along the far back wall were wigs of every length and color.

Loretta Swanson hadn't taken a day off for personal reasons. Loretta Swanson was waiting in the closet until John Hyatt decided to bring her out again.

John Hyatt and Loretta Swanson were the same person.

The pictures hadn't lied, and no one had been more surprised than me to look at those photographs and see that Loretta Swanson had a penis. Everyone in town was going to be surprised that John Hyatt spent his spare time dressing like a woman and making out with men in titty bars.

I poked through the room quickly because I knew my time was running out. I'd already been out of his sight for more than ten minutes composing myself. He'd be knocking on the bathroom door downstairs before too long.

I opened drawers along the walls and only felt the slight pull of jealousy as I saw the cashmere sweaters and expensive jewelry. Loretta Swanson had good taste for a man.

Sitting in a drawer with a diamond tennis bracelet and a broach the size of a hen's egg was a small pistol and a Swiss Army knife. I knew that with the photographs I'd taken and the new knowledge that Loretta Swanson had been at The Foxy Lady, Nick would have enough to get a warrant to search the premises.

I was satisfied that justice could now be done, so I closed and locked the door and slipped back to the bedroom. I realized only then that I was stuck on the second floor because my way back down was lying in a heap on the ground.

I listened at the bedroom door and opened it slowly. I looked both ways and slunk along the wall until I reached the stairs. I stopped when I heard the sound of John's voice speaking from somewhere in the house. I assumed John was on the telephone since I could only hear one side of his conversation.

"We've got serious problems here. I'm telling you she knows something," John Hyatt said into the phone. I had no idea who he was talking to, but I had a sneaking suspicion he was talking about me. As far as I could tell the conversation was coming from a room somewhere under the stairs. Probably his office.

"Listen, this is all your fault. You shouldn't have followed me."

There was silence while he listened.

"I don't know how she knows, but it's only a matter of time before the cops stumble onto the truth. Everybody knows that she can't keep her mouth shut."

I put my hands on my hips indignantly. I could keep a secret when I wanted to. It's just that there were very few secrets that weren't interesting enough to pass on to others.

"Just get over here," he demanded. "I'm tired of being the one who always has to get us out of these messes."

I hurried down the stairs and toward the front door as fast as my sore feet could carry me. I had no idea how I was going to explain my lack of shoes, but all I knew was I had to get out of the house. Now.

I stopped and tried to slow my breathing when I heard the distinct sound of the phone slamming down and footsteps on the tile. I picked up my purse from the table I'd set it on and prepared to give excuses why I had to run off.

I was standing behind a chair when he came into the room so my feet were hidden. "I'm sorry to fall apart on you like that," I said with a tremulous smile. I hoped my shaking voice was only in my imagination and not in reality. "I've just been through so much lately."

He looked me over like he was just seeing me for the first time. Did I look like someone who had just climbed a trellis and snooped through all his things? I had no idea, but his pensive look couldn't be a good sign.

"Thanks for hearing me out. I know I sounded crazy. It's been a difficult couple of weeks, and I don't know what I'm talking about." I backed away toward the entryway and thought this might be a good time for those plainclothes cops eating donuts in the dark blue sedan to make an appearance. "I've got to be going though. I've got an appointment I can't miss," I fibbed.

"Sure, sure. Let me walk you out," he said with a broad smile.

We were back in the cold marble entryway when I felt a cool rush of air against my neck and a sharp pain in the back of my skull.

I woke up crammed into a tiny box, and I could tell by the strong smell of cedar that it was some kind of keepsake chest like the one my mom used to have.

My head was pounding and the lack of oxygen wasn't making it better. I brought my arm up as best I could and touched the lump on the back of my head. The slippery wetness of blood between my fingers escalated my panic.

I didn't know if I was still inside the Hyatt mansion, but I could hear John's voice coming from somewhere. And then I heard the voice of a woman.

"What the hell are we going to do with her? There are cops sitting down the street watching our every move. They're not going to let us waltz out with a body and shove it in the trunk," the woman said.

"Did you move her car?" John asked.

"Yeah, I put on one of your dark wigs and took the keys out of her purse. I left the car at the park. I'm so sorry, John. I know this is all my fault, but I just love you so much."

"I love you, too, but there has to be a way to get out of this mess. You shouldn't have followed me to The Foxy Lady. Now three people are dead because of your jealousy."

"I did it to protect you. I thought you were starting to love Greg more than me, and when I saw the two of you together at that club I was just so angry. I knew the moment that principal looked at you he realized who you were, even with the disguise. I had to make sure your secret stayed safe. And this wouldn't even be an issue if Greg had just died like he was supposed to."

"I know, babe. You did what you thought you had to. And I did what I had to do to protect both of us, but there was no need for you to be jealous of Greg. He was a distraction. A one-time thing. You're the one I love."

"How could I not be jealous? I'm your fiancée. Why would I want to share you with anyone when what we have is so special, so unique?"

"Be that as it may, we have another problem on our hands. How did the Holmes girl get involved in this, and better yet, what are we going to do with her?"

"That's my fault," Fanny said, sounding as if she were near tears. "I hired a detective agency to keep tabs on you. If you'd cheat once then I was sure it was only a matter of time before it happened again."

"Wait. You hired a detective agency? Are you nuts?" John yelled. "Detective agencies are good at finding things out, Fanny. No wonder Addison Holmes has been snooping around. She mentioned she just started working for them last week. Even as inept as she is, there were bound to be one or two important details regarding our pastimes that would be impossible for her to miss."

"Well you shouldn't have cheated on me," Fanny yelled back. "I told you I wasn't thinking straight. I was upset. That's what happens when the person you love betrays you. Besides, I told her I changed my mind about the investigation. She was supposed to stop."

I groaned from the ache in my head and the fact that John Hyatt and Fanny Kimble were Cracker Jack crazy. From what I could understand John Hyatt dressed up as Loretta Swanson and Fanny Kimble dressed up as Loretta's main squeeze so they could spice up their sex life. The only problem was that John got a little carried away and used his alter ego to live a second life. One that didn't include Fanny.

"Be quiet for a second," John hissed. "Do you think she's waking up?"

I could practically hear them breathing as they leaned over the chest. I was as weak as a kitten and wasn't sure I'd be able to fight them off. The scrape of the key and the snick of the lock opening rang loud in my ears. I closed my eyes and feigned unconsciousness, while the pulse in the side of my neck beat frantically

"What should we do with her?" Fanny asked. "Do you think we could get her to promise not to say anything if we let her go?"

"You know we can't let her go. She won't be able to keep it to herself."

"But I don't want to kill her. There have already been too many deaths. And her mother would hound everybody in town until she had a search party gathered and every house searched. Can't you just bash her over the head hard enough so she gets amnesia?"

I could hear John sigh in frustration. "You know we have to get rid of her, Fanny. This will be the last time. I swear. We just have to figure out how to get her out of the house without anyone noticing."

John hoisted me over his shoulder and it was everything I could do not to groan in pain and give myself away. I took a quick glance around and noticed we were still in the living room before I closed my eyes again.

"I had to give my mother daily morphine injections before she died," John said. "I still have the syringes and medication. I'll just give her more than the normal dosage. It'll be quick and it won't be messy."

"Take her to the guest room," Fanny said. "We can keep her there until it gets dark and then we can move her."

John headed out of the living room with me, and I knew I'd never get out alive if I didn't do something quick. I hung limply with my arms hanging down his back, and when we passed a low table I grabbed a heavy candlestick and hit him in the back of the knee.

We both went down in a screaming heap, but I had fear on my side, so I kicked and clawed until his hands loosened their grip. Spots danced in front of my eyes and a thin sheen of sweat gathered over my clammy body. It wouldn't be long before I was passed out in a heap on the floor, so I scrambled off the ground and ran for my life.

Fanny stood her ground and blocked my way, so I squinted my eyes and channeled my inner middle linebacker before running right through her. We crashed over a table, and glass shattered around us. Pillows, overturned lamps, and a broken candy dish filled with sugared almonds littered the floor around us.

I had Fanny in a headlock and was trying to get her to stay down so I would have a chance to escape, but my palms were slicked with sweat and the blood that dripped down the back of my neck was more than a little distracting. John Hyatt came up behind me and pulled at my arms and legs like I was a human wishbone, and my screams echoed through the room.

"Let her go, you bitch! You're hurting her," he yelled.

I knew I was losing, so I let my body go slack. John gave a great heave as he threw me from Fanny's body. Everything seemed to go in slow motion from there. I flew through the air, and I knew when I landed it was going to hurt like hell. I got satisfaction in seeing a swarm of cops enter the room with guns drawn just before I hit the long expanse of glass windows at the back of the living room.

I tucked my head and tried to roll into a ball as the window gave and shattered at my back. My last thought was that I hoped the glass wouldn't leave scars.

"Addison—"

I heard the sound of my name in the distance, a persistent buzzing I wanted to ignore but found impossible to do.

"Let me die in peace," I said.

I lay spread eagle on the ground. My head hurt worse than it had a half hour ago, and I couldn't feel my legs. I didn't want to open my eyes and see the damage, but the annoying drone of my name being called didn't give me any other choice.

The flutter of the leaves on the trees above me was hypnotizing, and the ground was hard below me. In my imagination I was in a tropical paradise where there was no pain. I thought about swaying in the breeze on a hammock, a tall glass of lemonade in my hand and a half-naked man fanning me with giant palm leaves.

"Earth to Addison," the voice said again.

"I should've known it was you," I said to Nick.

His face looked strained and worried. "How many fingers?" he asked.

"A million. What happened to John and Fanny? Did they get away?"

Nick was doing some deep breathing exercises, and I realized he was as angry as I'd ever seen him before. I had a sinking suspicion he was angry with me.

"Please don't yell at me yet. I think I need some Tylenol first. I know you're angry," I said, licking my lips.

"Do ya think? I just watched your body fly twenty feet and crash through a plate glass window like you were on an episode of Smackdown. I ought to lock you up. Unfortunately we can't arrest people for being stupid."

"Don't call me stupid. I was trying to gather evidence so you could make an arrest since you seemed to be a little inept when it came to tracking down vicious killers. I was going to give you the information once I'd left here."

"I had a tap on his phone, and I was waiting for a warrant to come through to search the premises when you made your grand entrance. Fortunately, I'm aware of your tendency towards dumb luck and ordered the cops watching the house to let me know when and if you showed up."

I gasped at this admission. "You didn't trust me."

"Not as far as I could throw you. I've got everything I need to put these two away for a long time, and I had it all before you showed up. The only difference is my hands were tied because I had to go through legal channels."

My head was pounding, and I wanted nothing more than to go home and crawl under the covers for the rest of my life.

"I think I need to go home," I said, closing my tired eyes.

"From the looks of you, I think a trip to the hospital is the better choice. Let's have the paramedics check you out."

"Fine. Whatever. I'm too tired and sore to argue."

"That's a first. Hey," he said, brushing the hair back from my face. "For a minute there I was really worried. Maybe you can take up skydiving or NASCAR instead of hunting down criminals."

Nick was looking at me with an expression I'd never seen before, and if my head hadn't been pounding so badly I would have given it more thought. From the way my body was aching, I was pretty sure the craziest hobby I wanted to take up was knitting. Though with my luck I'd end up stabbing myself in the eye with one of the needles.

EPILOGUE

It took more than a week for me to be able to sit without a rubber donut or operate heavy machinery due to painkillers, but I hadn't been left out of the loop just because Nick was too busy cleaning up loose ends to fill me in. I'd had Kate and the rest of the town to keep me up to date.

John Hyatt and Fanny Kimble were both arrested and taken off to the jail in Savannah, both of them trying to place the blame on the other. I don't think there's much chance of their relationship lasting. Call me crazy. They did confess to the murders in front of a witness—me—so I'll be testifying at their upcoming trials.

On the personal front, things have gone to hell in a handbasket. Mostly. Rudy Bauer at the Gazette did some digging and found out I'd been stripping at The Foxy Lady the day of Mr. Butler's murder. My bad judgment made the front page of the weekly paper, sharing equal space with the story of John Hyatt dressing like a woman. Once the school board got word of my transgression, I was immediately put on probation pending a more thorough investigation, so I don't know if I'll have a job come fall or not.

The possibility of being unemployed has made up my mind about getting my private investigator's license. I found a correspondence course that was reasonably affordable, and Kate said she'd keep me on at her agency as a contract employee until I take my final test.

In less than a month's time, my apartment building will be no more than a pile of rubble. I have no idea where I'm going to go now that someone else has bought the house on Hutton Street, and there's a shortage of super cheap apartments in Whiskey Bayou, though my mother has offered my old room to me more than once. It makes me sick to do it, but I'm going to have to sell the Z once it's fixed and discontinue my underwear of the month club membership to make ends meet.

To make matters worse, I received a nice, thick envelope in the mail from Veronica Wade's attorney saying she was going to sue me for causing her public embarrassment and damaging her person. I'm not sure what I'm going to do about attorney's fees and court costs, but my mom always says, "You can't get blood out of a turnip."

I don't know what it means either, but it seems apt for my situation.

Things aren't all bad, though. Nick and I have decided to give our relationship a real shot since there are no more high-pressure situations or dead bodies to stumble over. We're determined for things to move nice and slow this time around. I don't really believe it's possible, and if we last another week before tearing each other's clothes off I'll be surprised.

Of course, the lives of an almost private investigator and

a big city homicide detective are always fraught with danger, so there's the possibility I could be wrong in my predictions. Only time will tell.

WHISKEY SOUR PREVIEW

IF YOU ENJOYED THE FIRST BOOK IN THE ADDISON HOLMES Series, make sure you check out book two, WHISKEY SOUR. Available now at all retailers.

HERE'S AN EXCERPT FROM WHISKEY SOUR!

CRIMINALS ARE MOSTLY DUMB. AT LEAST IN MY experience. And Walter Winthrop III, Noogey to his friends, was no exception to the rule.

I squatted behind a group of dumpsters at the Lone Ranger Trailer Park, ignoring the flies that swarmed around day old Hamburger Helper and dirty diapers. I was hard-pressed to tell the difference between the two and reminded myself to get my birth control prescription filled as soon as possible. Not that I was having a lot of sex or anything lately, but I didn't want to take any chances. I wasn't ready to be responsible for a child. I was barely responsible for myself.

Summer in Savannah wasn't forgiving, and it sure as hell wasn't for the faint of heart. It was barely eight o'clock in the morning and heat roiled in invisible waves off the pavement beneath me, baking the soles of my flip-flops and frizzing my hair, as the temperature pushed triple digits.

The air was thick with syrupy humidity. The breeze non-existent, the moss covered trees completely still. I hadn't heard a bird chirp in more than twenty minutes. I was pretty sure they were all dead—either from the heat or the stench—I couldn't be sure.

The Lone Ranger Trailer Park was located on the northwest side of Savannah, away from any tourists who might accidentally discover that not every part of the historic city was picturesque. The trailers were parked on a cleared off gravel lot, and if there was grass anywhere I'd yet to see it. Just miles of dirt and cement. The trailers sat haphazardly, a patchwork quilt of tin and rust, and bags of trash and old car parts littered the area.

I'd had no choice but to hide behind the dumpsters. The park was almost completely open unless I wanted to venture into the trees and marshland and set up camp— which I didn't, because twelve year old me knew from experience it wasn't fun to have a snake slither down your blouse.

Sweat gathered in places best left unmentioned, and I'd reached the point that the smell of my body no longer made my eyes water. Even raising the Long Range Nikon in my hands exerted more energy than I had left to give. Noogey Winthrop was going to have a lot to answer for if I ever got hold of him.

Six months ago, Noogey had been living the high life. He'd owned a mansion in Miami, a two hundred year old plantation house in Savannah, and three other homes across the world. He'd driven expensive cars and bought outrageous jewelry for his mistress. He had stocks and bonds and a thriving company, and he'd just gotten permission from NASA to have his ashes shot into space. But somewhere along the way, Noogey's luck changed.

When Noogey's wife caught wind of the mistress, she filed for divorce and decided to take half of everything he owned and then some, since there had been no prenuptial agreement. They had three kids between the ages of twelve and seventeen, and Mrs. Winthrop was going to make Noogey pay. More power to her. In my opinion, Noogey was lucky she hadn't run him down with a car or gone Lorena Bobbitt on his ass.

Unfortunately, getting taken to the cleaners wasn't sitting too well with Noogey. All of a sudden, his company wasn't turning a profit, his cars were being repossessed, and his debt almost doubled his net worth.

The theory going around was that all Noogey's money was really being siphoned into offshore accounts, and his wife had hired us to prove his guilt. My job should have been simple: Find evidence that Walter Noogey Winthrop was spending above his means. But I'd learned over the past months that hardly anything about my job was ever simple. At least when I did it.

Noogey was a tough nut to crack, and he and his mistress had moved into the Lone Ranger Trailer Park so their story would be more convincing. I had to admit I was pretty convinced. The smell alone would have made me confess to any crime after ten minutes.

I had a perfect view of Noogey's trailer from my crouched spot, and I'd gotten a couple of good shots of the primer gray rectangle. The knob on the front door hung precariously and a hole had been kicked in the bottom of the door. Their patch of concrete was empty except for a late model hatchback with a missing bumper and an oversized weathervane that looked as if it had fallen off the roof at some point.

I knew Noogey wasn't home. Kate McClean, my boss at the McClean Detective Agency and my best friend, had told me Noogey had left on an early flight to the Caymans on business. And he hadn't taken along Marika Dubois, his current ladylove.

I pulled out my phone and dialed Kate, hoping above all else that she needed me to come into the office and start work on another job besides this one. One that was more sanitary. And maybe one with sexy naked men.

"This job sucks, Kate," I said by way of greeting. "I'm going to have to bathe in bleach to get the smell off."

"I hear it's good for the skin. Kind of like arsenic. What's happening with Noogey?"

If I'd wanted a sympathetic ear, Kate was the last person I should've called. We balanced each other pretty well for the most part. I was prone to high drama and she kept me grounded (mostly). Sometimes keeping me grounded was like pissing in the wind, or so my mother liked to say. I liked to think I brought a little adventure to Kate's life. And I kept her in homemade baked goods when I felt like the scales were becoming unbalanced.

"Noogey's gone and there's been no sign of the girlfriend."

"She's still in there," Kate said. "Though rumor has it she's making Noogey pay for the inconvenience. I need you to get close to the trailer. See if you can get some shots of the inside through the windows. I bet the inside of that trailer looks like a palace."

"Sure thing, boss," I said, rolling my eyes. "I'll just

mosey on up and see if my x-ray camera lens can somehow see through the dirt coating the windows. No one will notice me skulking around in broad daylight."

"That's the spirit. I'm sure you'll think of something to get her out of there."

I sputtered in disbelief as Kate disconnected, and when I stood up to shove my phone back in my pocket I felt the squish beneath my feet.

I sighed and probably would have cried if I hadn't been so dehydrated. "At least it was the Hamburger Helper instead of the diaper," I said. Sally Sunshine, always looking on the positive side of things. That's me.

I pulled Noogey's file from my backpack and thumbed through it, hoping an idea of how to get Marika Dubois out of the trailer would magically appear in my mind.

Marika was a former model who was used to creature comforts. I knew without a doubt that the only thing keeping her around was Noogey's promise of the millions he'd somehow stashed away. A woman like Marika wouldn't live like this unless the payout was worth it.

A list of Marika's acquaintances were listed in alphabetical order on the back page of her profile. Kate was nothing if not efficient. An idea popped into my head and I picked a name at random. Sometimes my cleverness astounded me.

I grabbed my phone and dialed Marika's cell number, moving further behind the dumpsters just in case there were any nosy neighbors or Marika got suspicious.

"What?" Marika barked out, her French accent heavy with irritation.

"Marika, darling! It's been too long," I gushed, trying not to gag as I inhaled something especially foul.

"Who is zis?" I was still trying to figure out what *zis* was while she kept talking. "Zis is ze private number."

"It's Honey Rhodes." I thickened my accent to magnolia blossom proportions since I knew from the file that Honey was a local. "Don't tell me you don't recognize my voice. I'll just be crushed."

"I zought zou were in rehab. I haven't zeen zou in months."

I rolled my eyes, trying to interpret her sentences and wishing I'd taken French instead of Spanish. But any teenage girl would have made the same decision. The Spanish teacher at my high school had looked like Ricky Martin and he'd worn tight t-shirts that had barely fit around his biceps. My fantasies of him pretty much got me through high school.

I thought quickly, trying to decide how I wanted to handle the rehab news. "I've been back a few days," I said with a dramatic sigh. "I just needed to get away for a while. Life just gets crazy sometimes with all the parties and the social whirl. I figured rehab was the one place no one would bother me."

"Zen it's not true about ze story I read in ze paper? Zey said zou had cocaine and crashed ze Ferrari into ze pool."

Son of a bitch. I would have to impersonate the one friend on the list who'd had a high profile brush with the law.

"It was all a misunderstanding," I reassured her. "Now enough about me. I have rehab skin, and I think we need to treat ourselves to a day at the spa and a little shopping. We owe it to ourselves to stay beautiful for our men."

I hoped to God I wasn't overselling it, but the only examples of socialites I could think of were Paris Hilton and

Kim Kardashian, and I'd assumed it wasn't all that hard to be shallow and vacant.

"I'm not zeposed to shop," Marika said. "Ve have to be poor for a little while. Ze government is paying attention to our spending."

I made a sympathetic noise, trying not to gag. "Oh, sugar. It'll be my treat. I'm sure you need the break more than I do. I can't imagine having to live like a poor person."

"It is very difficult," Marika agreed. "Zey have nothing. No sexy cars or hot tubs. No body scrubs or shopping sprees. It is a dismal life. I'll be glad ven ve can collect our money."

I restrained the urge to march up to her front door and put my hands around her throat after her comments about being poor, choosing the mature route by making notes in the margin of the file about she and Noogey being able to collect their money soon.

"That's just terrible," I drawled. "How much longer are you going to have to live that way?"

"Not long, I zink. Walter promised me we'd be in Rio zipping zhampagne by the end of the month."

"Ooh, then you definitely need a spa day, sugar. You can't go to Rio with the smell of poor following you around."

"Zes, zou are right. I vill meet you at ze Green Door in half an hour."

Without so much as a goodbye, Marika disconnected and I shuffled my way back to the edge of the dumpster so I had a better view. I'd have to report the trip to Rio to the authorities. The judge hadn't demanded Noogey's passport because his lawyer had claimed Noogey needed to be able to deal with his foreign businesses in person, but this information would likely change that.

I smiled as the trailer door opened and Marika came trotting out in tiny shorts that showed off miles of tanned legs. Her long blond hair was pulled back in a ponytail and her breasts held up a halter-top of shimmering violet. Her feet were in strappy heels and a Yorkie stuck his head out of an oversized purse. I could see the disgust on her pouty lips from where I sat as she made her way to the hatchback with the missing bumper.

I shook my head in disgust. It was the most terrible attempt I'd ever seen at subterfuge. Marika made the worst poor person I'd ever seen. She kicked the tire once and let out an oath ripe enough to make a sailor blush. I zoomed in on the rock decorating her ring finger, taking several quick shots of the tacky diamond. It had to be at least ten carats, though she was wearing it on her right hand, so it wasn't an engagement ring. If Noogey and Marika were truly in financial trouble, that ring would have been the first thing to go.

Marika threw the car in reverse, the gears grinding and tires squealing, before she sped out of the trailer park. I waited a good five minutes to make sure she was gone before I unfolded from behind the dumpsters. The sun was brutal, and I could feel the burn on the back of my neck and my nose. I needed ice cream, a bottle of water and a shower. In that order.

The surrounding trailers were quiet as I crept toward Noogey's, most of them having left for work bright and early. The flimsy knob and hole in the front door were a nice diversion, considering it also had two sturdy deadbolts and the door was thick as a tree trunk. The windows were a heavy, double-paned glass, and I was willing to bet they were wired with a hell of a security system. They were coated with grime, dirt and a black film to keep anyone from being able to see in. Noogey was protecting something, that was for sure.

I walked the perimeter of the house and found a broken dog kennel by the back stairs that looked like it had been ground in a garbage disposal. I pushed it up to the window carefully, avoiding the sharp pieces of metal, and I climbed on top. I held on to the windowsill for balance, distributing my weight on each corner of the kennel as it creaked and wobbled beneath me.

My heart pounded in my chest and adrenaline coursed through my veins as I lifted the camera above my head. All I needed was a weak spot in their security and this job would be done. Maybe the camera would be able to see something I couldn't. I started clicking the shutter as the wobbling below me increased, and I found it harder and harder to keep my balance.

I'd just decided to get down and try another window when the face of a beast crashed against the window—snarling jowls and strings of snot hanging between razor sharp teeth.

I screamed as the kennel collapsed beneath me and I went sprawling on the concrete, my arms wrapped around the camera to protect it. I hit on my back with a *whoomph* and the air was knocked out of me. Something sharp had pierced my leg, but I barely noticed, my eyes wide and unfocused as I focused on getting my breath back.

"Ouch," I croaked out.

The growls intensified and the window shook as the beast rammed its head over and over against the glass. If that was a dog, it was unlike any kind I'd ever seen before. Unless you counted Cujo.

I inhaled air painfully into my lungs and rolled to my

hands and knees, looking around to make sure no one had witnessed my latest disaster. Granted, I'd gotten better at my job in the last few months, but that was probably along the same lines as telling Forrest Gump he was being promoted to remedial math.

The beast kept ramming its head against the window as I got to my feet. I gave it the middle finger because it made me feel better, and then I turned to head back to my car I'd left parked in a ditch near the marshland about a hundred yards away. My leg throbbed and blood coated the bottom part of my jeans. Good thing I'd already had a tetanus shot.

The growling and head butting stopped as suddenly as it began, and I breathed a sigh of relief. It was short lived, because the door of the trailer shook with a mighty force as the beast rammed against it. Apparently, he didn't like being flipped off, because his determination only seemed to intensify.

I shook my head in pity at his stupidity and kept limping in the direction of my car. The trailer house doors were reinforced just like the windows, and there was no way that dog was breaking through. Noogey was definitely hiding something inside that trailer.

I heard a yelp and then silence, wondering if the dog had knocked himself out, and then I heard a different kind of noise. One resembling a can opener peeling back a metal lid.

"Oh, shit," I said, staring wide-eyed as I realized what the beast was doing. Maybe he wasn't so dumb after all.

The doors and windows to the trailer were reinforced, but the trailer wasn't. Teeth ripped through plastic siding and insulation, and I saw the metal on the outside of the trailer bulge and bend grotesquely, reminding me weirdly enough of when the alien was trying to burst out of Sigourney Weaver.

I started to run, the adrenaline and fear masking the pain my body was in, and I didn't look back as I heard the metal give. Vicious barks and snarls gained on me with alarming speed. My car came into view—an old white Volvo that had about 300,000 miles on it.

I'd left the windows down because the air conditioner didn't work and I was tired of the cracked leather seats cooking my ass. I'd never been so grateful to see that stupid car in my whole life. I dived head first into the open window and turned back to roll it up just as the beast hit the side of my car.

Seeing him in his entirety was completely different then seeing his head through a window. He was the size of a horse and built like a monster truck. His fur was black with blotches of brown and gray and his paws were the size of dinner plates. It was safe to say the beast hadn't been neutered, considering he was half sprawled on my hood, humping the shit out of my side view mirror while he tried to eat his way through the metal to the inside of the car.

He changed positions and the passenger door caved in under his weight. I was trapped inside the Volvo oven, paralyzed with fear. Slobber and snot coated the car window, and all I could see was miles of snapping teeth and beady black eyes I'd see in my nightmares. My hands shook as I dug out the keys from my pocket, and it took me three tries before I was able to get the key in the ignition.

The car started easily, and I rammed it into drive, peeling out in a cloud of dust as I kept my foot on the accelerator. When I looked through the rearview mirror, the beast was still standing where I'd left him, his eyes intent on my car. With my luck, he was probably memorizing my license plate.

I rolled my windows back down to let the hot air out and decided I really needed a beer. Maybe a lot of beers. Unfortunately, there wasn't a drive-through beer store in the Savannah area. I was in no shape to go in anywhere. I'd have to settle for ice cream.

ABOUT THE AUTHOR

Liliana Hart is a *New York Times, USA Today,* and Publisher's Weekly bestselling author of more than sixty titles. After starting her first novel her freshman year of college, she immediately became addicted to writing and knew she'd found what she was meant to do with her life. She has no idea why she majored in music.

Since publishing in June 2011, Liliana has sold more than six-million books. All three of her series have made multiple appearances on the New York Times list.

Liliana can almost always be found at her computer writing, hauling five kids to various activities, or spending time with her husband. She calls Texas home.

If you enjoyed reading *this*, I would appreciate it if you would help others enjoy this book, too.

Lend it. This e-book is lending-enabled, so please, share it with a friend.

Recommend it. Please help other readers find this book by recommending it to friends, readers' groups and discussion boards.

Review it. Please tell other readers why you liked this book by reviewing. If you do write a review, please send me an email at lilianahartauthor@gmail.com, or visit me at http://www.lilianahart.com.

Connect with me online:
www.lilianahart.com
lilianahartauthor@gmail.com

f facebook.com/LilianaHart

y twitter.com/Liliana_Hart

◎ instagram.com/LilianaHart

BB bookbub.com/authors/liliana-hart

ALSO BY LILIANA HART

1001 Dark Nights: The Promise of Surrender

Sweet Surrender

Dawn of Surrender

The MacKenzie World (read in any order)

Trouble Maker

Bullet Proof

Deep Trouble

Delta Rescue

Desire and Ice

Rush

Spies and Stilettos

Wicked Hot

Hot Witness

Avenged

Never Surrender

JJ Graves Mystery Series

Dirty Little Secrets

A Dirty Shame

Dirty Rotten Scoundrel

Down and Dirty

Dirty Deeds

Dirty Laundry

Dirty Money

Addison Holmes Mystery Series

Whiskey Rebellion

Whiskey Sour

Whiskey For Breakfast

Whiskey, You're The Devil

Whiskey on the Rocks

Whiskey Tango Foxtrot

Whiskey and Gunpowder

The Gravediggers

The Darkest Corner

Gone to Dust

Say No More

Stand Alone Titles

Breath of Fire

Kill Shot

Catch Me If You Can

All About Eve

Paradise Disguised

Island Home

The Witching Hour

Books by Liliana Hart and Scott Silverii
The Harley and Davidson Mystery Series

The Farmer's Slaughter

A Tisket a Casket

I Saw Mommy Killing Santa Claus

Get Your Murder Running

Deceased and Desist

Malice In Wonderland

Tequila Mockingbird

Gone With the Sin